LAWN ORDER

A MARGARET AND BITSY MYSTERY

LAWN ORDER

MOLLY MACRAE

WHEELER PUBLISHING
A part of Gale, Cengage Learning

GALE
CENGAGE Learning

Detroit • New York • San Francisco • New Haven, Conn • Waterville, Maine • London

GALE
CENGAGE Learning™

Copyright © 2010 by Molly MacRae.
Wheeler Publishing, a part of Gale, Cengage Learning.

Wheeler Publishing Large Print Cozy Mystery.
The text of this Large Print edition is unabridged.
Other aspects of the book may vary from the original edition.
Set in 16 pt. Plantin.

LIBRARY OF CONGRESS CATALOGING-IN-PUBLICATION DATA

MacRae, Molly.
    Lawn order : a Margaret and Bitsy mystery / by Molly MacRae.
        p. cm. — (Wheeler Publishing large print cozy mystery)
    ISBN-13: 978-1-4104-3428-9 (pbk.)
    ISBN-10: 1-4104-3428-1 (pbk.)
    1. Sisters—Fiction. 2. Booksellers and bookselling—Fiction.
3. Attempted murder—Fiction. 4. Tennessee—Fiction. 5. Large type
books. I. Title.
PS3613.A2833L39 2011
813'.6—dc22   2010048904

Published in 2011 by arrangement with Tekno Books and Ed Gorman.

Printed in the United States of America
1 2 3 4 5 6 7 15 14 13 12 11

To The Book Place —
it was a great, good place

ACKNOWLEDGMENTS

With many thanks to Jenny MacRae Mc-Campbell for the flaming bathrobe — thank heavens Gary threw himself on top of you and you came through both the fire and the rescue in one piece; to Harriet Cone for the sinking soufflé — may all your soufflés stay risen from now on; to Cam MacRae for Rousseau; to Pat Crowley who shares Bertie's bright palette; and to Courtney McCampbell for the body in the sofa bed — a traumatic experience for you, a story for me.

Thank you to the MABs — Janice Harrington, Betsy Hearne, and Samira Didos, to Mystery Cat Sarah Wisseman, and to P.J. Coldren. I blew on your sparks of encouragement and look what happened.

CHAPTER 1

The morning my sister Bitsy flung a dead pigeon on my bookstore sales counter was the morning I decided to redefine my mission in life.

"Margaret," she demanded, "just look at that."

I was trying not to, but it was hard to miss, splayed as it was, like a bad joke, between the cash register and a display of *Elegant and Economic Dinners for Two*. I grabbed a bag, swiped the bird into it before the customers browsing the shelves saw it, and gave the counter a quick, disinfecting spritz. Taking a closer look at Bitsy I could see she wasn't going to be as easy to get rid of. The light of the fanatic burned in her eyes.

"Bitsy, what's gotten into you?"

"There are hundreds of them out there around the courthouse."

"So you, what . . . ?" I asked, trying for a calming tone of voice, "thought you'd do the town a favor and you shot one?"

"Don't be ridiculous." She leaned across the counter, beckoning me to do likewise. "It was poison."

"You poisoned it?" I recoiled, amazed. Reconciling this piece of news with the image I've always carried in my mind of Bitsy as the high priestess of the Latter Day June Cleaver Society wasn't going to be easy. How did this bit of toxic mania fit into the overall scheme of Bitsy as president of the Stonewall Garden Club, darling of the Stonewall Historical Society, happy alphabetizer of her medicine cabinet and linen closet? Actually, I don't know that she alphabetizes her linen closet, but she has that general air about her, and if I turn around fast enough, sometimes, there's a look in her eye that makes me think she's itching to have a go at mine, too.

But the look on my face now betrayed my mind wandering down a road best not taken. I've never been good at hiding errant thoughts from Bitsy. Her high-caliber voice snapped me back in line.

"Not me, Margaret. That swine."

"Shhh, Bitsy." One of my customers was beginning to look interested in our conversation. He re-shelved the Wodehouse first edition he'd been drooling over for twenty

10

minutes, moved closer, and took an unconvincing interest in the gazetteers at the end of the counter. "What swine?" I whispered, sliding down the counter in the opposite direction. I try to keep my business and my sister separate as much as possible for just this reason. A bookstore doesn't need to have the rarefied hush of a research library, but the din of a hyena's den gets on my nerves.

"That swine Douglas Everett," Bitsy failed to whisper back.

"Who?"

"You know very well who I mean."

"Well, yeah, Bitsy, of course I do. It's just that I'm dumbfounded. What did little Duckie Everett have against the pigeon?" I realized I was still holding the bag and handed it to her. She dropped it back on the counter.

"I don't want it. And for heaven's sake, Margaret," she said, brushing invisible pigeon specks from her blouse, "he's hardly 'little Duckie Everett' anymore. He's at least five years older than I am."

He's more like one year younger. Bitsy's cockeyed view of aging is grounded in some complicated formula involving mobiles, stabiles, and tangential slopes. It's similar to the theory of continental drift, the central doctrine being her age is the only stabile and everyone else's flows on by. Someday I expect to be five years older than she is, too, though I started out two years younger. Fifty-three will try catching up to her next month, but she already has plans to be out of town so she can avoid it.

"Bitsy, I sense there's more to this story than a dead pigeon. Why don't you go on back to the kitchen and make some tea. I'll take care of these customers and join you in a couple of minutes."

She stalked off in that direction and I sighed with relief. I do love my sister, but she can't carry on a conversation in anything but italics laced with exclamation points. Making tea has a soothing effect on her, though. Bitsy is one of those people for whom kitchen puttering is a tranquilizer.

In fact, I thought, as I rang up a magazine for one customer and the Wodehouse for the other, with that bit of inspired problem solving I'd killed two birds with one stone. But, as it turns out, that was an unfortunate turn of phrase to be thinking much less chuckling over. Too late, I remembered I hadn't done this morning's breakfast dishes, or any of yesterday's either.

"Oh, Margaret, really!" pierced the barrier of the kitchen door leaving all eardrums in its path quivering.

I sighed for a different reason this time, and after ringing up the last sale, I flipped the "welcome" sign on the door to its "back soon" side and went to join Bitsy in her idea of a domestic Superfund site.

The kitchen is the only part of my downstairs I keep private. I'm lucky enough to have what so many people dream of, a combination new and used bookstore in a great old house. Even better, Blue Plum Books and I live on tree-lined Main Street in Stonewall, my picturesque hometown, nestled in the foothills of the Tennessee Blue Ridge Mountains. That Stonewall's population manages to hover under whatever magic number would make it ripe for inundation by mega-merchants isn't bad, either.

The house my books and I share is a two story Craftsman foursquare built in 1913 with the style's characteristic shingle siding, rafters, brackets, and deep porch. The books take up most of the downstairs and I take up some of the upstairs. It's an arrangement that has customers leaning their elbows on the counter, looking moonstruck, and telling me this would be their idea of heaven. The reality is that living at work can be hell, but what the hell, it's mine and I like it.

I bought the house and business as a package deal after spending a fruitful and unhappy decade applying my MBA as an investment banker in Chicago. Those were bountiful years for the stock market, when moderate sums of money morphed into bulging nest eggs seemingly overnight. But banking and the windy Chicago winters left my heart cold. So on evenings and weekends I ignored blue-chips and bonds and warmed myself in bookstores and even ended up taking an evening job in my favorite one on Michigan Avenue. When Bitsy called to say Charlie Frank wanted to sell Blue Plum, I clapped my hands and packed my portfolio. I'd missed the hills and hollows of east Tennessee. I'd even missed Bitsy. But books were what thawed my soul and lured me home.

Charlie Frank was a little old gnome surrounded by his family of books. He'd owned the house with the shop forever and parted with them only at the insistence of his human children, who were themselves past retirement age. After reluctantly turning the keys and deed over to me, he was supposed to emigrate to Florida and move in with a daughter. Maybe he did, though maybe he eluded the daughter by slipping inside a conspiratorial book and is spending his retirement in a story with a more exciting ending.

I quite easily slipped into the house and business, and we've suited each other for almost twenty years now. That's not bad considering small independent bookstores have been on the endangered business list for about as long.

When I bought the place, Bitsy helped spruce it up, Charlie having spent more time chasing rare editions than repainting or deep cleaning. Bitsy was in her element, choosing paint colors (pleasing earthy greens and blues) and suggesting chintz for curtains (immediately vetoed). She also encouraged me to make the kitchen a part of the store and display the cookbooks there. Sort of like exhibiting zoo animals in their natural habitats. It was an appealing idea, but more appealing, instead, was being able to sit at the kitchen table in my pajamas not worrying about customer relations versus doing the dishes. Breakfast in pajamas and a lack of dish-doing are two of the differences between Bitsy and me. Once past our wren-brown hair, blue eyes, and general lack of height, several more differences lie in wait. Chintz curtains, for instance.

To make up for rejecting her kitchen and cookbook idea, I turned Bitsy loose on the front porch. Charlie had enclosed it for more floor space and included lovely windows in the remodel. But then he proceeded to cover the windows with a ramshackle collection of tall bookcases, creating a dark entryway with a piecemeal look. Bitsy saw the possibilities, though, and convinced me to have new shelves built around the windows. Now the porch walls are lined with bookcases and there are window seats for geraniums and enrapt readers. There are also several low, free standing units with shelves on all four sides and space on their table-tops for displays. Bitsy suggested moving the gardening and craft books to the porch and I did.

Bitsy stood, now, in the middle of the kitchen, teacup artfully aloft in her right hand.

"There were so many of them, Margaret." Her moue, comprised of equal parts distaste, aggrievedness, and belligerence looked as though it had been professionally applied. I wasn't sure which was causing her present unhappiness — the hundreds of poisoned pigeons flapping and dying around the downtown square or the dozen or so dirty dishes lounging shamelessly on the counter

16

behind her. She looked poised to flee if the pots in the sink made a sudden move in her direction. There wasn't much I was willing to do about the kitchen at the moment, though, so I tackled the pigeons.

"Why couldn't you just tell me about them without bringing one along as a visual aid, Bitsy?"

"What?" She was leveling a bent eye at a sticky saucer on the stove and had lost the thread of the conversation.

"Why did you bring me a dead pigeon?"

"It was still alive and suffering and you're closer than the vet since he made that stupid move out to the highway. Why do so many people think progress means paving over the countryside and throwing up metal buildings?" Now she had the thread of the conversation, but if she headed off any further in that direction it was going to unravel.

"But Bitsy, I don't know anything about dying birds."

"No, but you have all those books out there."

"Oh, right. I'll go check my Dead Pigeon section. I think I squeezed it in between Classics and Children's Picture Books."

"There's no need to be sarcastic, Margaret. You know very well you've got books on all kinds of things."

"The library has more and you passed it on your way here."

Her moue got a little mouier and her eyes reflected her further pain. Bitsy had a run-in with the librarians several years ago when they converted to an automated self-checkout system. I don't know for certain why she hasn't set foot inside the library since then, but it's either a self-inflicted banishment or something the librarians voted on and wrote into an official addendum to library policy.

"You're always bragging about the books you can find for people that no other bookstore seems to be able to. Like that book on glass wigwam boats you found for that woman and then bored us all to death with for weeks."

"It was *Glaswegian Shipbuilding: 1830–1920.* Out of print. Rare."

"Whatever. You found it and so I thought a small thing like help for a suffering pigeon would be something you could handle. You've got the *Mayo Clinic Guide to Family Medicine* out there. Surely you have something along those lines for pets."

"Oh, but Bitsy, wild birds are different."

"And it's dead now, anyway, so what's the use." She dumped herself into a chair at the

18

table and it was an indication of how upset she was that she didn't brush off the toast crumbs first.

"Has anyone called the street department or whoever it is who picks up dead animals?"

"Who knows?" Bitsy does despondent almost as well as she does aggrieved.

"Someone probably already has by now but maybe you should call anyway to make sure. So then, uh, how exactly do you know Doug poisoned them?"

"Well, they aren't like lemmings, Margaret. They didn't all just take it into their heads to jump off the courthouse without flapping their wings."

"I mean, how do you know Doug is responsible? That's kind of hard to believe."

"Isn't it obvious?"

The only thing obvious to me was that talking Bitsy through this crisis was going to take longer than I'd expected. Though why, I muttered to myself as I scrounged around for a clean cup, I should ever expect any crisis of Bitsy's to die a quick, clean death I don't know. Maybe it's my eternal optimism that keeps bubbling up. A bit of misplaced *joie de vivre.*

Bitsy made a face when I sat down across from her with my tea and took a sip. She hates my "Eat More Possum" mug. "It's obvious because he's a member of the Progress through Paving Party," she sniffed.

"You know that isn't its name."

"It might as well be."

"And how does that tie in with poisoning pigeons?"

"Don't you see?" she asked, impatient with my denseness. "It's all part of the plan. Kill off business downtown so people will go out to those new places along the highway to shop."

"By killing off the pigeons?"

"Would you take your children downtown to shop if they were going to see pigeons dying on the sidewalks?"

"But, Bitsy, doesn't Doug own buildings downtown? Why would he sabotage his own businesses?"

"He thinks pigeons are a nuisance and hates the mess they make on his window ledges. He says they're like rats with wings."

"Rats are probably smarter. But Bitsy, first you said he was sabotaging downtown and now you're saying he's doing some sort of cockeyed community service project. Which is it? And how do you know it was him?"

"Anyone would know it was him."

"But do you have any proof? Did anyone see him sitting on a bench passing around poisoned popcorn?"

"Margaret, I assumed you would be on my side in this matter."

"What side, Bitsy? It was a gross and nasty thing to do but you don't really know who did it. Maybe it was the town, they've come up with dumber ideas. But if you've got proof it was Doug, go to the police. There's bound to be a law against wasting winged rats."

"Margaret. It is not a joke."

"No, you're right. I'm sorry. But you've got to be careful about assuming you know who did it and very careful about going around saying you know for a fact he did it."

She was very careful as she put her teacup on the table. "Douglas Everett and his buddies are not good for this town. I am not assuming this. I've heard enough reports from reliable sources to know this for a fact. You, Margaret, as a small business owner should be more aware of, and certainly more concerned about, what's going on. Things are changing in Stonewall and not necessarily for the better. But there are some of us who have our eyes on Mr. Everett and we will fight him. That's the side I assumed you would be on."

She gathered herself and her shrouds of

21

glory and stood to leave. "And Margaret, I'll take the bag with the pigeon. I'm afraid if I left it here you might lose it amongst the dishes and not find it again until next month."

I usually let Bitsy have the last word in situations like this. It gets her out of my hair sooner. Besides, she knows how to make a good exit and why rob her of an opportunity?

Which brings me back to the redefinition of my mission in life as precipitated by Bitsy and her ex-bird. Oddly enough, almost any time I redefine it, Bitsy ends up getting a mention. I haven't analyzed this phenomenon and I'm not sure I ought to. Some mysteries are best left in their own dark corners.

Having a mission in life isn't something I spend a lot of time brooding over. But occasionally giving it definition seems to give my life a sense of direction. Or maybe it's just that it gives me a sense of control as I wallow along in the river of life. "Lock all doors and windows anytime you see Bitsy coming," for instance, gave me a wonderful feeling of empowerment for a short time last spring.

I was waxing nostalgic over that memory when the regrettably unlocked kitchen door opened. I jumped, sloshing tea across the table. But it wasn't Bitsy back to blight my day further. It was our elderly cousin Leona. She has an uncanny talent for slipping through the front door without jingling the bell.

"I didn't think that was your trouble, Margaret," she said, surveying the scene. She tottered over to the sink and unearthed a dishrag and handed it across to me.

"What? Being a slob?"

"No dear, that hasn't ever slowed you down. But you're not usually the nervous type. Why so jumpy?"

"Bitsy threw a dead pigeon at me this morning."

One of the reasons I like my late mother's cousin is she doesn't ask me to explain statements like the one I'd just made or offer reproof. She confines her comments to monosyllables. They encapsulate volumes of accumulated observations of the Welch girls, which she's never lacked opportunities to collect. As children, Bitsy and I were in and out of Leona's house almost as much as our own several blocks away. Her ethnologic study really took wing, though, when I bought Blue Plum. Her house is conveniently next door.

"Hmph," she said, "your 'back soon' sign

is on the front door."

"Oops."

I sent the dishrag on a half-hearted flight toward the sink and Leona followed me back out front. I flipped the sign on the door so that Tom Kitten was once again welcoming people to the bookstore.

"Have you been downtown yet this morning, Cousin Leona?"

"Yes, dear. I always walk down to Bertie's for a cup of coffee at eight o'clock. It makes me feel as though I'm getting a head start on the day. You should try it."

"Maybe I will sometime. Did you see anything unusual?" I stuck my head out the door and peered down the street toward the courthouse. My place is four blocks from downtown proper. The pigeons tend to hang out down there where they can catch up on courthouse gossip and panhandle on the square. There weren't any staggering in my direction.

"Like what, dear?"

"Like . . ." I turned around to answer her, but instead of finding Leona of the comforting shirtwaist ready to give my worries perspective, I was surprised by a man I didn't know standing at the sales counter staring at me.

CHAPTER 2

Perhaps not staring. Openly gazing? I returned the look, whatever it was. He had on a nice red plaid flannel shirt. He looked fairly settled in, leaning there with his arms crossed, and I found myself admiring the way he didn't seem to care that the foot casually cocked across his other ankle wore a shoe whose sole obviously needed attention. Only his eyes gave me an uneasy feeling. He had the look of a mental health expert called in on consultation.

"Well?" he prompted.

I felt like asking "Well, what?" but my better business sense kicked in. "I'm sorry, I didn't know you were waiting. How can I help you?" I tried to sound efficient and welcoming, anything other than the eccentric or paranoid his eyes seemed to suggest I might be.

He smiled and a bit of the devil crept into the professional gaze. "What was the unusual thing you thought we might see down-town?"

"I think she was wondering about dead pigeons." Leona tottered into view from somewhere in the Literature section. "This is Mr. Mashburn, Margaret. We had coffee together at Bertie's and he gave me a ride here."

"She made me go around the block three times, first."

"He has a blue sports car. It corners well."

I looked from one to the other. I opened my mouth to comment, and on second thought closed it again. Instead, I walked around behind the counter, an old booksell-er's ploy for gaining the upper hand in uncertain situations. "So, what can I do for you, Mr. Mashburn?"

"I saw dead pigeons. Well, dying pigeons. They're probably dead, now, though. It reminded me of that Tom Lehrer song. Do you know it? 'Poisoning Pigeons in the Park.' " And here he broke into a strangled rendition of what I guess was that song.

Leona coughed politely. Then less politely. "Mr. Mashburn," she finally got through to him.

"Please, call me Gene."

"Gene. Don't sing."

"Oh, sorry, little early in the day, isn't it?

Catch me some evening after a few beers and I can sing anything. Anyway, what's with the pigeons? There are other ways of dealing with nuisance animals than poisoning them. Was this the town's idea?"

"I don't know," I said, suddenly tired of the whole topic. "The first and last I've heard about it, or want to hear about it, was when my sister threw one at me shortly before you came in."

"Why did she do that?" He looked genuinely concerned and I liked him for that. And for his flannel shirt. But Leona stepped in before I could work on developing this bond.

"Margaret, dear, you're exaggerating. Surely she didn't throw it at you."

I thought about arguing the point but then something else occurred to me. "Bitsy huffed out of here just before you came in. Didn't she stop you and make you look at her pigeon and harangue you with her theories?"

"We must have missed her, dear."

"Oh, wait," Mr. Mashburn, Gene, snapped his fingers. "Was that the woman we saw coming out as we were pulling up? She looked mad enough to bite the heads off snakes and she was carrying a bag like maybe it had the snakes still in it." He turned to Leona. "That was when you told me to peel out and go around the block one more time."

"Mmph. I'm sure I don't know what you're talking about."

"So did you peel out?" I asked.

Leona had stalked off home but Gene Mashburn stayed behind and was dithering in the Mystery section. He appeared to be stuck between choosing a Dick Francis and a Kinky Friedman, weighing one of each in his hands.

"Sorry?"

"When Leona asked you to, did you peel out?"

"Oh, no. Never. I'm a sober and sedate driver. Not that your cousin didn't try to get me to punch it. Has she always had a thing for fast cars?"

"Beats me where it comes from, but the older she gets the faster she likes them. If you don't mind me saying so, you don't look like the kind of guy who drives a, what is that, anyway?"

"Lamborghini," he said, "and I'm not. I used to drive a VW Rabbit."

I raised my left eyebrow, a move I've been practicing, hoping to use it to good effect someday on Bitsy. It was having a pretty good effect on Gene Mashburn and he came over to the counter still carrying both books.

"A client of mine couldn't pay me for a job so he gave me his car instead. So far it's working out. It's a symbiotic relationship."

"You and the client?"

"No, me and the car. We keep each other in one piece. Which of these do you recommend?" He shoved both books across the counter. *Driving Force* and *Roadkill*.

"Hmm, tough choice. Maybe your car has an opinion?"

He turned around and looked out the front windows at the car. If he went out and started talking to it, I decided I would lock the door and not worry about this particular sale. But he turned back and that bit of devil was in his eyes again. "I don't know. We're not that close yet."

"That's okay, these things take time. Do you ride or like horse racing?"

"Never been to a race. I used to ride but I haven't been on a horse in years."

"And I bet you haven't been singing country and western lately, either."

"I can't tell you how many times I've been asked not to," he said.

"Leona would certainly ask you not to. Of course, you don't need to sing or even like

29

country and western to enjoy a Kinky Friedman and you can do your riding and racing vicariously through Dick Francis."

"Better living through books. Maybe I'd better take them both."

"Good decision." I rang him up, slipping one of my free bookmarks into each book. "Would you like a bag?"

"Got any more with pigeons in them?"

"Sorry, relatives only. Special perks. Here's a feather, though." A wispy gray one was still lurking next to the register and I swiped it up, wondering if I should disinfect the whole counter, again. Then, without thinking, I reached across and tucked the feather in his shirt pocket.

Now that surprised me. I'm not a very forward person. I tend to prefer, as Bitsy would say, to keep my nose either stuck in a book or in my bookstore. So what made me do that? Maybe it was the flannel shirt. My cheeks were about as warm and red as it was, now. Or maybe it was that bit of devil.

But I missed whatever Gene Mashburn's reaction to all that was because — speak of the devil — Doug Everett walked in.

CHAPTER 3

Doug stopped inside the door and peered around, looking disoriented.

"The Wildlife and Pets section is in the other room, Doug."

"Huh? Oh, Margaret, hey." He flapped a hand in my direction. "Hey, Mashburn. Good to see you." Doug knows everyone.

He approached the counter, casting looks left and right, managing to appear both reluctant and impatient. Doug is someone a mental health expert should diagnose as suffering from biblio-aversion. He apparently leaves book buying up to his wife, Diane, who comes in every couple of weeks. Doug makes it once or twice a decade. Maybe it has something to do with the way he dresses. Tailored Suits, as a rule, aren't browsers, even if they retain their boyish good looks as Doug has.

"Someone told me you have books on local history," he said.

"Sure, let me show you."

I led him into what had been the dining room, where I shelve the local, regional, and state history. It's a room popular with area history buffs and genealogists. I even get the occasional bus full of heritage tourists stopping to browse. East Tennessee history is full of characters and tales, both true and tall. Davy Crockett and Daniel Boone kicked around these parts in their early days. Nolichucky Jack, who was more formally known as John Sevier and became the first governor of Tennessee, lived here, too. If bookselling hadn't beguiled me away from banking, a graduate degree specializing in the area's history might have seduced me.

Doug stepped into the room and his eyes glazed over at the sight of so many volumes on so many shelves. Seeing the droop to his shoulders, the tilt of his head, and the big, sad eyes, I almost laughed. He'd used that little-boy-lost look to good advantage with the various mothers in the neighborhood when we were kids. It must have been endearing in an eight-year-old and it usually got him what he wanted. I suppose it was still mildly endearing in a fifty-something.

He seemed to be waiting for some direction so I pulled a copy of *The City of Stone-*

wall: a Pictorial History from a shelf. It's a local bestseller, full of maps, drawings and old photographs. Smiling encouragingly, I put it in his hand.

He sank into a chair and I left him, wanting to either pat his head or shake mine. But being a slave to customer relations, the backbone of small businesses, I settled for another smile. Although it's hard sometimes, I try to save other gestures for after hours. Or for Bitsy.

When I got back to the front counter, Gene Mashburn was gone. What a shame, but just as well because there was work to do.

Gene Mashburn and his flannel shirt had only been a pleasant diversion, I told myself firmly as I gathered the weekly sales report and most recent book catalogues. So what if there were any number of nosy questions running around inside my head? Like, how long had he been in town? What sort of work did he do that he had clients with spare exotic sports cars? And did he also have that flannel shirt in shades of blue to match his eyes? Be still my fleeting curiosity. Time to concentrate on organizing the weekly book order.

People seem to cherish the idea of a bookstore as the perfect refuge, a quiet corner they can count on for sanctuary in their busy lives. It's a lovely image and I try not to tarnish it. But translating that image into reality is what keeps the bookseller busy. One doesn't find oneself idling the hours away discussing Proust or settling down in a comfortable chair with the latest bestseller.

I'd just sat down on the hard, wooden stool behind the counter with the list of bestsellers I needed to order when Doug returned.

"Must be nice," he said. "Great job if you can get it, sitting around all day reading."

"Best job in the world, Doug. Did you find what you were looking for?"

"No."

"Oh. Well, can you give me a more specific idea of what you want?"

"Old records. Information about buildings."

"Not the kind of information you can get at the courthouse?"

"No, no." He started drumming his fingers on the counter. He looked like a man trying to be patient while inspiration dawdled somewhere in the wings.

"And you looked through the other books back there and didn't see what you want?"

"Yeah, I looked and no, I didn't find

anything. So, okay, look, someone said you've got things like . . . ," he waved his hand around as though that might describe something I would recognize. Next he'd be telling me what color it was. Actually, sometimes that helps.

"What kind of buildings, Doug? Commercial? Residential?"

"Commercial. I want to know, like, what businesses have been in, say, Hauck's Drug Store. Or some of the other buildings on Main Street. Over the years."

"That kind of information isn't at the courthouse somewhere?"

"No." The expression on his face added, "you idiot." Funny, he wasn't even mildly endearing now.

"Oh. Well, there is a nifty book called *A Walk Through Time*. It was written in nineteen sixteen, though, and it's anecdotal."

"Anec what?"

"Stories, hearsay. Not necessarily unreliable, but you've got to take it all with a grain of salt. Harker Grundy wrote it when he was in his seventies. It's his memories of Main Street from eighteen fifty when he was ten until the turn of the century. It's not any kind of official record, but it's fairly interesting."

"I'll take it."

"Gosh, I haven't had a copy of that for sale for months."

"Well, Jesus, Margaret."

"Sorry, Doug, I wish I did. It's rare, though, out of print. It's not the kind of book I can order from the distributors." And even though I personally owned a copy, it also wasn't the kind of book I'd lend to a jerk, even if I'd had a crush on him when I was six. "I can search for a copy, if you'd like, but in the meantime the Historical Society has one. You can't check it out to take home or anything, but they've got a reading room. They're always helpful over there."

"Hah. The Hysterical Society. Right. I bet a few of them wish I was history."

I wasn't about to argue with that after Bitsy's tirade this morning. Bitsy. Aha. There was shy inspiration flitting past and I caught it on the wing.

"Doug, here's what you do. Give Bitsy a call. I'll write her number down for you. She's a member of the Historical Society and she'll be happy to take you over there and show you the book. I'll write the title down for you, too. Here. It's *A Walk Through Time* by Harker Grundy."

I handed him the paper, not even tempted to tuck it in the pocket of his suit coat. He was nodding his head, now, to some staccato beat I was glad I couldn't hear.

"Hm. Okay. Sounds good. And Bitsy's not like some of those people. She's always liked me. Thanks, Margaret, you've been a great help. Sorry for being out of line a minute ago. You've got a great shop here. It was great seeing you. Bye." With a flash of teeth he was gone.

"Great, bye."

I settled back down to the book order with contentment. The satisfactions in this job are many. On the one hand Bitsy brought me a poisoned pigeon, on the other I sent her a pigeon poisoner. It's hard to beat that kind of symmetry.

The rest of the morning maintained that sense of balance and proportion. Customers flowed in; books flowed out. I finished the paperwork for the new book order. Last week's order arrived via UPS right on schedule. I paid some outstanding bills and the mailman brought me new ones. The sun was shining brightly on my pigeon-free stretch of Main Street. The phone rang and I answered it.

"Margaret!"

CHAPTER 4

I almost slammed the phone down again. Instead, I smiled so she could hear it. "Hi, Bitsy."

Bitsy had quite a lot to say. As I stood there listening to her say it, I practiced the art of Not Making Faces That Will Alarm the Customers, an important skill for business people dealing with the public. I don't lack for opportunities to practice.

As I was getting ready to wrap up this particular drill session, the bell over the front door jingled. Gene Mashburn was back. I listened to Bitsy for about ten more seconds then gently hung up.

"I didn't mean to interrupt your phone call," he said.

"Oh, you didn't."

"You didn't say goodbye." He pointed at the phone and his eyes had that consulting mental health expert look about them again. "Were you on one of those interminable holds?"

"In a manner of speaking."

He lifted one eyebrow to a height I only dream of attaining.

"That was my sister."

"Is she safer over the phone?"

"In a manner of speaking."

"You're going to strangle it." He nodded at the poor pen dying a surrogate death in my white-knuckled grip.

I laid it down. "What can I do for you?"

"I thought you'd like to know the pigeons have finished dying and they've all been picked up by the street crew."

"Why?"

"Would you rather they hadn't been picked up?" That notion affected him somehow, but having just met the man I couldn't read the innuendoes of his body language. Was he showing signs of alarm or professional interest?

"Oh, no, I'm glad they've been taken care of," I rushed to assure him. "I was wondering why you took the trouble to come tell me."

That smile and those eyes again. "So you won't have to cringe every time your sister comes near you with a paper bag."

"That does reduce my stress level, thank you. Though, according to her, the pigeons were expeditiously 'disappeared' to get rid of the evidence."

"Evidence of what?"

"Oh, she's got several theories. A few of which she was sharing with me on the phone. None of which I'll repeat, if you don't mind." If he were an itinerant shrink, I'd probably already tainted his view of the family psyche. Adding Bitsy's particular manias to the picture wasn't likely to make it any prettier. "How well do you know Doug Everett?" I asked instead.

"Not very. I know more about his businesses than I do about him."

"Like what?"

"He recently bought the old mercantile downtown. Says he's going to make it into a climbing center or whatever they call those places. Doing some other developing around town. Got his fingers in a lot of pies."

"Pigeon pie?"

At that he folded his arms across his chest and the fingers of his left hand strayed to his bearded chin. It was a nice beard and a nice chin and his fingers looked at home stroking it.

"Have you always had a thing about pigeons or did your sister really traumatize you this morning? Of course," he continued, "what you're suggesting is that Doug had a hand in poisoning the pigeons. Do you think he did?"

"Are you humoring me?"

"What?" He looked surprised. "No. If Everett did it, he should be reported."

"That's exactly what I told Bitsy."

He cocked an eyebrow again.

"My sister. Her name is Bitsy."

"Oh, yeah." His smile struggled briefly with a grimace but came out on top again. "I hope Bitsy's short for something."

"Elizabeth."

"Do you have a nickname?" he asked with the slightest hint of unease.

"No."

"Good."

"Doug does. When we were kids we misunderstood the nickname his mother used and thought she was calling him Duckie."

"That probably scarred him for life and he developed an insane hatred for anything with wings."

"Now that's a theory even Bitsy wasn't crazy enough to come up with," I laughed.

"Thank you, Margaret," Bitsy said, materializing behind me. Of course, she doesn't need to carry a bag with a dead pigeon in it to make me flinch. Her voice carries the crucial cringe factor all by itself. And it's not just me. Other people are affected the

41

same way. Even Gene Mashburn, who'd suffered no previous conditioning, managed a credible cringe at this, his first full exposure to her.

She must have been over at Cousin Leona's when she called and then cut across the yards to come through my kitchen door. She blessed me now with a look dripping with long suffering before sliding past me to the phone.

"We got cut off," she explained as she lifted the receiver. "I was worried."

"Why didn't you just call back?"

Apparently reassured by the dial tone, she re-cradled the receiver. "Margaret, of course I rushed over. What if something had happened?"

"Like what?"

"I don't know. A fall? An avalanche of books? Robbery?" Here she looked sideways at Gene, who appeared to be hypnotized by her the way people are who come face to face with a swaying cobra.

To give Bitsy her due, though, she does worry. Irrationally, maybe, but honestly and thoroughly. And if a situation ever did turn out to be dire, she wouldn't hesitate to wade in to save my life, as long as she could do it without getting something icky on her shoes.

"Thank you, Bitsy. I'm attracting solicitude from all over today. By the way, this is Gene Mashburn. Mr. Mashburn, meet my sister, Bitsy Decker." They bared their teeth in facsimiles of smiles.

"Oh, yes, Cousin Leona mentioned something about you," Bitsy said. "You and your car."

Cousin Leona has a clear field of vision from her living room window to the small parking area in front of my store. Bitsy's solicitude was beginning to look as though it had an ulterior motive and I wondered what her interest was. A fast lap or two in the beautiful, blue car?

"Well, Bitsy, thanks for checking up on me. I've got some work to get back to now, though . . ."

"Oh?" She glanced around at the general lack of customers. The counter could have been ten deep in customers jockeying for position with armloads of books and she wouldn't have sounded any less skeptical.

"I should get out of your hair, too. Nice to see you again." Gene was backing toward the door.

"Oh, but wait." Bitsy fairly leapt over the counter after him. He was obviously a quick study and the way he cringed this time made up in style for what it lacked in subtlety. "Mr. Mashburn, judging from the

43

conversation I interrupted when I came in, you also have an interest in the plight of the downtown pigeons."

"Only peripherally."

Bitsy brushed aside that hedge and pressed on. "I'd certainly be interested in hearing your theory, even if Margaret was rude enough to dismiss it. I'm acting," she said, puffing up a bit, "in my capacity as a member of the Townscape Committee. We feel this was an outrage and would very much appreciate any input you can give."

"The committee's met already?" I asked. "That was fast work."

"No, we haven't met yet. Not officially. But I know I can speak for the rest of the committee on this."

"But is poisoning pigeons something for the Townscape Committee to address?"

"Yes. When dead pigeons become a part of our landscape, they are definitely something the committee should address. Douglas Everett has taken things into his own hands once too often. We will find out how he perpetrated this outrage and he will be stopped."

She glanced at her watch and flicked her eyes back to me. "I assume you thought you were being funny by telling Doug to call me, Margaret. Well, we'll see who has the last laugh. I'm due to meet him at the Historical Society in a few minutes. Mr. Mashburn, it's been a pleasure. I'm sure we'll run into each other again and you can tell me your pigeon theory then."

With that she marched out the door, clearly a woman on a mission. Gene stared after her open-mouthed.

"Isn't she great?" I asked.

He turned his open-mouthed stare on me.

"I'll probably end up strangling her someday, but you've got to admit she's got style. Can't you picture her practicing speeches like that in front of a mirror?"

He appeared to be trying, with mixed results. "Tell me something," he finally said, "if I handed you a pecan right now and you ate it, would you feel like a cannibal?"

"What? Why?"

"Because I think maybe you're nuts." He looked pained to be making such a bald diagnosis in a semi-public place. "Almost certainly your sister is, anyway. What, uh, what exactly do you think she's planning to do?"

The poor guy seemed genuinely concerned and not a little shaken up over his first encounter with Bitsy. And to think he'd only stopped by out of kindness to sow the seeds of serenity. Look what we'd reduced him to.

It was at this point that my duty became clear. I owed it to myself and to this man who'd only been trying to help.

"You know what?" I said, planting my hands on my hips and raising my head to look the whole world straight in the eye, "I'm not even going to try to guess what she's planning to do."

"Oh." He looked more hopeful. "Those sound like wise words."

"Damn right and that's my new mission in life: 'Never assume anything as far as Bitsy is concerned.' And just for kicks I'll throw in this as a footnote: 'Always get the facts.' "

"Very proactive."

"Well, she was casting aspersions this morning on my community involvement."

"You're not going to run out and join the Townscape Committee or anything, are you?"

"Oh, god, no. But, and it pains me to admit this, Bitsy's right. How could it hurt to pay more attention to what's going on around town?"

And they say there are no stupid questions.

CHAPTER 5

Eunice, one half of my part-time bookselling staff, arrived shortly after one. She works weekends and two afternoons and isn't the shrunken, ninety-year-old dear her name suggests. She's a six foot, tattooed twenty-five-year-old who has dropped out of school while she gathers her thoughts. She has the three Rs down. That is she reads, she's reliable, and she's got retail experience. But she's also restless and I don't expect she'll stay much past next spring.

"You going to the bank or me?" she asked by way of greeting.

"I think I'll go. Are you okay?"

She already had her hand out for the bank bag but recovered smoothly, sticking her hand in her low slung hip pocket and shrugging her shoulder. "Yeah." She yawned. "Late night, early morning, and not much sleep in between. Archie kept me up. But I

47

can cope. See?" She pulled a half smile from somewhere and added a few lumens of bright interest to her eyes. "Hi, anything I can help you find? We have a special today on dead white guys in the biography section."

I laughed. Archie is her teenaged cat. The way she talks about him some people think he's a live-in boyfriend. She and Archie look as though they're related, having the same tawny hair and rangy grace. He's developed a late night fetish for pouncing on her toes.

"Good enough. Say, Eunice, do you belong to any clubs or organizations?"

"You mean, like, groups? I belong to some online groups, yeah."

"Anything local? Young Citizens Involved in Something-or-other?"

She draped herself over the counter and yawned again. "Who's got time? Actually, I've thought a lot about joining a monastery, but I don't suppose one of those really fits the definition of a club or organization."

"I guess not. Or local. There aren't any monasteries around here, are there?"

"I'm thinking of Minnesota."

"Hm, well, keep me posted. In the meantime, new books are in and you can start shelving. I'll be back in a few, if anyone's looking for me."

Waking my fifteen-year-old Toyota from its dreams of retirement in a sun drenched desert junkyard occasionally requires patience. Today it coughed a few times, sounding like Archie's great grandmother hacking up a hairball. We recovered, though, and headed out.

Up until three years ago, running to the bank meant a brisk walk down Main Street. Then my bank uprooted and moved to the slowly spreading outskirts of town. It's only a short drive away, but its defection from downtown is a source of minor irritation. Loyalty to Nancy Umphrey, a good bank manager and friend, keeps me from transferring my accounts to the rival bank still on Main. But over the past year I've fallen into the habit of letting Eunice make the deposits.

The new bank is up on the four-lane, opposite Holston Heritage Antiques. Holston Heritage Antiques, written in ornate script on a faux colonial pediment, is a highfaluting name for a flea market housed in a cavernous metal building. The building and its acre of parking stand on more level ground than naturally occurs in east Tennessee. A couple of small hills and the hollow between gave their lives to provide it. Another lovely wooded knoll was shaved flat for the bank. Standing at the near edge of the bank's parking lot, facing travelers wending their way into town, is a marquee, massively framed in slabs of limestone, with the town's catchy new slogan "Welcome to Stonewall. We're sure glad you're here."

Nancy Umphrey is somewhere in her late fifties and dresses the way I might if I hadn't taken up the book habit. The difference is, she makes heels and nifty little jackets look fun and comfortable. She looked up from watering a pot of rosemary when I walked in the bank. The rosemary, resplendent on a walnut sideboard, was enormous. The posh sideboard had clearly never played with the waifs across the street at the flea market. "Margaret! It's been ages. Here, smell this."

I leaned close, closed my eyes, and inhaled. "Mmmmm. I could live in that smell."

"They were Mother's, and I don't have room for them at home."

"They look good here. Even the loan brochures look more inviting."

"Speaking of which, when are you going to let me arrange a car loan so we can bury that heap?" she asked, tsking out the window.

"That baby purrs like a new kitten, Nancy."

"You're hopeless," she laughed. "Come on in my office, though. Something I want to tell you."

She led the way past the tellers and down a wide, carpeted hall. Former bank officers gazed from portraits hanging at intervals along both walls. Their sober eyes followed us to the door of Nancy's corner office. Nancy closed the door behind us and crossed to her desk. Instead of sitting down, though, she tucked the chair in and stood with her back to me, looking out the window across a rumpled cow pasture and beyond the fringe of woods to the folds of our mountains. Each receding ridge shaded to a deeper green until the furthest were lost in purple and then black. Moving the bank out of downtown had probably been worth it for this view, alone. Nancy turned around with a grin on her face.

"I'm retiring."

"Nancy . . ."

"And I can hardly wait I am so excited. I'm moving to Santa Fe. I haven't formally resigned, yet, and haven't told the staff, so please don't breathe a word."

"Holy cow." I sat down. "Isn't this kind of sudden? When will it be official?"

"End of next week. I've been going back and forth in my mind for some time. When

51

Mother died I thought I'd be devastated, but it turns out I feel liberated. I need to tie up some details before I make it official, but it's been bubbling up inside me for days and when I saw you drive up in that wonderful, horrible car of yours I knew you were the right person to tell before I explode."

"Mum Margaret, that's me. Woman of zipped lips. But I had no idea. All the way to Santa Fe? Knoxville's not far enough west for you?"

"Remember that walking tour I did out there two years ago? I absolutely fell in love with the landscape, the colors, the light, the space, the people, the art. Everything. East Tennessee mountains brood. Have you ever noticed that? I've felt claustrophobic ever since."

"Wow, well, congratulations. That's wonderful. But I'm sad. Who'll I eat lunch with, now?"

"Plenty of people."

The notion of eating lunch with Gene Mashburn flitted through my head. "Could be. Huh."

We parted on promises to grab a bite soon. I left her staring out the window, bouncing on her toes, humming something that sounded like "Home on the Range." I made my deposit, a bit dazed by the news, then brushed my hand over the rosemary for another whiff before leaving.

Nancy felt liberated and I was feeling prematurely bereft. I sucked in a lungful of *eau de diesel* from a passing semi, coughed, and glared after the offending truck as it belched its way up the short rise out of town. And it hit me. Not the truck, but the realization I was liberated, too. When Nancy went west, I could transfer my accounts to the bank on the courthouse square guilt-free.

As that small consolation cheered me, a faded red pickup crested the rise. Ray Jenkins, former mayor of Stonewall, tooted his horn and waved. I waved back. But something went wrong. Ray's truck seemed to hesitate, then it veered off the road. Ray's eyes goggled. He picked up speed. I leapt aside and Ray plowed straight into the stone-framed marquee.

CHAPTER 6

"Ray! Ray, are you okay?" I sounded like a cheerleader as I ran toward the truck. "Ray?"

Ray didn't answer, but with a groan and a shriek, the truck's sprung hood wrenched itself open. Steam spewed from the radiator. The engine had died on impact.

"Did that crazy old loon try to hit you?" someone shouted from across the parking lot.

"No. Call 911!" I yelled over my shoulder. I turned back to Ray.

"Ray, can you hear me?" His window was down and he didn't appear as crumpled as his truck. No blood I could see. Maybe he was in shock. "Ray? Mayor Jenkins?"

He turned toward my voice but his eyes didn't look focused.

"He okay?" a voice behind me asked, huffing as he ran. Several others joined me, including Nancy, who must have run across the lot in her heels.

"Ambulance is on the way," Nancy said. "Should we get him out? Is it going to explode or something?"

"He didn't hit it that hard," the puffer behind me said. "He hasn't driven over twenty-five since he turned ninety. Old truck is totaled, though. Ray, you old fool, what happened?" He kicked Ray's rear tire. The back bumper fell off.

I reached in the window and touched Ray on the shoulder. He looked as though he were trying to remember where he was going. When I gave his shoulder a little squeeze he startled and his eyes refocused.

"Well, hello Margaret Welch. I just saw you a minute ago. Some one of these days I'm going to write a book for you to sell. Now, what's all this?" He smiled at the anxious faces crowding around. "What's going on? Wait a second. There was something . . ." he broke off and searched the cab for whatever he'd remembered, finally noticing the hood blocking his view through the windshield. "What . . . Wait, I know . . ." Agitated, now, he fumbled with his seatbelt. "Why those sorry . . ."

"Take it easy, Ray," Nancy said. "Sit tight till the paramedics get here."

"You might've hit your head," I said.

"Had a stroke or something," the puffer added.

Sirens screamed up the hill from town, but Ray wasn't listening to them or our helpful chorus. He got the door open, pushing aside hands reaching to steady him.

"Nothing wrong with me," he said as the paramedics arrived and tried to take control. "Ain't nothing wrong with me, I tell you, but look at that!"

He shoved around to the front of his truck and we looked where he pointed. Someone had altered the slogan on the marquee. Instead of welcoming the world to Stonewall, it now said in loopy, congratulatory green paint "Well done, Stone Sprawl."

CHAPTER 7

"Hooligans!" Ray howled. Then he had a coughing fit and succumbed to the paramedic's ministrations.

By then the police and a fire truck had also arrived. The fire truck might have been overkill, but they hosed down the pickup and the area, anyway. Aside from its altered message, the stone-solid marquee was undamaged. Ray's truck, on the other hand, was a goner. When Ray realized that, he started howling again. The paramedics, impressed by his agility and lung power, eventually stowed their gear and left. I stuck around long enough to see I wasn't needed to answer any questions and returned to the bookstore, wondering how Nancy could think of leaving such an exciting place.

And that reminded me of my earlier question. How could it hurt to pay more attention to what goes on around town? A better question might be how I planned to accomplish that, short of being in the right place when it's time to leap clear of a berserk pickup truck. Not that I'm isolationist by nature, but I don't have much of a life away from the store. Keeping my business afloat pretty much ties me down, unlike Bitsy who flits from project to cause to meeting. She "flits," but only in the sense of happy, free movement. She is otherwise perfectly serious about her involvements, having embraced the life of a volunteer and committeewoman from the day she married Rodney twenty-five years ago and quit teaching seventh grade math. She thrives on organizational minutiae and motions seconded. But then Bitsy has always been more of a doer than I have. I like to think of myself as the more contemplative sister.

"Margaret, dear, you're daydreaming again."

I brought the bookstore back into focus and hoped I was smiling pleasantly at Cousin Leona. An unnecessary glance at the clock assured me she was punctual as ever. She totters over from next door most afternoons shortly after Eunice leaves, when business is winding down for the day. "I was meditating on the benefits of community involvement, Cousin Leona."

"You were about to fall asleep. That's your

trouble, Margaret. Too much wool gathering. You should get out and exercise more. Dancing, maybe. With Gene Mashburn."

Leona has the innocent wrinkles of the eighty-five-year-old retired spinster schoolteacher she is. But if you look closely, you can see the lascivious smirk that adds sparkle to her eyes when she says things like that. She is forever trying to fix me up with likely single men, most of them being pretty unlikely.

"He somehow doesn't strike me as a dancer, Cousin Leona."

"The Texas two-step."

"Hm?"

"His favorite dance, dear. He told me this morning when we were having coffee together."

"Oh. Right. Well, I did a bit of the Tennessee two-step earlier this afternoon." And I told her about Ray and his runaway truck.

"Hmph. I'm glad no one was hurt," she said. "They'll probably take his license away from him."

"I'd like to see them try. Now, would you like a cup of tea?"

"Oh, no, I don't think so, dear."

This is our usual routine. "I've got some made, won't take a second to pour you a cup."

"That would be nice, then. I'll sit over here where I won't be in your way."

She settled into one of the rockers I keep along with a few over-stuffed chairs tucked here and there. The rockers tend to squeak and the old blue slipcovers are worn on the armchairs but they give the place a lived-in look and a feeling the megachains can't quite conjure. One man comes in every Saturday and regularly falls asleep in the corner chair under the window with Gibbon's *History of the Decline and Fall of the Roman Empire.* At the rate he's sleepwalking through it he'll be a customer for another dozen years.

"So, what's this about community involvement?" Leona asked, after taking a sip from the mug I handed her.

"I don't know if involvement is the right word."

"And that's your trouble, Margaret. Afraid to get involved. Lack of commitment." Cousin Leona has a way of sounding like Bitsy sometimes, or maybe it's vice versa, but there is one important difference. Leona doesn't expect to change the world with her pronouncements and then take the inevitable lack of results as a personal insult. She just hasn't quite lost the schoolmarm habit of straightening spines and rapping the occasional knuckle. "So what has Bitsy got you talked into this time?"

"What makes you think she's talked me into anything?" I asked, settling back on my stool behind the counter.

"Hmph."

"Cousin Leona, I do have a spine and a mind of my own." Leona merely looked at me. "Oh, all right. Bitsy thinks I don't take enough interest in what goes on in town." I shrugged. "I've been thinking she's right."

"Will wonders never cease. Though I don't suppose you let her know you think she's right."

It wasn't really a question so I didn't bother to answer. She was apparently content to mull unceasing wonders and sip her tea while I waited on customers.

Late afternoon sunshine streamed in through the front windows and parents trickled in through the door looking for the books their children should have read and had in class yesterday. This week it was copies of *A Separate Peace,* which they variously asked for as "One Piece," "A Segregated Peace," and "A Little Separate Prince."

"Bless their hearts," Leona said during a lull. "Could they possibly tangle that title any further?"

"Oh, let me count the ways."

"What's the most garbled title you've ever deciphered?"

"Hm, let's see. Oh, yeah, a classic. A parent came in with a summer reading list, fairly gnashing his teeth and railing at the poor library, because they didn't have any books by the author Evan Froman."

"And you did?" she asked.

"Me? No. I'd be surprised if anyone did. But I did have a copy of a book by Edith Wharton."

Leona's brow creased in mild pain. "*Ethan Frome*. Bless their hearts. You'd make a good detective, Margaret."

"In my own limited way."

"I'm serious, dear. You're analytical. You have the mind of a puzzle solver and isn't that what a detective is?"

"I haven't a clue."

"And that's your trouble, Margaret. Rather than accept a sincere compliment you make a joke. You should take some things more seriously."

"Been talking to Bitsy?" She didn't answer because I hadn't asked it out loud. She would only have hmphed at me. And besides, I've never really wanted to know how often the two of them casually discuss my many failings, some of which I'm even happy to admit to.

So we sipped our tea, smiling somewhat insincerely at each other. I waited on the few last-minute customers. Leona flipped through the new issue of *The Skeptic*. She was still engrossed in it when I locked the front door behind the last straggler who'd been happy to find a copy of "A Celibate Piece."

Leona sighed and levered herself out of the rocking chair. "I always feel refreshed after reading that magazine," she said, tucking it back with the others in the rack. "Skepticism can be a healthy thing, don't you think, dear?"

"I don't know about that."

"Oh, stop it, Margaret. Sometimes I think you're very wicked."

"Speaking of wickedness and skepticism, what do you think of the pigeon poisoning? Do you think it was selfishly deliberate or more like some cockeyed community service project, or . . . ?"

"Or maybe a mistake? No, dear. I very much hate to say it, but I think it was deliberate. And I'd be surprised if the police agree with Ray Jenkins about the welcome sign being defaced by high school hooligans."

"Why not?"

"It's one more instance, isn't it?"

"Instance of what?"

"Vandalism, pure and simple," she said.

"One more instance? What do you mean? What else has been going on?"

"Oh, a dumpster behind one of the businesses downtown was filled with manure. And then there was that crosswalk in front of the veterinarian's new office, though I rather liked that."

"Depending on whose dumpster it was, I kind of like that, too. But what crosswalk are you talking about?" I tried picturing Dr. Hoff's new office, part of the highway sprawl on the other end of town from the bank. Between being petless these days and trying to do most of my shopping downtown in an effort at small business solidarity, I probably haven't been past his new building more than a couple of times. But I couldn't picture a crosswalk out there on the four lane. "What crosswalk? And what happened to it?" I asked.

"That's just it, there wasn't one until someone went out in the middle of the night and made one. With paint. It was a lovely shade of green."

"A homemade crosswalk?"

"A guerrilla crosswalk." One of Leona's rare jokes. Dr. Hoff started out as a zoo vet.

"Oh, that is good. Yeah, I like that, one, too. But neither of those things, or the welcome sign, is in the same league as killing several hundred pigeons."

"They are vandalism all the same, Margaret. The intention might not have been for someone to go gaga and run off the road, but the vandals certainly were looking for some kind of reaction. Ray might have been very badly hurt. And then the attack on Hattie McKinney's garden was an out and out crime."

Cousin Leona can be very fierce and judging from the snap in her eyes now, dire consequences for garden vandals were playing out in her mind. Absently, she picked a pencil up from the counter and started slapping it in her palm as though it were the sturdiest of twelve inch rulers and she was waiting for the villain to drag his knuckles forward for a good whacking.

"Hattie McKinney's garden," I said hoping to bring her back to the here and now. "Okay, I'll bite. What happened to Hattie's garden?" I pictured decapitated garden gnomes and gutted plaster deer.

But Leona was rigid with suppressed emotion. "Someone used weed killer on the flower beds and then wrote something across the lawn with it. The entire garden,

65

Margaret. Harriet's been working on that garden for fifty years. Some of the plants were cuttings from her mother's garden. It is an almost total loss."

"Oh my gosh. Leona, that's horrible. That's beyond horrible. It's completely sick. How's poor Harriet?"

"I think it about killed her."

"Geez, I can imagine. So, um, what was written on the lawn?"

"Harriet wouldn't tell me."

"But you've found out, since, haven't you?" I could tell from the pink burning in her cheeks that she had. "What did it say?"

"Words I have never in my life uttered and will not now." She looked at the pencil still in her hand and put it down. "I won't write them out, either."

"That's all right, Cousin Leona, I get the idea. Why didn't you tell me about this before?"

"Because it was too monstrous."

"Why don't you sit down?"

"I'm fine."

I went about settling my cash register as quietly as I could, glancing over at her from time to time. I didn't think she had high blood pressure or anything, but she was obviously suffering on her old friend's behalf and I hadn't seen her so riled up in a

66

long time.

"I wonder if I might ask you a favor, dear," she finally said. Her breathing was calming and her color was better.

"Of course."

"The Garden Club is holding a dinner for Harriet tomorrow night at the Bank Tavern and you know how I hate to walk alone or drive at night these days . . ."

"Really?" News to me, though welcome. She's getting scary after dark.

"Don't interrupt, Margaret. I was wondering if you would mind giving me a ride there and back afterwards."

"Sure, I'd be happy to take you. But isn't Bitsy going?"

"Yes, but she's in charge of something or other and I don't like to bother her. Quarter of seven, then? I'll come over here."

"I can come get you."

"No, that's all right, dear. You just be ready at a quarter to seven."

Sometime I wish she'd just warn me not to be such putty in her hands and be done with it.

CHAPTER 8

That evening a frosty Heineken and a crisp new Carl Hiaasen tempted me to curl up on the sofa, ignoring pigeons, pickups, and vandalized gardens. The beer and the book would have won, too, except, annoyingly enough, for my redefined mission in life. Why hadn't it developed along lines more suitable to lounging in my pajamas after a long day? Instead it was kicking me in my conscience.

"Always get the facts," I'd said. Sure. How? Images of the five acts of vandalism circled each other warily in my head threatening a sleepless night. How were they connected? Were they connected? Was there a band of eco-vandals operating in town? Why? And why should I care?

Those thoughts and a few others entertained me as I waited out on the front stoop in the cooling evening air. I'd surprised myself by calling Bitsy and asking her if she wanted to go for a walk.

"You, Margaret?" she'd asked. "Why?"

"It's a nice evening. People take walks on nice evenings."

"When was the last time you took a walk?"

"I'm taking your advice to heart, Bitsy. You're right, I should take more of an interest in things. I thought taking a walk might be a way to sort of, I don't know, reconnect with the old neighborhood."

There was a grinding noise in my ear and I wondered if it were the wheels in her mind turning that thought over. Then I realized she was crunching ice cubes.

"Speaking of taking an interest in things, did Doug happen to tell you why he wanted to see that book?" She sounded calm enough, so maybe there weren't any fireworks when they met up at the Historical Society this afternoon.

"No."

"Didn't you ask him?"

"No."

"Why not?"

"Book buyer confidentiality, Bitsy."

"You're actually saying that with a straight face?"

"It's something I believe in."

"Oh for Pete's sake." She crunched more ice.

"Was it what he was looking for, do you think?"

"Oh, fine, now you show interest," she sniffed. "I don't know. I found it for him, stepped out of the room for five minutes to talk to Betty Grundy and when I went back, he was already gone."

"So after all the work I went to, arranging it so you could tackle him with your questions, so you could call him out for pistols at dawn, he managed to slip through your fingers?"

"Don't get carried away, Margaret. And don't worry either. I'll catch up to him and believe you me, he'll know it when I do."

"Don't you get carried away, Bitsy."

"Hmph." She took another swallow of whatever she was drinking. "How about I pop by in, say, fifteen minutes? The walk, remember?"

"I'll be waiting out front."

And so I was. From my front steps, if I look to the right, I can follow the sidewalk as it trips over the roots of a few enormous oaks and a line of silver maples that have seen better days, past some of the oldest houses and on downtown. There's a bit of a rise and then a dip so I can't see the courthouse, but it sits in the middle of downtown, offering a couple of benches under an ancient willow tree for anyone with the leisure to sit and watch whatever goes on. Mostly that's lawyers and their clients coming and going and people renewing their car tags, or pigeons flapping to their deaths, that kind of thing.

The willow tree is large enough and old enough to worry the town council about liability in case it comes crashing down during the next wind or ice storm. According to legend the tree was grown from a cutting taken from a willow planted by Napoleon. In certain circles that story isn't open for debate. Once a new member of the Historical Society tried tracing the willow's family tree, but either she gave up or her findings were hushed up. She left the Historical Society and joined the local chapter of the Sierra Club.

Looking to the left, the sidewalk passes Leona's house and continues on toward the elementary school where she taught fifth grade for fifty years. The school is boarded up now and looks lonely. A new school sprouted up somewhere between two of the classier subdivisions on the southern edge of town.

I haven't asked Leona how she feels about her school left derelict like that. She's seen a lot of change over the years, most of it probably inevitable and some of it completely regrettable. I was in danger of waxing maudlin about the shifting landscape around us and the limits of personal tolerance to change when Bitsy showed up. Saved by the belle.

Bitsy knows how to dress cute. She was wearing a pink sweat suit and dainty white shoes. Bitsy calls them tennies. I would call them gym shoes or sneakers but, then, I wouldn't be wearing them in the first place. Being on my feet much of the day, I find that shoes from the Nurse Ratchet Collection of Footwear make more sense. They're not unattractive, just more robust than dainty. Great for standing all day, great for walking. They also go with any combination of blue jeans and T-shirts I throw at them. As much as Bitsy and I look like sisters, and aside from my more comfortable build, no one ever mistakes us one for the other.

"Great, let's go," I said as Bitsy hopped out of her car.

"You're going like that?"

"I thought you wanted to walk around the old neighborhood," Bitsy said, as I took the lead and headed toward the east side of town. "I thought you wanted to 'reconnect.' "

"And then I decided why think small? You said it yourself, it's the whole town I need to take more interest in. But I've got to start somewhere, so I flipped a coin and the east side won. I figure I'll work my way around to the other neighborhoods in the days and weeks to come, probably going clockwise because we're in the Northern Hemisphere." I looked at her out of the corner of my eye to see how that was going down. Pretty well, apparently. Bitsy likes a well thought out plan of attack.

She also likes to walk at a pretty fair clip. Things were rosy between us for the time being, though, so rather than complain I stopped somewhere in each block to make appreciative comments about a roof line or window shape or a cat surveying its yard. Not to be outdone, she started pointing out flowers and gardens and foundation plantings she admired and in no time at all we were moving along at a more reasonable pace.

"It's different on foot, isn't it, Margaret? Funny how you lose track of the details when all you do is drive by."

"Drive-by-living. You'd think we evolved with radial tires instead of feet." A yellow cat sauntered down a front walk to greet us.

73

It accepted an ear rub then returned to its porch. "How long's it been since you walked around our old neighborhood?" I asked.

"Gosh, I can't remember the last time. I was looking forward to that tonight."

"Well, heck, let's forget that clockwise malarkey and do the old neighborhood tomorrow night."

"Why not now?"

I shrugged. "As long as we're here, we might as well keep going. Gosh, look at the size of that magnolia. Tomorrow will be soon enough for a tour of memory lane, don't you think?"

"Sure, that'll be great. Oh, wait, no. The Garden Club . . ."

"Whoops, I almost forgot."

"Forgot what?"

"The Garden Club dinner. I'm giving Leona a lift. She says she doesn't like driving or walking alone after dark these days."

Bitsy stopped short. "Talk about malarkey. What's she up to?"

"Who knows?"

I'd continued on and she had to skip to catch up. The mass of black-eyed Susans in the next yard was lost on her. From the vacant look in her eyes, she'd slipped into some sort of fugue state, probably trying to make sense of the mystifying machinations of Leona's aging mind. I would have told her it wasn't worth the effort but instead took the opportunity to steer us around the next corner onto Monticello Avenue. This is a street I've heard described as one where the big possums trot.

"You know, she was pretty upset this afternoon," I threw over my shoulder to Bitsy. Her brow was furrowed, her mind still at work. "She said something about Hettie Wainthrop's garden."

"What?" Bitsy spared a moment from her cogitating to shoot me a look of incomprehension.

"Oh, no, not Hettie Wainthrop. Where's my head? Hettie Wainthrop is a character in one of those British mysteries on TV. Hattie. It was Hattie somebody's garden."

"Margaret," Bitsy screeched us to a halt, figuratively and literally. "Don't tell me you haven't heard about Hattie McKinney's garden?"

She grabbed hold of my arm, and in case my ears weren't adequately detecting how appalled she was, she telegraphed it in a pulsing death grip. She took off up the street, dragging me with her. Half way down the block she stopped and I yanked my arm free.

"For heaven's sake, Bitsy, I'll have bruises

for weeks. What's gotten into you?" She didn't answer, just stood, arm extended and finger pointing. I turned to look.

Leona's description of the vandalism hadn't gone far enough. Her rigid-with-anger reaction did more justice to the reality of it. But standing there with Bitsy on that soft evening, on that graceful, sleepy street plucked right from the pages of *House Beautiful,* I found the viciousness of the attack unbelievable. For Hattie, it must have been unbearable.

I could smell it, whatever chemicals they'd used, anyway. And maybe it was the power of suggestion, but the scent of tortured and dying flowers and bushes seemed to hang in the air, too. I could almost taste it. The whole scene made me feel like I should go home and take a decontaminating shower and probably burn my clothes. I certainly didn't want to touch any of it.

The lawn was gouged and dug up in a wide area. Nothing remained of whatever message had been written.

"When did this happen, Bitsy?"

"Over the weekend. While Harriet and Ed were away. I think Harriet came close to having a stroke when she saw it."

"But who would do this? This wasn't just dumb kids, was it? And why would anyone do it?" She shook her head. "What did it say on the lawn?" She shook her head again then turned to look at me. Something was going on again behind her unblinking eyes.

"You did know about this," she said.

"I told you, Leona was talking about it this afternoon. Frankly, I'm surprised you let her scoop you with the news. But, wow, now I can see why she was so upset. This is like something out of a nightmare collaboration between Salvador Dali and Hieronymus Bosch. Ugh." I felt like a gawker at the scene of an accident or someone who couldn't tear her eyes away from the smoldering ashes of a house fire.

Bitsy only had eyes for me, but I ignored her and instead wondered what weed killer the vandals could have used to melt down the garden so thoroughly and efficiently.

"Have you got a quarter I can borrow?" she asked.

"Hm?" Maybe they used something like bleach. Would that work?

"I said, have you got any change?"

"Sorry, all I've got is my keys and a tissue."

"You skunk," she said.

"I beg your pardon?"

"Reconnecting, my foot. Working your way around the neighborhoods in a clockwise direction because we're in the Northern Hemisphere. Talk about malarkey. You didn't flip any coin. You haven't even got one in your pocket to flip. You planned on coming here all along. Why didn't you just say you wanted to come over here? I'll tell you why. Because you're a weasel."

"Actually, I was trying more for ferret." That had the double virtue of quelling her spate and being the truth. Bitsy crossed her arms. The tilt of her head invited me to continue; the lightning smoldering in her eyes cautioned me to watch my step. "I was sort of combining your advice with something Leona said this afternoon. She said I'd make a good detective so I was trying to be. . . ."

"Sneaky?"

"I wouldn't call it that."

"I would. Margaret, why didn't you just ask me?"

Telling Bitsy that I was no longer assuming anything as far as she was concerned, including that she would tell me the truth, didn't strike me as the best idea. This time I went for weasel and succeeded.

"I wanted to see the damage for myself and I wanted to see your candid reaction to it." I raised my eyebrows and smiled, a look I've used on her before and like to think of as disarming.

She weighed the answer and the look and grudgingly found them adequate. "I suppose at least you are taking an interest. But I still say you're a rat."

"Are weasels rodents?"

"How should I know?" she asked. "Why?"

"Weasel, ferret, rat. At least I'd be keeping it all in one family."

"You're such a nut."

"You're the second person today who's said that, and you know comments like that could begin to shake a person's self esteem. If I hear it again, I might start believing it."

"Heaven forbid. Who was the first one?"

"It was . . ." By now we were facing each other rather than the McKinney's yard, the better to heckle each other. And in one of those moments that lend coincidence more meaning than it deserves, Gene Mashburn hove into view riding a bicycle down the middle of Monticello Avenue. ". . . Gene Mashburn."

"Evening ladies." Catching sight of us, he saluted with one hand and nearly ran into the curb on the opposite side of the street as he overcompensated and pulled the handlebars too far aport.

It was hard to tell whether he was an incompetent cyclist or too encumbered by the gas can tucked under his left arm. He managed a tight turn at the last minute and peddled across the street to stop in front of us.

"Fancy almost running over you two. Small world. Itsy bitsy world. Bitsy." He hiccuped. "Why, Bitsy, that's you, isn't it? And is this your garden?" A sweeping gesture of his arm almost carried him off the bike. "It's lovely. Suits you. Can't say I like it much myself because I tend to like 'em greener." He beamed and wobbled off down the middle of the street. We gazed after him, wincing when he bounced through a pothole.

"What a strange person," Bitsy said.

"If he's not careful he'll get a ticket for operating a bicycle under the influence."

"You think he was drunk?" she asked. "I thought maybe he was light-headed. Fumes from that gas can or something."

"Oh, I think if we'd been standing closer we'd have caught a few other fumes. But you're right. He's not your run-of-the-mill Stonewallian."

"Leona seems to have taken an interest in him. What do you know about him?"

"He does the Texas two-step." Bitsy looked at me as though maybe I, too, was strange. "It's some kind of dance. Leona told me.

80

She thinks the two of us should go out together. Dancing."

"She's getting goofier than I thought," she sniffed.

"Oh, I don't know, Bitsy. He seemed okay earlier. We should give him the benefit of the doubt, at least."

"Mm. How long has he been in town?"

"No idea. Long enough to meet Doug Everett. But then Doug seems to know everybody. Why?"

She turned on a 100-watt smirk. "I think I'll take a leaf out of your bookstore and do a little ferreting myself."

CHAPTER 9

" 'Lo, Margaret."

"Hi, George."

George always 'los me and I always hi
him. It doesn't help. George Buckles travels
under a perpetual personal rain cloud. A
real live Eeyore. He comes into the bookstore to look for used copies of works by
depressing philosophers, but I think he's
happier when he doesn't find what he's
looking for. The thrill of disappointment
after a fruitless search rubs him right
somehow. He's a police sergeant, the one
they call Officer Friendly and send around
to talk to all the school kids.

"What's new on the beat, George?"

"Do you really care?"

"Yes, I do, George. In fact, I've got a question for you."

George had moped his way up to the
counter but now backed off, hands raised
to ward me off, a stricken look on his sweet,

square face.

"Oh, no, Margaret. You know I'll buy books from you, but don't ask me to . . ."

"Not that, George, I promise. Now come on over here. I won't ask you to do that ever again. I've told you that. How many times do I have to say I'm sorry?"

"Yeah, well, I have you to thank for this." He unbuttoned his uniform shirt and pulled it open.

"Oh, dear, George. I had no idea. I am so sorry. Do you have to wear it?"

"Hell yes, I have to wear it. You don't know what it's like."

"How's Sergeant Lambert getting on?" I asked in a properly subdued voice.

"Depressed. What do you expect?" He re-buttoned his uniform shirt and plodded off into the next room to rummage and rumi-nate on people who'd done him and his partner wrong. Me being the current num-ber one suspect.

George, in addition to being Officer Friendly, is the town's canine officer. Ser-geant Lambert is his canine partner. They make a cute couple, their matching hangdog expressions adding a lot to the effect. George has been a bit hangdoggier, though, since doing me a favor a few months ago.

The trouble started when I asked them to

be special guests at Saturday morning story hour. They've won awards for their team-work. And, Buckles being a good old name in town, what could be more appropriate than inviting George and Lambert to story hour when we read the Caldecott Medal-winning book *Officer Buckle and Gloria,* a charming picture book about another canine officer and his partner?

They were a hit. George wore his crisp blue uniform. Sergeant Lambert wore his no-nonsense red and black collar. George hid various small packages around the store and Lambert found every one of them. Lambert sat. He stayed. He growled. He lunged. He leapt back and forth over the front counter like a deer. He shook hands like an officer and a gentledog. George and Lambert both let the children hug them and then they sat on the floor while I read the book. They'll never live down their success.

Lambert, according to George, has lost his self-confidence and is suffering an identity crisis. Not only is he incapable of standing on his head or flashing cue cards like the glorious storybook canine, but everywhere he goes now he's addressed as "Gloria." Even by fellow officers. I would feel worse about it except that no one else has noticed a personality change in either of them. George has always been morose, and if his partner's doggy smile and lolling tongue are any indication, Lambert is as happy and feeling up to wuff as ever.

The latest repercussion, though, is what George flashed at me before moping off into the other room to hunt up a bit of nihilist bedtime reading. Luckily I'd already heard about it so I was able to commiserate solemnly when he unbuttoned his shirt. It would have hurt his feelings if I'd grinned.

The third graders at the new elementary school had a poster contest as part of an "Our Community" unit. The teacher was so tickled with the winning entry, a portrait of Officer George Buckles and his faithful partner, that she had it made into a T-shirt. The students all signed it and then presented it to their special buddies George and Gloria.

It's adorable. George hates it. And he'll wear it because he can't bear to disappoint the children. George Buckles will always be one of my heroes.

He feels like I set him and poor Lambert up but he keeps coming into the bookstore anyway. He says it's because he can't help himself, that it's part of being an existentialist or a nihilist.

There are two things I've known about

George since high school. He has always liked used books and he has always had a soft spot for me. He got married after I disappeared into my banking phase for those years in Chicago, but that fell apart the way police marriages often do. My coming home and buying the store reignited his spark for both me and books. The books I can help him with. For the rest, over the years and after teetering in one direction and then the other, we've come to a mostly easy understanding. He looks at me with his doggy brown eyes from time to time and I tell him I'm sorry. He buys a book or two and I wish love could be that simple.

He made his way back to the counter, a Sartre volume tucked under one arm.

"What was your question?" he asked. He didn't look any happier than when he'd come in. There wasn't any more spring to his step. But he did remember that I'd had a question for him so maybe he was pleased with his find.

"Oh, yeah. You know about Harriet McKinney's yard?"

He nodded. "Mom helped organize the dinner for her tonight at Bertie's."

"But as a policeman, George, what's your take on it? And these other things, like the pigeons and the welcome sign, and what else was it?"

"Exploding fish ponds?"

"I'm serious, George."

"So am I. Someone blew up Doug Everett's fish pond last night."

"Oh come on."

"Big fat goldfish blown sky high. Came down all over his yard. Some landed on that oversized Macho Honcho Fantasy Whatever-it-is he drives. You should have seen the cats and crows fighting over the scavenging rights." A smile played around the edges of his rain cloud.

"Retaliation for pigeons, do you think?" He shrugged and I realized I didn't want to explore that possibility any further with him, considering who might be responsible. Not that Bitsy has ever shown terrorist tendencies, but if I was following through in the true spirit of my new mission in life, how could I assume she wouldn't go off half-cocked, half-baked, half nuts and blow up Doug's fish? "So, George," I rushed to ask before he wondered why I'd begun to sweat, "then why aren't you and Sergeant Lambert out there with your fellow officers sniffing out clues?"

"Goats."

I'd never heard the word "goats" said in quite that way before. It sort of struggled out of the back of his throat, burdened with emotions not normally associated with goats. Maybe he hadn't said "goats." It's unlike George to be anything more vibrant than mildly depressed so maybe the situation with *Officer Buckle and Gloria* was worse than I thought. Maybe instead of "goats" he'd said something rude. In Swedish? I cocked an eyebrow at him.

"And a bull." He tossed Sartre down on the counter. That action alone told me how upset he was. George usually treats books like the children he's never had. "C'mon outside for a minute and I'll show you."

I could see Sergeant Lambert waiting stoically, as always, in the patrol car. A squirrel halfway up the maple George parked under was making faces and calling Lambert names. No British Guardsman ever ignored hecklers better.

"Lambert's a fine dog, George." I take every opportunity to tell him that. Part of my self-inflicted penance.

"The car, Margaret. Look at the car." He crossed his arms and looked everywhere but at the car. It must have physically pained him to be seen driving it in that condition. The hood was covered in dings and scratches. So was the roof. Gravel damage? Hail?

"What happened?" I asked.

"I told you, goats. They jumped up on the car. Three of them. Jesus, they can do a lot of damage with those little hooves."

"And the bull?"

"I was exaggerating about the bull. Oh, there was a bull, all right, but it turns out Lambert is a pretty good bull dog and we didn't have any real trouble there."

"Where?"

"Corner out there near the highway. There at Franklin and Walnut. Couple acres for sale. Got some trees, bit of a hollow. Guy was supposed to start clearing it and leveling this morning, make it more salable. Called 911 about seven. Someone got cute and put half a dozen goats, herd of cows and a bull out there. It's all fenced in. Guy with the bulldozer was afraid they'd attack him or something and I don't blame him. That billy was mean. And look what they did to my car."

"But who did all that?"

A volcanic red blossomed on George's cheeks, rapidly engulfing his ears and neck. He manfully held his breath in an effort to maintain decorum. When he finally exploded, I knew the words he uttered hadn't included "goats." And foreign though the words sounded on George Buckles's tongue, they weren't Swedish.

"Is that something like what it said on Harriet's lawn?" I asked after George had given himself a shake and walked me back inside.

"A lot of raw Anglo-Saxon, yeah, and some Elvira Gulch thrown in for good measure."

"Elvira Gulch?"

"Rude suggestions," he said, "followed by 'and your little dog, too.' "

"That's a lot of nastiness. Especially on one lawn."

"Big lawn."

"So what's going on in town, George? Who's behind all this and are all these things connected?"

"Why, what've you heard?"

"Nothing," I said. "That's just it. Nothing but rumors and innuendoes."

"Well, I don't think it's anything for you to worry about, Margaret. Couple of bored kids, some fool with a grudge, a full moon and high gas prices. Who knows what combination of things'll get people crazy? Tell you the truth, I'm surprised more of it doesn't go on."

The word according to Saint George of Perpetual Pessimism. He paid for his book, sighed heavily at nothing in particular and returned to his depressed dog and goat-ravaged patrol car.

I returned to straightening books on shelves and the sad thought that Fran, the other half of my part-time bookselling staff, was still out of town. Her widowed and increasingly fragile mother had broken her hip and Fran was doing her daughterly bit. She'd called this morning to say she'd be another day or two. Eunice was out of pocket, as well, having gone over the mountains to Asheville. Their absence wasn't a big problem because it's not difficult running the store solo on quiet days. But it can be lonely. Besides, Fran isn't just a good bookseller. She's also a wise friend who would listen to my questions and come up with a few of her own.

Questions like who would leave such a foul message burned into the McKinneys' lawn? Someone went to a lot of effort to so thoroughly wreck the yard and Harriet's prized garden. Was the message intended particularly for them? For both of them or just one of them? Did they even own a dog? I tried to think what I knew about Harriet or Ed. Not a lot. So how was I going to find out anything, tucked away here in the shop like an abandoned bookmark?

The Garden Club dinner. There was a

thought. After indulging Leona's latest eccentricity by escorting her to the Bank Tavern, I'd planned on sticking around anyway, indulging my fat tooth with one of Bertie's hamburgers and the best onion rings this side of Saturn. Maybe instead I should gussy myself up and crash the dinner in the private room. How hard could it be to subtly pump a bunch of gardeners for information?

"Good morning, Margaret." William DeAngelis had oozed in the door. "I'm looking for books of an explosive nature. Got anything that tells how to make bombs? Haha, got you! You should see your face. You don't get that question everyday, do you?"

William has the sort of personality most people outgrow. It's the kind that's barely forgivable in raw youth and annoying as hell in someone over forty. There are extenuating circumstances in his case, though. His mother, Eleanor, was the high school French teacher. Very dramatic, larger than life. She didn't so much teach French as swoop down on unsuspecting classes and inject it into their blood streams. William must be what happens when that's also used as a parenting technique. It doesn't help that he looks like everyone's idea of an undertaker — tall and pasty with lank black hair — and also happens to be one.

"I can get you a copy of *The Anarchist's Cookbook,* William."

He looked blank. "Are we on the same wave length here?"

"Bombs, yeah. Why?"

"Oh, of course, right. I get it. Hah, bloody, hah. You know, Margaret, just because I shocked you with my question, which happened by the way to be facetious, as in a joke, doesn't mean you have to try to get back at me in some juvenile tit for tat way and pretend I was looking for a French cookbook. As if. Like I'm going to spend my time hanging around in the kitchen whipping up a *bombe.* Now, what I really came here for is a copy of 'Silent Peace,' which I have to take over to the library because they insist Desiree lost theirs. So please tell me you have a copy, that I may go fling it in the face of that battle ax they call a public servant."

Desiree is William's daughter. Before she was born, a joke went around that a collection should be taken up in lieu of throwing a baby shower, with the money ear-marked for the psychotherapy the poor kid was going to end up needing. So far she hasn't needed the collection. Probably because

William's wife divorced him early on and won primary custody. It's anyone's guess why she didn't also take Desiree and move to the opposite end of the country.

I rang up a copy of *A Separate Peace* for him. "Would you like a bag for that, William?"

"Need you ask? In fact, why do you ask?"

"Not everyone wants one, William."

"The way I see it, Margaret, the purchase is not official without the bag. In fact, let me have an extra large bag. I'm feeling expansive today. Explosive, you might even say. By the way, did you appreciate the significance of my joke? You do know that Everett's fish folly blew sky high last night, don't you?"

I'd forgotten that on top of everything else, William is an inveterate gossip. If I wanted to get anything useful from the Garden Club, a little practice now in gleaning fact from fiction couldn't hurt. "I heard something about it but not much. What happened?"

"Ka-flooom! Fish fertilizer. That's what happened."

"But what was it? A prank?"

"A piscine prank, pray tell? Possibly, possibly."

This was getting nauseating. "Do they

have any idea who did it?"

"They, Margaret? They who did it know who did it. And they who think Everett is an ass wouldn't say if they did know who did it. Get it? Now we've got it," he held up his bag and shook it, "so we will say good-bye."

"Money first, please, William."

"Put it on my tab," he said, heading for the door.

"You know there aren't any tabs."

"Show a little charity, then, and start one because I seem to have blown all my cash. And watch that blood pressure, Margaret. We can't have you exploding, too." He let the door slam behind him.

A headache blossomed in the middle of my brain as the bell over the door jingled again.

"You look like you could use some coffee," a quiet voice said.

That should have been my line last night. Gene Mashburn stood just inside the door with two paper cups, steam rising from the blowholes in the middle of the lids.

"Why? Are my brains so obviously leaking out my ears?"

"Are you always suspicious of people's motives?" he asked.

"Part of my charm," I said. He continued

95

to stand just inside the door, apparently happy surveying the store with two cups of cooling coffee in his hands. "You know, I wouldn't mind drinking that while it's still hot."

"Oh, right." He came the rest of the way in and handed me one of the cups.

I pried the lid off, closed my eyes and inhaled deeply, feeling the soothing fingers of caffeine vapor already massaging ragged nerves.

"Rats," he muttered.

Rats? Was someone after rats now? What a lot of wildlife in my peaceful world all of a sudden. "Rats, goats, pigeons, fish, ferrets . . . ," I murmured. A glance at his face and I caged the rest of the litany. "Sorry, you were saying?"

"The whipped cream melted," he said. "And the sprinkles all went to the bottom."

"It was mocha?"

"Well, it still is, just without the whipped cream and the sprinkles."

"Well, rats. But if it makes you feel any better, I always let the whipped cream melt, anyway. That way I don't wait on customers with a white mustache. By the way, thank you. This is awfully nice of you. What happened, no date with Leona this morning?"

"Oh, sure." He'd wandered over to the

magazines and was leafing through a copy of *Cigar Aficionado.* "It was time for a break, though. And another cup certainly couldn't hurt after last night." I hoped David Letterman was a good listener because Gene was addressing these remarks to his picture in the magazine.

"Where was your car?"

"The gas gauge is broken and every once in a while I lose track of how many miles I've gone and end up hoofing it to the nearest gas station."

"Or wobbling as the case may be." A quirk pulled at his mouth and was gone. Hard to tell if it was the corner of a smile or a twinge of conscience. "Bitsy thought you were goofy on fumes from your gas can."

"Am I right in remembering I insulted her?" he asked.

"She just thinks you're strange, so join the club."

"You know what Groucho Marx said about joining clubs, don't you?"

"Oh, god, please. You're not going to turn out to be another Eeyore, are you? Quick, tell me, is your cup half empty or half full?"

He turned from the magazine rack with his professional assessment look in place again. Then he grinned. "On the other hand that might be an organization right up my alley. When I join, do I get a code book so I know what you're talking about?"

"Hell no."

He laughed and shook his head, put the magazine back in the rack. "See you later."

On the whole, that sounded encouraging. But before I could say goodbye, he was out the door. Always disappearing, this Gene Mashburn. What was his story?

CHAPTER 10

Dithering over my wardrobe that evening, wondering what a seasoned sleuth might wear for mingling at the Garden Club dinner, didn't take long. My wardrobe has three distinct strata. At the down-to-earth level is my collection of blue jeans and corduroys, fine for work-a-day bookselling, but not high tone enough for this affair. Then there is the lone high flyer, my small black, so called because it's small whenever I'm not. It's a stunning number but too dressy and probably smaller than usual these days. This left several pairs of stylish, yet unpretentious, tailored trousers and a few skirts. I decided on my favorite skirt, a mid-length, indigo blue swirly sort of thing. It's seen me through thick and thin, literally. It's comfortable and draws no particular attention to itself. Paired with a slightly darker indigo twin set, it was perfect for my detecting debut.

A glance in the mirror on the back of my closet door startled me. Thank god I didn't own a pair of saddle shoes. With those and a string of pearls I'd look like a middle-aged Nancy Drew. I slipped into a pair of dark brown, open-toed huaraches and left the pearls behind.

"My goodness, you look lovely, dear. I'm so glad. An excellent choice for dinner." Leona was in an unusually complimentary mood. She patted my arm and fairly beamed at me. That probably should have made me suspicious but didn't because, really, I need every encouragement I can get.

"Thank you, Leona. You look pretty spiffy yourself. Shall we go?"

She took my arm and we tripped lightly down the stairs. I started us around back toward the car. In vehicle years it must be about Leona's age but on the whole I'd say she's got more muscle.

"Ow." She pulled me up short with a yank on my elbow.

"Let's walk, dear. It's such a pleasant evening."

"I thought you were worried about the uneven sidewalks in the dark."

"It's not quite dark, yet. And besides, that's why I have you, dear. Come along, neither one of us wants to be late."

Neither one of us? My suspicious nature definitely gave a twitch that time. Except that Leona's a smart old bird. Obviously she'd guessed what I was up to and she was right. If I wanted to gather information, I didn't want to be late. If we got there soon enough it could be useful to plant a few seeds among the gardeners before we sat down to eat. Then afterwards I could see what thoughts had sprouted before we all said our final good nights.

She was right, too, about the pleasant evening. I was proud of myself for getting out two nights in a row, now, communing with my community. Stonewall isn't a bad little place. It's had its hiccups and setbacks, the decision to tear down the red brick Victorian train station to make a parking lot being notable among these. But the town survived and the new Historic Zoning Ordinance should curb future demolition-by-idiocy.

"So how many of the Garden Club's finest do you expect to turn out this evening?"

"Oh, all of them, dear," Leona said. "It's Hattie, you see."

"Good, that's certainly a tribute to her. I saw what's left of her garden last night." I felt a shudder pass through Leona. "Do you think it'll ever recover?"

"No. Not to its glory, not in Hattie's lifetime, anyway. But she has always been generous, sharing cuttings and bulbs and seeds. The lilac at the back of the house, dear, that was from Hattie and hers came from her mother. And that lovely deep purple St. Peter's Pence that blooms early in the spring out along the alley. That's Hattie's, too."

"So you can all return her favors and she can start over."

"If she has the energy." We were passing the old Turner place and Leona nodded toward it. "You've seen Ida's bearded irises? Hattie's. Most of the day lilies, too. There is probably some of Hattie and a lot of Hattie's mother in half the gardens of Stonewall. I think she'll find the energy somewhere. I hope so. Now, here we are and let me look at you again. Smile, Margaret. Not like that, that's perfectly ghastly. Hmph. Why I bother, I don't know. But you'll do. Come along."

I would do? My suspicious nature made a grab at my skirt hem. When it's that insistent, I've learned to listen. I hesitated as Leona stepped up to the restaurant door. "Ouch."

And so we entered Bertie's Bank Tavern, Leona with a smug grin on her old puss and her hand like a vice grip on my arm.

Bertie's is great. It's on the corner of Main and Maple so Bertie uses "MmMm" as her address. She's in the old First State Bank building and keeps her wine in the original vault. There's a table for two in there as well, very romantic, reservations only. But the vault is the only vestige of the original interior.

If you walk in the door off Main Street you find yourself in the main dining room. The happy clatter of cutlery on china mixes with scattered conversations and you're hit immediately with the life-giving aromas of strong black coffee, grilling hamburgers, thick bean soup, apple pie and onion rings.

The room is an ell, maybe thirty feet down one leg to the corner where you can duck into the kitchen and Bertie will yell at you to clear out, and another fifteen feet along the other leg. The ceiling is twenty feet high, pressed tin. The impression you get is of being in a wide hallway with dark wood booths back to back running down each side and around the corner. There's plenty of room to walk between the two rows of booths but not enough for a row of tables.

Open the door from Maple Street and you're in a different world. This is the tavern — dim, smoky, and smelling of beer and whiskey. The bar itself is a lovely, long, curved, wooden affair, polished for so many years that it glows. Any sunshine that manages to find its way in through the row of small windows high up near the ceiling looks pallid and insecure by the time it tries to cast light on that wonder of a bar. There's no TV and no pool table. There is a green canoe hanging over the door but no one remembers why. Dusky music is piped in from somewhere and it would take longer than I've ever spent in the tavern to locate the source. I don't think it's the kind of place where you drop a quarter in the slot to make your own selection, anyway.

A swing door connects the restaurant and the tavern. You can easily pass from one to the other, though most people don't take their children through the tavern. You can eat in either room but only beer and wine make it into the restaurant.

The boardroom upstairs was converted into a private dining room for large parties. That's where Leona and I were headed, me still attached to her iron claw and wondering what it is about me that makes my relatives think they can or need to manhandle me like this. She pulled up short at a booth half way down the long leg of the ell and I did some fancy footwork to avoid flattening her. Gene Mashburn stood up from the booth, smiling.

"Wow, you look great," he said.

"Of course she does," Leona said. "Didn't you believe me?"

He had the grace to look uncomfortable over this remarkable exchange. He even shuffled his feet and coughed into his hand, a couple of those gestures polite people make in an effort to cover social embarrassments. They had the interesting effect of making this whole situation look fishier than hell.

"Well," he said brightly, under the obvious delusion that he'd put things back on the right track, "perfect timing, too. It's almost seven fifteen."

Leona gave me a shove toward the booth. "As long as you're here, dear, why don't you two have dinner together?"

"I was planning to join you."

"Out of the question. Members only. That's your trouble, Margaret. If you were a member you would know these things." She disengaged her grip from my arm, shaking her head over my lack of attention to important details. "Let me go, now, dear. I don't want to be late."

She gave me one more shove toward the booth but didn't get any satisfaction because

I was ready for it this time and had braced myself. I crossed my arms and watched her disappear around the corner, tip tapping along in her little old lady sensible heels, perfectly happy with herself and her meddling.

"She has no conscience," I said.

"Sorry, I thought you knew."

"No. I've been bushwhacked." I looked toward the door wondering which I'd rather do, stalk out feeling self-righteous and still hungry, or stay, feeling manipulated but replete.

Garden Club members were trickling in. The booths were filling, too, as various members of their families followed them in, not willing to fend for themselves at home. George came in with his mother. Doug and his wife, Diane, arrived with Hattie and Ed McKinney. It was interesting to see that Hattie seemed to be showing more resilience than Ed, though I hadn't seen him in a while and maybe it was age getting the better of him. Some discussion developed between Diane and Doug, maybe over whether the two men should escort the women upstairs. Ed didn't look as though he wanted to let go of Hattie. Finally Hattie gave Ed a peck on the cheek and pulled away.

I was somewhat surprised to see Bertie's granddaughter, Claire, playing waitress for the evening. She usually handles the bar or whatever function is taking place in the boardroom. Claire is somewhere in her mid twenties and looks as though she should be on a runway. Not the kind with 747s. But apparently the restaurant business runs true in her blood. She came here from Asheville where, according to her doting grandmother, she made her mark in the fern bar world. Tonight she was stunning in an unpretentious white number that on anyone else would have looked like a waitress uniform.

"Hi, Margaret. Be right with you guys." She winked at Gene and went to give menus to the new arrivals.

Bitsy breezed in followed by Rodney, her husband. He kissed her and sat down with George. Catching sight of me, she gave me a bit of the old once over, then turned to say something to the two men in their booth. They, subtle souls that they are, immediately leaned out of the booth to stare.

"What's the festive occasion, Margaret?" she asked, advancing down the room. "The last time you broke out Old Faithful, there, was for Frances Ledford's funeral." At least she'd waited until she was a booth away before making this announcement.

"Thank you for noticing, Bitsy. Bye, now. Wouldn't want you to be late." I turned back toward the door and she flounced off.

I'd already admitted to myself that I thought this guy was attractive. So what was keeping me from plopping down and enjoying myself, other than I don't like being tricked by conniving cousins?

"Are you going to sit down?"

I glanced over my shoulder at him. Poor polite guy, he was still standing.

Just then Eleanor DeAngelis flapped in. Eleanor never needs to say a word when she makes an entrance. Her appearance does that for her. She is close to six feet tall and habitually wears black. Tonight she also wore her long black wool cape. Heads turned toward her and she nodded her way down the room.

"Margaret Welch, how wonderful to see you. You are joining us this evening, perhaps?"

"Hi, Mrs. DeAngelis. No, much as I would like to join you, it turns out I have other plans. Have you met Gene Mashburn? Gene, this is Mrs. Eleanor DeAngelis. Mrs. DeAngelis, Gene Mashburn."

She enveloped his hand in both of hers. "So charming to meet you. You are the architect, about whom I have been hearing so much, are you not? I think that is fascinating work. I hope we will be seeing more of you around town. *Bon appétit.*" She let go his hand with some reluctance and I saw him surreptitiously wipe it on his pant leg.

"Which do you suppose she meant, more architects around town or more of me?" he asked.

"You're an architect?"

"Are you going to sit down?"

We sat and I stared at him, probably with my mouth unbecomingly open. He gazed back.

"There, now, you see that look you're giving me?" I asked him. "Why do you do that if you're an architect? I thought you were some sort of mental health professional."

"That's insane," he said. "Are you disappointed?"

"More like relieved. Now I can relax."

"Is that why you've been so suspicious? You thought I've been making notes in a case file labeled 'Nuts I've Known'?"

I grinned and wondered if the devil ever creeps into my blue eyes the way it does his. "It's just that I've been getting dizzy looking over my shoulder for the men in white coats with the long net."

"Hm. Interesting. And architects don't

make you nervous?"

Claire appeared with a laden tray. "You were right, Hon," she said to Gene. She started unloading the tray and turned to me. "You know, I told him, I said, how can you be sure she won't get tied up somewhere, like, what if you had to stop and get gas or something but he said no she'll be here and be sure and bring the food out at seven fifteen. So here y'are. Enjoy." A constrained silence settled over the table at her departure.

"Nervous might not exactly be the word I would use," I said. "Would you like me to start making a list of the words I would use? No, I didn't think so. So, tell me, seeing as neither of you had the courtesy to tell me earlier, when did you and Leona cook up this ambush?"

He colored nicely. "I really did think you knew." And then a thought struck him, probably like a two-by-four between the eyes. "She's not entirely honest, is she?"

"Honest but not trustworthy. You should remember that and never leave your car keys where she can find them."

"I often leave them where I can't find them, but thanks for the warning. So, er, what made you finally decide to join me?"

"I'm still not sure I should have but I'm

conducting an experiment."

The same conniving cousin who lured me here must have whispered in his ear exactly what to order. Claire had brought two hamburgers on dark pumpernickel, two sweet teas, and the main focus of my attention, a steaming, golden loaf of Bank Tavern onion rings. Bertie's recipe should go down in whatever annals there are for classics of American cuisine. Freshly sliced onions are battered for each order and quickly fried. When they're done they come out in the shape of the fry baskets she uses. Every other time I'd eaten them they were perfection. But would their crunch be as crisp, each strand of onion be as savory, the smell waft as sweet . . .

"What's the experiment?" Gene asked.

I held up a finger to shush him, then deftly separated one of the smaller rings from the rest of the pack. It was still too hot so I juggled it back and forth for a minute. Over the years I've eaten these onion rings under all kinds of conditions — disappointment, elation, frustration, everyday run-of-the-mill camaraderie, boredom — and through everything they've stood the test of time. But as far as I could remember I'd never eaten them feeling this particular combination of irritation, humiliation, and the effrontery of being suckered into a date.

Judging the temperature optimum, I popped the ring in my mouth.

"Oh, mmm, that's all right then. Mm, mm, mm," I said, shaking my head. "That Bertie is a wonder. These are fabulous, as always. Would you like some?"

He turned out to be a multitasking kind of guy. Maybe that's typical of architects. Where as I would have been happy attacking the food first and saving the get-to-know-you type questions for later, he started right in on both.

"So tell me about the book business."

"You know, I'd be willing to bet you already know a bit about the book business, or at least my little corner of it. I get the feeling my life hasn't been my own between you and Leona." I took a sip of tea. "So how about you tell me about the architect business instead."

"Fair enough," he said. "What do you want to know?"

"Do you like what you do?"

"Very much."

"What kind of buildings do you design?"

"Bit of this, bit of that." He was stacking graduating sizes of onion rings on his plate and looked up when I didn't ask another question. "What? You want specifics?"

"Sure. You got to look at the books on my shelves."

"I've done the corporate bit, hotels, that kind of thing. I didn't like it much. But I was lucky and got into working on redesigning existing structures for alternative uses."

"Like this place. Cool."

"Your place, too," he said. "It's very nice. Pleasant use of space."

"Thanks. So what's been your favorite redesign?"

"The best one I ever worked on was a decommissioned lighthouse for a guy who wanted to live in it." Forget the multitasking at this point. Memories of the lighthouse turned him on and his hands flew, describing the building, its foundation, the original construction, the site, and the beach below it. They were probably itching to make a model of it right there on his plate. And then I realized they already had. His stack of onion rings stood sentry next to a small sea of ketchup. He could hardly talk fast enough to keep up with himself. "Here, I've got a picture of it in my wallet." He pulled his wallet out and flipped it open. "But you're laughing at me."

"No, I'm not, I'm enchanted. You're in love and that's really nice to see." I took the picture from his hand. "Wow. No wonder you're in love."

"I pretended the whole time I was doing it for myself." He took the picture back, cradling it in the palm of his hand, then put it away and rededicated himself to his hamburger. He was kind enough to leave the lion's share of the un-constructed rings for me.

"So then what brings you to land-locked Stonewall?"

"Gotta go where the jobs are."

"An itinerant architect. Are there jobs in Stonewall?"

"The old elementary school," he said. "A consortium bought it and I got the bid to redesign it. Condominiums."

"Huh." Visions of square rooms of institutional green and yellow done up in Martha Stewart chic swam through my head. He must have a better imagination. "Neat. I can't quite picture it but I'm glad they're not tearing it down. But, see, that's something that's been bugging me. It's not like I'm a total recluse, but why don't I hear these things? I've been wondering what's going on with the school ever since they boarded it up."

"This just happened."

"It couldn't have 'just' happened. Obviously people must have worked on getting the consortium together and putting out a call for bids on the work. That takes time. And Eleanor DeAngelis knew who you were so word must be out there somewhere. Bitsy must be right and I don't pay enough attention. Although, come to think of it, she didn't know who you were, either."

"I've only been in town a few days and I'm kind of a low profile guy."

"Driving a car like that? Huh. Maybe I don't get the right kind of people with the right kind of gossip coming into the store."

"Or maybe you don't ask the right questions when they do come in."

I pointed my dill spear at him. "And that's something I intend to work on. I'm not looking for gossipy gossip, though."

"What kinds of things do you want to know?" he asked.

"There's strange things been going on. Like the pigeons. Like Harriet McKinney's garden. That was her yard where Bitsy and I were when you saw us last night."

"Oh, yes, I vaguely remember it looking dreadful and dead," he said.

"Or Duckie's fishpond blowing up, for god's sake. Did you hear about that? What's with all this stuff? But I don't want to know what people assume happened."

"Good luck. What people know and what

people think are often two different things."

"Mm. And just because it's blatted out at ear shattering decibels doesn't make it the truth."

"You're right," he nodded. "More people should take time to remember that, if they ever knew it in the first place. What are you going to do with whatever you find out when you do find it out?"

"Do with it?" I hadn't thought that far.

Gene shrugged and waved his last onion ring around. "You don't have to do anything with it." The onion ring was about to break and would have been flung off into space so I saved it. And ate it.

"I probably won't do anything with it. I'm not much of a doer."

"Except when it comes to taking a man's last onion ring."

"Sorry. Probably about all I'll do with any information I get is brandish it like a silver cross anytime Bitsy comes in and starts throwing around wild assumptions. Hold it up in a blaze of truth and glory to ward her off."

Gene had spent the first half of this exchange casting frequent and increasingly uneasy glances over my shoulder toward the door end of the room. For the second half he'd gradually slid along the bench until he was propped in the corner of the booth and invisible to anyone except me and the couple directly across from us who were more interested in sucking ketchup off each other's fingers.

"I don't want you to get dizzy looking over your shoulder, or alarm you, because I think you're a touch paranoid, but there's a guy sitting in a booth on the other side, near the door, and he's been staring over here ever since he finished eating what looked like three whole chickens."

CHAPTER 11

"That would be George staring over here," I said, not bothering to check.

"Aren't you're falling into your own trap by assuming that's who it is?" Gene asked. "How can you know without looking?"

"Trust me, that's one thing I do know. There aren't that many people who spend their time staring at me."

"How do you know he's not staring at me?"

"Now who's paranoid? Though come to think of it he could be staring at you, too, because you're with me. Oh, hi, George."

" 'Lo, Margaret."

"George, I'd like you to meet Gene Mashburn. Gene, George, George, Gene."

Claire showed up again with two pieces of warm apple pie, sharp cheddar on the side. Exactly what I would have ordered if anyone had asked.

"You joining them for dessert, George?"

Claire asked. "Pie's hot."

"Sure. Hey, Rodney," he called over his shoulder. "C'mon over. Pie."

I sighed and scootched over and George plumped down next to me. Rodney arrived and settled in next to Gene who managed to be both pleasant and polite about the intrusion.

George stuck out his hand for Gene to shake. "George Buckles. I'm a cop." Gene shook his hand and turned to Rodney.

"This is my sister Bitsy's husband, Rodney Decker," I said. "Rodney, Gene Mashburn."

"Oh, yeah," Rodney said, "I heard something about you." Gene's eyebrows rose. Rodney didn't elaborate. Elaboration isn't something Rodney does. He's an insurance salesman but that might not have anything to do with it.

"You the guy living upstairs?" George asked.

"Yeah, for the time being."

"Drive the Lamborghini? What kind of mileage you get on that thing?"

"What kind of insurance you got on that thing?" Rodney asked.

This was turning into a scintillating conversation. "Excuse me, guys," I said. "I'm going to skip to the loo."

Claire came back with two more pieces of pie.

"You leaving, Margaret?" she asked. "You haven't had your pie."

"I'll be right back, Claire. Move, please, George. In the meantime why don't you guys talk to your hearts' content about insurance and mileage and tire treads and. . . ." I headed for the restroom shaking my head.

Actually, the bit about Gene living upstairs was interesting. That was something we hadn't gotten around to in our conversation. I'd forgotten there even was an apartment above the boardroom and wondered what it was like. The view of Main Street from up there was probably worth checking out. Well, maybe I'd get a chance to do that. Maybe Leona's shenanigans weren't all bad, though I was loath to encourage her by telling her so.

Leona was in the bathroom when I got there. I gave her a beady look and brushed past her. Diane Everett was there, too, reapplying her lipstick.

"That's a becoming shade, Diane," Leona said to my back as I disappeared into a stall. "More women should wear crimson lipstick, don't you think?"

"Why thank you, Miss Leona." Diane

always says things brightly. The world has been her oyster from the time she always got the lead in school plays right on through her tenure as head cheerleader and down to the present day where she is a regular member of the local Realtors' Million Dollar Club. But tonight she sounded tired. It was interesting to hear her sounding human.

"How's the dinner going, ladies?" I called.

"A lovely dinner, dear. How are you doing? Margaret is here on a date, you know." This last she was confiding to Diane, unless half a dozen others had wandered in and she was making a general announcement.

"For heaven's sake why?" Diane laughed.

"What?" I joined them at the sinks and looked at Diane in the mirror. This was Diane venturing beyond sounding human and approaching bitter.

"Sometimes I think you're the smartest one of us all, Margaret," she said. "Marriage isn't all it's cracked up to be."

"It takes a lot of work," Leona added her sage two bits. "Margaret wouldn't appreciate that, not ever having been married."

"Leona knows these things because she's been married five times."

Diane looked confused.

"That was a joke," I said.

121

"Oh, yes, well sometimes it is a joke. And sometimes I wonder if it's worth the effort," Diane said. She smacked her lips several times at herself in the mirror and patted her hair, bright smile back in place. She still looked plastic and perfect but this was a more interesting Diane. She snapped her purse shut and she and Leona turned to go.

"Let me know when you're ready to leave, Leona," I said.

"No need, dear. Diane kindly offered to drive me home."

"That's nice. Is there anything else I should know?"

"Yes, sarcasm isn't becoming, Margaret."

I returned to the booth to find the three men and four empty dessert plates.

"Well, we should get back to our booth and let you two be," said Rodney. He's a sweet guy. George made no move to get up.

"Too late, Rod. William took over your booth." I sat down next to George.

George groaned. "He's probably looking for me. I'd better go talk to him."

"No, looks like he's eating a hamburger," Rodney said.

"Why go talk to him and ruin a perfectly good meal?" George turned his doleful eyes on me. "I meant yours, George, not his."

"You don't want to go over there, anyway,"

Rodney said. "Doug just sat down, too, and he's been in a crappy mood all evening. Probably give you indigestion."

"Who's William?" Gene asked.

"Pain in the ass," said George.

"William DeAngelis," Rodney said in sepulchral tones, "funeral director."

"Eleanor DeAngelis's son. You remember," I said, "she melted all over your hand earlier. 'A great, flapping, black vulture of a woman.' " The other two looked startled and George moaned again. "There's nothing to be ashamed of, George. It was a good poem."

"Right."

"Something he was inspired to write back in high school," I explained to Gene and Rodney. "Anyway, what's William need a cop for?"

"He owns the goat-infested lot."

"Really?" I asked. "Since when is William into real estate? I mean other than the eternal kind."

George shrugged.

"I think he bought it off Doug," Rodney said. "Or maybe not bought. Doug bought the old mercantile off William and maybe the lot was part of the deal. Something like that. Maybe not such a good deal for William, though. There's talk about rezoning it as green space and I bet Doug won't admit he ever heard a whisper of that before the transaction with William."

"Green space is nice," I said.

"William's probably dreaming of green cash," Rodney said.

"Oh. So who owned the goats, the cows, and the bull?"

"Ben Jaspers," George said. "But he didn't truck 'em into town. We're still working on how they got there."

"Do you always have this much trouble with animals in Stonewall?" Gene asked.

"No, some animals are very well behaved," I said. "You should meet George's canine partner, Sergeant Lambert."

"Yeah, how is Gloria these days?" Rodney asked.

George's eyes went a shade more morose. A jab like that is usually beneath Rodney but George and Lambert are such inviting targets. With a hurt look at Rodney, he turned to Gene. "So, how's a guy like you keep a car like that in one piece?"

Gene gave George an odd sort of half smile, crossed his arms, looked at nothing in particular in the middle distance, looked back at George and said, "I'm very careful."

"George could take some lessons in that department," I threw in, wondering what

I'd missed that might shed some light on that last bit of dialogue. "The renegade goats in William's lot used his squad car as a dance floor."

Gene gave me a genuine smile at that. Rodney quietly mouthed "goats" to himself several times, apparently lost in contemplation of the intricacies of an insurance claim involving city owned vehicles, private property, and livestock. George drank the rest of his coffee, looking deflated.

"Ready?" Gene asked me.

For what, I wondered? "Sure. Bye, you guys."

CHAPTER 12

Whatever we were ready for had to wait, though. First, for Claire to finish the conversation she was having at Doug and William's booth. She finally turned from them with the glassy smile of someone stifling the urge to strangle someone. Probably William. Then Gene caught her eye and we settled up, said goodbye to George and Rodney again, and turned to go only to find William blocking the aisle.

"I've been waiting to have a word with you," he said.

"What about, William?"

"Not you, Margaret. You can always be found. Look in any corner full of dusty and forgotten tomes. That's the sort of place that Margaret feels at home. I want to know where I can find your beau, *Monsieur le Architect.*" He made a shooing motion at me with his hand and said to Gene, "I might have some business to throw your way. In fact, we might already be in business together if certain parties hadn't kept the school consortium private. Water under the bridge at this point, though, I suppose." He gusted a sigh in Doug's direction. "Anyway, where might I find you tomorrow so we can discuss my proposition?"

"Look in any corner of a dusty edifice, that's the sort of place I'm at my best." Gene flashed his teeth at William and we pushed past him.

But before we cleared the door, Doug flagged us down.

"Hey, Margaret, how you doing? Great tip on that book, by the way."

"Anytime, Doug."

"Well, so, thanks. I owe you one. Mashburn, got a minute?"

I'd had enough socializing by then, waved good night to Doug, and told Gene I'd wait for him outside. He came out a few minutes later and we made our way over to sit on one of the benches under the courthouse willow. The willow's leaves rattled, hinting at crisp fall weather to come.

"You get Doug squared away as neatly as you did William?" I asked.

"Hm? Oh, yeah, guess I was kind of rude to the guy, wasn't I?"

"Don't worry. William's skin is thicker

than most. He probably didn't even notice."

"Everett had some nice things to say about you, though," he said. "He thinks we make a nice looking couple."

"That's what he wanted to talk about?"

"No, he wanted a few tips on treasure hunting."

"Have you done much treasure hunting?"

"Not really." He seemed content to leave it at that and I noticed his arm making its nonchalant way across the back of the bench behind my shoulders.

"Sorry about George and Rodney crashing the party back there," I said.

"Kind of rounded out the evening, though, don't you think? There was a sense of balance to it. First you were bushwhacked by me and your cousin, then came a pleasant interlude during which you ate most of the onion rings but seemed to be enjoying yourself so I didn't complain, and then the jolly fuzz and your stolid brother-in-law bushwhacked me. There's something to be said for good old symmetry."

"Ooh, symmetry, my favorite. Is that architect talk?"

"Yeah, you like that?"

I liked the way his arm had finally found my shoulders, too.

"You know, something else Leona left

out," he mumbled into my hair somewhere nice behind my ear, "she didn't tell me that you've been seeing George."

"That's because I haven't been seeing George for several years."

"Does George know that?" he asked.

"Was he giving you a hard time while I was in the bathroom?"

"No. He seems like an okay guy. Maybe a little suicidal but then as it turns out I'm no mental health expert."

"Nah, that's just George."

We spent some time looking at the moon shining down on Main Street. Then he chuckled a pleasant, low chuckle. "It's perfect," he said.

"What?"

"I finally figured it out. And so you know, most of the time it's half full."

"What, your stomach? Your dance card?"

"My cup," he said. "George is Eeyore and this morning you wanted to know if I was another one." He turned and looked me in the eyes. "I'm not. There are a lot of things I am, but not that."

Intense was obviously one of the things he was. I was first to blink.

"Well. Time I headed home," I said.

"So soon?"

The Garden Club dinner had broken up

and we'd watched the members and their happily-fed families departing. Leona and Diane were among the last to leave. They didn't see us under the willow or Leona might have come over to supervise.

"It's almost Leona's bedtime and she'll expect me to call her."

"You always do everything she expects?" he asked.

"No, and that's my trouble." He hadn't heard that line enough yet to know I was spoofing Leona. "But I know she's going to wait up until I call. And if she's up much past her bedtime she'll be cranky tomorrow."

"Is this going to happen every time we go out on a date?"

"Are we going out on more dates?"

"I don't know," he said. "What do you think?"

"Let me see." I studied him for a moment or two then kissed him for another. "Yeah," I said, "probably. And no, it won't happen every time because from now on we won't be arranging our dates through Leona, will we?"

I didn't let him walk me home. For several reasons. If Leona were watching out her window, which I had no doubt she was, I didn't want to give her the satisfaction of seeing us bidding each other a sweet good night. The other consideration was that it might have been too tempting not to bid him good night at all.

The phone rang before I even had a chance to kick my shoes off.

"Why didn't you let him walk you home and then invite him in?" Leona asked.

"Invite who in?"

"That attitude might explain a lot."

"Leona, if I tell you we had a nice time and we'll probably go out again, that so far he's an interesting person, but I don't know a whole lot about him and it's a good idea to take these things slowly, will you back off?"

"Do I detect a hint of antagonism, dear?"

"Gosh, no. Why do you ask?"

"It's just that, next time, if you're going to shout you might open the window and not bother with the phone at all. But I'm glad you had a nice time. Far be it for me to interfere in your life . . ."

"Heaven forbid."

"But there was something about him the first time I saw him at Bertie's that intrigued me."

"His car," I said. "You can't wait to get your hands on it."

"It's not just the car, dear, there was something about him that made me think of you."

"It was that red plaid shirt."

"And then he talked to me, Margaret. We had a conversation. An exchange of thoughts. Do you know how rarely that happens in a casual encounter between two strangers of such different ages? I go to Bertie's for coffee because I run into people my age who have time to talk. We're invisible to most people, you know. People with busy lives, always rushing somewhere to do something. That's just the way it is. I'm not complaining. But here was this nice younger man and he took the time to talk to me. And when you're not too busy being flippant or sarcastic, that's the way you are, too. So I thought the two of you might hit it off."

"And for now at least we have. And thanks for telling me that about him. I like that and I'm glad you told me. But Cousin Leona?"

"Yes, dear?"

"Let me take it from here, okay?"

"I wouldn't dream of interfering. Let me go now, dear, it's past my bedtime."

I was brushing my teeth, sorting through

the thoughts and emotions padding around inside my head after spending the evening with Gene, basking in the memory of his glow as he'd rhapsodized over his light-house. Not everyone gets so caught up in their work. According to Bitsy, I run on sometimes about the book business, but I'm glad I still feel that way about it. I've never heard Rodney wax eloquent over insurance. Maybe he does, but only among other insur-ance agents. It's possible that William gets that way, but anytime he starts explaining the joys of undertaking, I find an excuse to leave the room. Nope, Gene Mashburn looked like something special.

I rinsed and spit and realized that some-thing was tickling the back molars of my memory. About how Gene had ended up in Stonewall. Following the jobs? He was an itinerant architect. Oh. I spit again. Rats.

Still, he was here now, and if that wasn't a cup half full, I didn't know what was. I ignored the bathroom scale, doused the lights and crawled under the covers feeling warmer and fuzzier than I had for some time. Usually I curl up with a good book for half an hour or so before drifting off. Tonight I curled up with sweet dreams.

My dreams ended at three A.M. when the

phone rang. Even a wrong number at that hour would have been bad news because I hate being dragged awake. But Bitsy's news was worse than that.

"There's a fire downtown. It's Bertie's."

CHAPTER 13

And what do you say then? My god. Are you sure? But we were just there. How could it? Did everyone get out?

"Margaret, did you hear me?"

"Yeah. Yeah, geez. I'm going down there."

"Margaret I don't think you should. . . ." At least I guess that's what she was saying but I'd already put the phone down.

I wasn't sure what I was throwing on except I know I put on my shoes because I wanted to run. My brain was with it enough to know another car in the area would cause more problems. Another person might, too, but that wasn't computing. I didn't even lock the door behind me.

Half a block from home I could already smell the smoke. I'm not ordinarily a ghoul. I don't slow down and stare at traffic accidents, and I don't relish the tragedies reported on the evening news or watch reality TV disaster shows. But that whiff of smoke hit some primitive nerve I didn't know I had, curling around and brushing against my panic button.

I ran faster, wanting to get there in time to do something even though I had no idea what, and I ended up flying when I tripped on the uneven sidewalk and skidded to a landing on one knee and an elbow. That woke me up. I took a couple of deep breaths, picked myself back up, and eased into a lopsided sort of lope from there.

Lines from books occur to me at inappropriate times. One of the curses of being a book person, maybe. Running through my head now were words from a picture book I'd feared and loved as a child, *Five Little Firemen* by Margaret Wise Brown. In it, a house catches fire in the night. A flame, like a little mouse, darts in and out of a hole in the hall closet as the family sleeps. An alert policeman smells it.

That little mouse of flame, so playful, so benign, and so insidious was the perfect representation of a monster that might really come calling on unsuspecting people in their beds. I'd loved the shiver of fear it gave me as a small child. I always wondered if that policeman would smell it in time.

I hoped to god one had this time.

I couldn't see flames shooting up into the

night sky as I limped up the bit of rise between my house and downtown and that gave me a small surge of hope. But there it all was as I came down the other side. A corner of Main Street tipped into a nightmare. Fire engines and flashing lights and people staring and straining from across the street and flames licking greedily around the edges of Bertie's windows. I ran the rest of the way.

It wasn't chaos. I could see that. In fact, they probably had the fire under control, no great gouts of flame were tearing away the roof; walls weren't collapsing. But it smelled like chaos and it felt like it. The street around the trucks vibrated with the growling of their engines as they blasted water through the hoses. The vibrations came up through the soles of my feet and made my blood fizz like I'd had ten cups of coffee. Above it all the flames crackled and roared and billows of black and yellow smoke poured out of Bertie's in choking clouds where the water shot in.

I didn't see Gene anywhere.

The firefighters performed as though choreographed. There was nothing frantic in their movements, just concentration and steadiness. They poured water through the windows and sprayed the roof from the hook and ladder truck. They hosed down the adjacent buildings. Police were there to keep people back. An ambulance stood ready.

I didn't see anyone being rescued from the third floor apartment.

"Margaret." Bitsy peeled away from a cluster of others who'd been drawn from their beds by the flames. "You're bleeding," she said, joining me closer to the makeshift cordon.

"Doesn't matter. Do you know what's going on? Did everyone get out? Did they get anyone out?"

"Well it'll certainly make the morning news. Claire barely got out. If the pictures turn out they'll burn up the AP wires."

"Claire? Is she okay? Who was taking pictures, for god's sake? Bitsy, listen, are they looking for anyone else? Is George here? I'm going to find him."

"No, Margaret, wait, wait." She caught my sleeve. "It's all right. There was no one else there; it was already closed for the night. Claire must've been upstairs in the apartment. She was in her bathrobe and it was on fire by the time she got down but they got her on the ground and got it out and she's okay."

"What do you mean 'it was on fire,' you

mean her bathrobe was on fire?"

"She was so freaked out she didn't even know it and the whole back of it was in flames but one of the firemen tackled her and rolled on top of her and she's okay. It's okay, Margaret."

"Bitsy, it's not okay. That's Gene Mashburn's apartment and I don't see him anywhere. Did he get out?" I could tell by her face she didn't know and couldn't believe he had. "I'm going to find out."

"But Margaret, if Claire was there and in her bathrobe doesn't that tell you something?"

"Jesus, Bitsy, it doesn't tell me to let him burn," I pulled away from her and ran down the cordon to where a policeman stood staring, as mesmerized by the fire as the people he was supposed to be keeping back.

"Did anyone go in?"

"Huh? Lady, it's a fire. People don't go in burning buildings. They come out of them."

"Yeah, and if they don't come out, don't you guys go in and get them out?"

"Not me, lady. Hey, hey, look, calm down. Is there someone else in there?"

"The guy who lives there."

"Hey, you can't go over there."

I'd have to try that maneuver next time Bitsy or Leona made a grab at my arm. I dodged over to where a couple of people in more serious looking gear stood and caught their attention by slithering into one of them through a puddle and a patch of mud.

"Ma'am? You all right? I'm sorry, but I'm going to have to ask you to move back across the barrier."

"There might be someone in the apartment, third floor. Has anyone checked?" They exchanged looks that were a foreign language to me.

"If you're referring to the young lady, she's safe."

"No, there's a guy who rents the apartment." I was getting tired of this. "I haven't seen him down here. Did you send anyone in to search?"

"Yes, ma'am, we did. Now if you'll move back. Buckles, take her." And solid George was there.

" 'Lo, Margaret." Together we made our way beyond the cordon, me not so much aware of moving my feet across the ground as feeling a lurching void opening up in front of them.

Some bit of excitement shivered through the gapers in front of us. It swelled the undercurrent of their nervous conversations and then hushed them altogether. George and I turned to see what was happening.

Two firefighters with oxygen tanks and masks were easing down the ladder on one of the trucks. Somehow between them they got a third person down the ladder. He was beyond helping himself.

"I can't believe it." Bitsy said, joining us. "What if it had started while we were all there eating dinner?"

"It wouldn't have happened that way," I said.

"My god, it's like one of those plane crashes where you should have been on it but you missed the flight because thanks to your guardian angel you got caught in traffic." She heaved a throbbing sigh. "We all could have died."

"It's not like that."

"How can you say that, Margaret?"

"It wouldn't have happened, Bitsy. What, you think some god of Garden Clubs was watching out for you? It doesn't work that way. You're not on the receiving end of some karmic burp."

"Well if you're going to put it like that."

"If it had started earlier someone would have noticed it. Everyone would have gotten out."

"Margaret, you're crying."

"I'm not."

"George, don't stand there looking hopeless, do something."

"Margaret, listen to me." George put a heavy arm around me. "The guy was a loser. He was an alcoholic."

I'd been wondering what it felt like to be in shock and if what I was feeling was anything like it. No, I decided, because then George's statement probably wouldn't have come across with such blazing monstrosity.

"How do you know that?" I pulled away from him. "And, so, what do you mean? He deserved to die?"

"I didn't mean that, Margaret, I only meant . . ."

"Is he dead?" We both looked at Bitsy. "Well, we don't know, do we? Maybe he was overcome by smoke. Someone ought to go check." She poked George in the chest. "George."

He went.

"Thank you, Bitsy."

"There isn't much point in getting bent out of shape until we know if there's something to be bent out of shape about." That sounded awfully reasonable to be coming from Bitsy. Maybe *she* was in shock. Whatever it was, I was glad she was there to lean against for the time being. "But if you stop and think about it, Margaret, maybe you'll see that there isn't so much to be bent out of shape about, anyway. I mean, you've got to look at the facts, there was Claire, in her bathrobe . . ."

This sounded more like Bitsy. I closed my eyes, something I've often wished also closed my ears. My head was in enough of its own muddle sorting through what I thought and what I felt and what I didn't want to know and what I didn't want to believe. Bitsy's contributions agitated it all to the point where my brains felt like suds.

". . . and George is a good man, Margaret. I've never understood why you two haven't been able to make it stick. Do you suppose Leona knew that about this Mashburn?"

"What, Bitsy? Did she know what about him? So what if George thinks he knows something. When it comes right down to it we don't know anything about him."

"And that's my point exactly."

She was happy with this point gained. I let her revel in her triumph and turned to look for George. He'd disappeared in the tangle of emergency vehicles. He didn't need to come back to tell us anything, though. No ambulance, siren wailing, had raced off into the night. That was answer enough. Maybe I'd just wander home.

"Bitsy, I'll see you. I'm going home." She didn't say anything so I turned to look back at her. Her face was transfixed. Then it melted into disbelief.

"Hi, Bitsy," a quiet voice said. At that she experienced sensory overload and emitted a thin, piercing squeal. I wasn't much better after hearing that quiet voice, but at least I didn't assault anyone's eardrums. "Hi, Margaret. This is a hell of thing, isn't it? Anyone seen Doug?"

CHAPTER 14

"But I don't understand," Bitsy ululated. "Who was in the apartment?"

Gene had leaned his bicycle against his hip. He was sagging a bit himself and it might be that the bike was the more stable of the two. He righted himself when he saw George bearing down on us. It was George who answered Bitsy, but he only had eyes for Gene.

"It was Doug Everett. He's dead. Mashburn, where you been? Out riding your bike in the middle of the night?"

"Yeah, yeah, I was. Jesus, look at that." He was having trouble dragging his eyes away from the fire to concentrate on George's questions.

"Bike's got a flat."

"Hm?" He focused on George's finger pointing out the flat front tire.

"Yeah, I picked up a nail or something and didn't have the repair kit with me. I spent most of the time walking back home. What the hell happened here? How'd this get started? Everett's dead? Jesus."

"We'll probably have some answers in the morning. Probably have more than a few questions, too. You got any place to go? You want me to drop you at a motel?"

"I don't know. I," he shook his head as though that might clear it. "No, thanks."

"I'll be around for a while you change your mind." He fixed his eye on Gene until he gave a glum nod indicating he'd heard and maybe understood, then headed back to the action.

Bitsy looked confused or possibly disappointed. Maybe both. The outcome was a furrowed brow and an unpleasant twist to her mouth. I decided to give her the benefit of the doubt.

"You look tired, Bitsy. Why don't you go on home? Thanks for calling. Thanks for being here."

"Mr. Mashburn, why were you out riding your bike in the middle of the night?" It wasn't the first question springing into my mind to ask a man whose home and possessions were drifting by as ashes on the breeze. But I have trouble sometimes understanding what passes for logical thought in Bitsy's mind.

"Keeps me off the streets."

She looked less than satisfied with that answer and more than a little something else.

"Well," I said, jumping in, hoping to divert whatever train of thought she was boarding. But then I couldn't think of anything worth adding to that and ended up clearing my throat in a lame sort of way. Adrenaline withdrawal was setting in. "Okay, I'm heading home. Maybe I'll see you in the morning, Bitsy. Hope you get some sleep." I turned to say goodbye to Gene.

"How about I walk you home?"

This time I let him and we left Bitsy sputtering along with what was left of the fire.

"You're limping," he said.

I waved off his concern. "So's your bike."

"Did you notice that your sister was dressed like she was on her way to a luncheon meeting?"

"She can't help it."

"You look more like . . . ," We stopped under a street light and both looked at what I'd thrown on in my mad dash. It wasn't hard to see why he was at a loss to say exactly what I looked like — one blue sock, one red, a pair of green corduroys now sporting a ripped and bloody knee and the only orange T-shirt I've ever owned.

"Charming, isn't it? It's what all the fashion unconscious will be wearing to fires this season." I studied the T-shirt. "You know, for the life of me, I cannot figure out why I own this shirt. I don't even like orange."

"If you're lucky, the blood from your elbow won't wash out of it and then you can get rid of it. What happened?"

"I don't know. Grease fire? I don't even know where it started." The details of that scene were still sparking and popping in my head. The nightmare glow of flames and the flashing lights. The thick yellow smoke. The roar of both the fire and my fears. But he'd seen it; he didn't need a description of it from me. Then I caught a whiff from my horrible orange shirt. The fabric was permeated with the smells of the fire, as though I'd dipped it in a well of smoke and wrung it out and put it back on. As though *it* had been on fire. Aroma shock therapy. "Oh, god, Claire . . ." And I told him about Claire and her flaming bathrobe. "Probably a miracle she didn't go up like a torch."

"She was lucky."

"Not poor Duckie." I shivered.

"Nope."

"Why was he in your apartment?"

"Tiff with his wife."

148

"Are those Duckie's words?" He shrugged. "A tiff. Poor Diane. She was congratulating me tonight on being smart enough to avoid marriage. She wasn't recommending it."

"My ex-wife probably wouldn't recommend it either."

Ex-wife? "Oh well, at least she's not feeling guilty because you went up in flames right after she gave you the evil eye."

We walked in silence for a while. Then he said, "Before, when I asked you what happened, I meant your knee and your elbow. Are you all right? What happened?"

"I thought you were dead."

He looked up into the branches of the maple we were passing under. Whether to admire it or to find inspiration to deal with that non sequitur, I don't know. "And you must have thought I'd been with Claire."

I sighed. "No, I think I've expanded my mission in life beyond Bitsy and now I'm not making any assumptions about anyone."

He gave that some thought. I wasn't sure it merited any. All I'd been doing was giving myself a verbal kick in the pants for jumping to conclusions. But his thinking was interesting to watch. It didn't look anything like Bitsy's. When she thinks, she narrows her eyes, and I imagine her views until she pounces on the answer she wants.

Gene's eyes were studying the question from all angles.

"But don't we depend on assumptions," he asked, "as a matter of course, to get through the day? I know the first thing I do every morning is assume I'll be able to find a cup of good strong black coffee. And if I couldn't trust that assumption, you'd either find me gibbering in my bed with the covers over my ears or threatening someone with my T square and a fistful of sharpened pencils at their throat."

"So I'll exclude logical assumptions."

"It would have been logical to assume I was fooling around with Claire."

"Bitsy seemed to think so. I heard some other things about you tonight."

"Probably all true," he said pleasantly.

"They weren't especially flattering. George says you're a loser and an alcoholic."

"Huh."

By now we were in front of my house and all I could think of was my bed. I'd lost all sense of time, hadn't worn my watch. Felt heavy. Beat.

"Look, you haven't got any place to go and I've got a sofa that isn't too bad. It's not much but you're welcome to it. I'm all in and if I don't get some sleep soon, I'm going to die." I started up the steps. He stayed at the bottom. When I glanced back he looked up from whatever he'd been seeing there in the dark. "You can put your bike in the kitchen."

I dug sheets and a blanket out of the linen closet for him. Found a spare toothbrush. Asked him if he wanted to take a shower.

"Oh, sorry," I said when he answered politely that yes, he'd appreciate it, "you'll have to wait. I've got to get this smell off me right now. Ugh, it's in my hair. It's in my teeth."

"You need to clean that knee and elbow, too. Have you got gauze and tape? You never did tell me what happened."

"I tripped. Running. Downtown. You want to borrow some pajamas?"

"No, Margaret, I'll be fine."

"Good night, then."

"Night. Margaret?"

I stopped, drooping against the wall. "Hm?"

"Thanks for running."

"Night, Gene."

CHAPTER 15

When the radio came on the next morning at its preset time, I was barely able to stop myself from snarling at Bob Edwards delivering his breezy, bottom-of-the-hour news item. The idea of removing myself from my warm nest of blankets and standing upright on the cold floor did not appeal. Thank goodness Sylvia Poggioli reported in from somewhere in Eastern Europe. The sound of her voice gave strength to my limp brain.

Still, I lay there, with all the night's ghastly images floating by in a smoky haze. I shivered and pulled the covers closer around me. Then I took a tentative sniff of the air to see if I'd brought anymore of the nightmare home with me, to see if I'd gotten it scrubbed off my skin and out of my hair. I smelled coffee.

Gene was reading the morning paper when I stumbled, bleary eyed, down to the kitchen. He had the paper in one hand, a steaming mug in the other and a look of total absorption on his face. I brushed past him and poured myself a cup of the coffee he'd made. He barely twitched. Standing there in the middle of the room, his posture was so rigid it looked as though he didn't fold in the right places to sit in a chair. Maybe my sofa hadn't agreed with him. I plumped myself down at the table and started absorbing my first cup of morning energizer.

After inhaling half the cup, my eyes were able to focus better. I took them on a test run, casting a glance over to Gene. He was still engrossed in the paper. Somehow he managed to look appealing even in the dishevelment of having slept in his clothes. He wasn't especially tall, maybe five nine, probably not. More on the wiry side than solid. Nice square shoulders, though. And his hair curled here and there in an off hand way I couldn't help smiling at.

I lost myself in those details for a while, then I gave myself a quick shake to dispel any burgeoning dreams and glanced around the rest of the room. That gave me a severe case of over-the-rainbow. This didn't look like my kitchen anymore. It was spotless. The floor, which happens to be yellow, though not brick, had been washed and everything else was spit-shined beyond words. The bike leaning against the stove added a jaunty touch. I drank the rest of my coffee more slowly and wondered what all this meant. Finally I cleared my throat. He looked up.

"Hi," I said. It wasn't the sort of "hi" that means "lovely morning and how splendid to see you." It was a caustic "hi" and I was hoping it would come across as "so, you want to tell me what's going on?" From the look on his face, though, it had sounded more like "what the hell?" Which is why I always try to avoid entertaining first thing in the morning because, really, I'm not at my best. "Sorry."

"More coffee?"

"Please. Fast."

He topped my cup and retreated behind the paper until I made noises that were less threatening. Then he folded the paper and tentatively joined me at the table. "You don't want to read about the fire, do you?"

I shuddered. "No, maybe later. Bitsy said someone took a picture of Claire." He held up the front page. "Wow. If it weren't so scary it might be festive. It looks like the Feast of St. Claire. Do you think they would've run it if she'd died?"

"Probably. But bigger."

"If some is good more is better. Wow. But, so, what are you going to do?"

"I draw the line at cleaning your kitchen. You'll have to fend for yourself for the rest of the place."

"Listen, wise guy . . ."

"Hey, I didn't mean to disturb whatever environmental statement you were bent on making here but I needed to make some coffee. In order to make coffee I had to wash the pot, in order to wash the pot I had to empty the sink. One thing led to another."

"Funny, I've never particularly noticed that." I waved my hand around at the sparkling expanse of my kitchen. "It must have taken you awhile."

"Couldn't sleep."

"Oh, sorry about the sofa."

"Sofa was fine."

"Did you lose everything?"

"Compared to Doug, no." He leaned on his elbows, his hands clasping the top of his skull, trying to keep his thoughts from flying apart, I guess. "I've been trying to think. And trying not to think. I started a list of what I had up there. Keys to the car were up there."

"Your designs for the school?"

"No, thank god. I've been working in a

155

room over there, at the school, I mean. And a lot of my stuff is in storage." He looked up briefly, with a crooked smile. "I've been traveling light. But I had drawings and photographs and books and . . ."

"And now part of you is gone forever."

"Yeah." He got up and poured himself more coffee. I shook my head when he tried to put more in my cup. By now I was as awake as I wanted to be. No point in entering small dog phase. "Well," he said, leaning against the counter and rubbing a hand through his beard, "maybe it wasn't the best part of me anyway."

"I would have thought that in traveling light you'd have some of the best parts with you."

"Who knows."

"At least some of your favorite things. You know, favorite books, favorite clothes, pictures that really meant something to you." He shrugged and I stopped listing the things he might be regretting. It obviously wasn't going to make him feel better. "Gosh, poor Bertie and poor everyone whose favorite place that was. Oh my god," I jumped up, knocking my chair over. "Leona, geez, what if she didn't read her paper this morning and gaily walked down there for her cup of coffee?" I was in a complete lather and reaching for the phone when he put one hand over mine and his other on my shoulder.

"Hey, it's all right. She knows. I went over there as soon as I saw a light come on this morning."

"How'd she take it?"

"She's glad no one else was hurt. She has an idea the fire is somehow part of the string of vandalisms and I told her it pretty certainly wasn't. And she was worried about you."

"Me? Why?"

"She says you're a 'sensitive little creature.' "

"Oh for god's sake. Swell. Now I'll have her fluttering around all day." Speaking of fluttering. He still had one hand on mine and the other on my shoulder and my heart was giving me a demonstration of what must be the Texas two-step. His hands were warm. There was a whiff of the fire about his clothes but his skin smelled good. Like lemon fresh kitchen.

"Leona doesn't really strike me as someone who flutters," he said.

"I guess not. She flaps sometimes, though. And badgers a lot. Thanks for going over there."

"Margaret?"

"Hm?"

"Thanks for putting me up last night."

"Looks to me like I got the better end of that deal. I got some sleep and a clean kitchen. I could get used to doing that kind of favor." I could get used to this, too. Too bad the books were calling. "The public probably isn't really awaiting, but I've got to open the store."

"Yeah, I need to get going, too. The building, at least, wasn't a total loss. The stuff inside's another question. Maybe I can get in and see if there's anything worth salvaging. And I guess I ought to show up somewhere and see if they've got any questions I can answer." He gave my ear a bit of a nuzzle before I slipped away.

Bitsy was pulling up as I fit the key into the front door. She saw me there or I might have ducked. That never works because she has built in sonar capability for locating me. Resigned to a rehashing of our night at the fire, I unlocked the door and flipped the open sign. I drew the line at holding the door open for her but the lingering glow of Gene's nuzzle put a smile on my face. It irritated her.

"I don't know what you think there is to be happy about."

"Nice to see you, too, Bitsy." She didn't

return the greeting. She was caught up in assessing my comportment, an unnerving process. I retreated behind the counter. "Did you get any sleep?"

She ignored that, too. When she'd reached her conclusion, she leveled a finger at me. "You haven't read this morning's paper."

"I saw the picture of Claire and didn't have the stomach to read the rest of it. Why?"

"You amaze me, Margaret, you really do. All this talk about taking an interest, being more involved, and you didn't even bother to read the paper."

"Bitsy, I was there. I saw them bring Doug down the ladder. I couldn't have gotten much more involved unless I was a volunteer with the EMS. The whole thing was horrible and I wish it hadn't happened, but accidents do, and me sitting and pouring over the details in the newspaper isn't going to change anything."

"But that's just it," she said. "It wasn't."

"What wasn't what?"

"It wasn't an accident."

"Oh come on."

"A fire of suspicious origins." She enunciated this with both hands, turning the words into a blaring headline hanging in the air between us.

159

"Give me a break. Who'd want to burn down the Bank Tavern? Not Bertie. Not Claire. They loved the place. You've heard Claire talk about her plans. And she was in her bathrobe for god's sake. And don't tell me they think it was Duckie?" This was making me sick. "What's he supposed to have done, start the fire then panic and lose his way in the smoke?" I groped for the stool and sat on it.

"And those are only some of the questions, aren't they?" She planted her headline hands on the counter and leaned closer. "I can think of a few others. Like what was Claire doing there in the first place? Who exactly was she there visiting in her bathrobe? Or was she even visiting? Maybe she'd moved in with someone, if you know what I mean. And where was Bertie last night? Surely someone called her. Why wasn't she at the scene? And most of all, and think about this Margaret, what was Gene Mashburn doing with a can of gasoline the other night? Maybe the fire was suspicious but not intentional. Maybe it was a suspicious accident caused by an alcoholic with a can of gas who then conveniently left the scene and took a ride on a bike with a flat tire."

When Bitsy gets excited, she gets loud. Incrementally. By the time she'd finished

160

accosting me with her list of questions she was fairly crowing.

"And furthermore, Margaret, I saw George this morning. And that information about Mr. Mashburn isn't merely supposition. And they're wondering where he is this morning. Don't you think that's interesting? That he seems to have disappeared?"

"Oh, I don't think he's disappeared, Bitsy."

"I wouldn't be so sure about that."

"I would." We had a sisterly stare down. We're both experts at that kind of competition and neither of us blinked.

The kitchen door behind me opened.

"Hi, Bitsy," Gene's quiet voice said. "Margaret, mind if I leave the bike in the kitchen? I'll fix the tire and get it out of there this evening."

Bitsy did her fish imitation. It's one of my favorites.

"Sure, leave it as long as you need to," I said.

"Thanks. Want me to bring you a sandwich at lunch?"

"If you can get away."

"Man's gotta eat."

"Bird's gotta fly, too, but in this town that doesn't always work out. If you can make it, that'll be great. Eunice comes in at noon

161

and I can break anytime after that. Bye."

He gave a wide berth to Bitsy who pivoted, keeping an eye on him as he skirted her. They made quite a picture, neither one of them sure what the other might do, the possibilities apparently endless in their mutually suspicious minds. The bell over the door jingled and Bitsy's head snapped back to me.

"Margaret, are you harboring him?"

"Harboring? Bitsy, the man lost his home and all his possessions last night. He's not a criminal. He spent what was left of the night on the sofa. Actually he spent it in the kitchen, cleaning. He's very domestic. You should go take a look."

"And you should have your head examined."

She was quite possibly right, but rather than start down that path I deflected her with a question.

"Did George say what they think happened?"

"Well," she carefully squared all the edges of the stack of cookbooks next to the cash register, "no. Not exactly, but . . ."

Bitsy is an interesting combination of exactitude and illusion. She likes precision in her surroundings, hence her penchant for straightening my counter. Balance that with her tendency to let her rational thought processes take wing for parts unknown, and you have the admixture I call Bitso-mania.

"But what, Bitsy? What didn't George exactly tell you?" Considering my new mission in life, I was leery of listening to her analysis. On the other hand it might be good to know what theories she'd either heard and was repeating or was happily gleaning from her own flights of fancy. It might work like an inoculation and I'd be protecting myself from stepping in any further assumptions myself.

"Do you remember the last time a restaurant in town burned down?" she asked.

"No."

"The Corner Cupboard?"

"That was more than forty years ago."

She shrugged that off as insignificant. "Do you remember the prevailing theory behind that fire?"

"It was a grease fire. It started in the kitchen and the place was so pickled in grease fumes, it went up like a torch."

"Margaret, you don't pickle things in grease. And besides," she said, shaking her head, "it wasn't the grease, or at least not just the grease. It was the Mafia."

I can picture the succession of expressions that crossed my face then. Surprise. Disbelief. Dumbfoundedness. A bit of wicked pleasure sifting down from across the years. Guilt. "Bitsy, it wasn't the Mafia."

"You're so sure? Everyone heard the whispers about it at the time. People still talk about it. Maybe the authorities never admitted it. Maybe nothing was ever proven, but that doesn't mean those shadowy relations of the DeAngelis' . . ."

"Yes, it does. Bitsy, really, it does."

"This is a revelation, Margaret. You? Toeing the establishment line? Is this some residual effect from your days of dating George? In fact, you were the one who told me about it in the first place."

That would be true because I was the one who had made it up in the first place. Maybe this is why I don't trust rumors. "Bitsy . . ."

"Don't you remember? I had the flu or something and couldn't go see the smoking ruins and I was so mad I cried. And you got to go and when you came back you sat on the end of the bed and told me all about it. And you kept bouncing up and down because you were excited and you wouldn't quit and I threw up. Remember?"

"Yes, that brings it all back up nicely. Thank you."

"You were squeamish back then, too."

Time to get the conversation off that track. "Poor Diane. And the girls. I can't even think how old they are now. They came in every Saturday for story time when they were little."

"They're in high school. Christa was homecoming queen this year."

"Oh God, poor Duckie. So terrible."

"I called and talked to Diane's mother. I'm going over there later this morning." Bitsy's good that way. She doesn't always know what not to say but she usually knows what a person should say and do at a time like this. Where I'm left tongue-tied or blathering like an idiot, she steps in with grace and a gentle shoulder. Another one of the enigmas that make up my exasperating sister.

"I talked to her last night," I said, "in the bathroom at Bertie's. She actually seemed human."

"What's that supposed to mean?"

"You know what she's like. What she was like in school, too. You know what I mean. Everything about her is perfect. The hair, the teeth, the figure, the clothes, the husband, the kids, the house, the job. She probably waxes her driveway." I suddenly wondered who I was describing, Diane or Bitsy? Except Bitsy and Rodney don't have any

165

children. I flicked a glance at her, but she was busy straightening the bookmarks.

"Anyway, last night she was telling me how smart I was for never getting married. Of course that was part of her being perfect, too, because she always knows what to say to make a person feel good." I looked at Bitsy again. She'd left off the bookmarks and was giving me the kind of look a rat terrier must have when it spots that first tremulous whisker testing the air at the opening of the warren or wherever rat terriers do their sniffing.

"Were she and Doug having problems?" she asked, eyes agleam.

"I don't know."

"What exactly did she say?"

"I don't remember."

"Come on, Margaret. In your own words, she was more human last night. She must have been showing cracks in something and it sure wasn't her makeup. Claire really was there visiting Duckie, wasn't she?" I shrugged, sorry I'd brought up that conversation. "Or," she gave that simple word about ten seconds more than it needed, "she was there because she's been shacking up with this Mashburn character and Doug stopped by and one thing led to another and Mashburn caught them at it and . . ."

"Mrs. DeAngelis."

"Mrs. DeAngelis caught them at it? What sense does that make unless Claire was two-timing William, of all people, or maybe three-timing him if you throw Mashburn back into it. Anyway, I thought you were pooh-poohing the Angel of Death and Mafia link."

I'm not sure I would have kicked her to alert her even if I could have and that's the kind of moral lapse I should probably work on. Eleanor DeAngelis swept into the store on the tail of the Mafia comment.

"Hi, what can I do for you, Mrs. DeAngelis?"

Bitsy froze for one brief moment before recovering and flashing a smile. "*Bonjour, Madame.* I'll go start the tea, then, shall I, Margaret?" And she glided around the end of the counter and on into the kitchen, cheeks pink but head held high.

CHAPTER 16

Eleanor DeAngelis didn't stay for tea. Mostly because it took Bitsy longer than usual to trot it out. Otherwise I think she might have joined us. She was in a chatty mood.

Bitsy probably had trouble finding things like the teapot and tea bags and cups because they weren't strewn across the counters or huddling in a sink of cold water. Or maybe she spent some time being dazzled by her reflection in every single shiny surface of my newly spiffed kitchen. She might have been too mortified to face Eleanor after her Angel of Death and Mafia crack, but I've seen Bitsy bluff her way out of more ticklish situations. Whatever the case, she missed Eleanor at her best.

"Margaret, my book angel. I'm sure this horror has everyone not thinking clearly. But you, I can always count on you. Isn't it all too awful for words? And so I shall not try to find them and shall simply tell you what I need. A book. Ah, but you knew that, didn't you? The book I am looking for is something I want to give Douglas and Diane's daughters. You know, it is something my husband used to keep before he turned the business over to William. It helps the child to understand the so sad death of a parent. As much as that can ever be understood. So very sad. You do know what I mean, don't you?"

I always find myself falling into Eleanor DeAngelis's deep eyes and wanting to agree with her. Everything about her is mesmerizing. Her sweeping gestures, her faux French syntax, the black drapery that I'm never sure is actual clothing. She's easily nine inches taller than I am, which leaves me permanently feeling like the student to her *professeur. "Mais oui, Madame"* is the automatic answer I have to stifle every time she asks a question.

"There are several good books like that. Do you know the title of the one you're looking for?"

"Ah, no."

Ah, well. "Let me see what we've got in stock, then." She trailed behind me looking like one of Edward Gorey's pen and ink femmes fatales. I found myself longing for silk scarves and wondered briefly what they might do to improve my small black. How eye-catching might that be? And for whose eyes?

"And your Mr. Mashburn?" she said, making me jump. "How is he after this tragedy? He was so kind to give Douglas a place to stay while he and Diane worked through their problems. Mr. Mashburn was not there to escape from the fire, so I hear?"

"Apparently not."

"Bad timing then for Douglas. Good timing for your friend."

Calculated timing? That thought popped to the surface of the quagmire I call my mind, though I'd been working pretty hard to keep it submerged. A shiver ran up my spine along with it. It was one thing to have Bitsy throwing around ideas about gasoline cans and midnight rides. I'm used to dismissing her imaginings. But if questions like calculated timing were swimming unbidden into my head, then . . .

"Do you know when the funeral is, Mrs. DeAngelis?" I asked, hastily stuffing the question into a dark corner. "Is William handling it?"

"I'm sure he is but I do not know the details. There are some questions, still, I believe. But William and Douglas were such friends and of course Diane and William are cousins so I am sure she will want him to make all the final arrangements. Now, what books do you have for me?" She took the books I pulled from the shelf and settled herself in a chair to look them over.

I left her with them and settled myself into the never-ending chore of straightening books. It's a good job for when you want to avoid thinking about anything else, which struck me as desirable right about then.

I put my feeble brain power to work checking over the mystery shelves. Maybe I was subconsciously hoping that questions about last night would sort themselves out neatly like a plot in one of the pleasanter British village mysteries. Cozy answers might volunteer themselves for Cousin Leona as an erstwhile Miss Marple. But soon enough more customers wandered in out of the bright, mocking sunshine and I made my way back to the front counter to look cheerful and hope for sales.

In between ringing up a Jamaican barbecue cookbook and the new Stephen King, my brain shook itself off and started thinking again.

Diane and William were cousins. I'd forgotten that. They were certainly never kissing cousins. In fact, I remember her calling him Wee Willy and making him cry. In middle school. And since when were William and Doug such buddies? William hadn't made it sound as though they were yesterday. Not unless he regularly calls his friends asses. But maybe he does. I would never pick him out of a line up and label him normal.

"This one, I think, Margaret." Eleanor had chosen one I would have recommended for younger children, though I don't know that any book could explain this particular situation to anyone. And I shuddered at the thought of Eleanor, looking like a vulture, swooping down on Doug's daughters with tears and sympathy and *The Fall of Freddie the Leaf*. "That is wonderful, Margaret. I so appreciate your help. You always know so exactly the thing. I depend on you, you know. Goodbye."

"Thanks, Mrs. DeAngelis. Bye, now." She's a bit over the top. I refrained from blowing her kisses but couldn't help a largish wave.

"So what did *Madame Defarge* want?"

"Bitsy, shhh." There were still other customers in the store. My staff and I are careful not to talk about customers in front of other customers. If only my sister would be so good.

She'd brought the tea on a tray I vaguely recognized as one I'd last seen next to the back door holding my muddy boots. Turns out it was fairly attractive. So now where were my boots? I ignored Bitsy and rang up sales. She wandered off into the local history room blowing on her tea.

"Is Fran around?" A young woman approached the counter with a copy of *Dr. Spock's Baby and Child Care.*

"She should be back tomorrow. She's looking after her mother for a few days."

"I'm going to be a mother soon," the woman said unnecessarily. She lovingly rubbed her protruding tummy that looked at least ten months pregnant. "Will you tell her I went to the library like she recommended? And I spent all afternoon looking through all the guides, there's so many of them, and I finally decided on this one. She was really helpful."

"Thanks, I'll tell her." I held my breath when she left, hoping she'd at least make it back into her car before going into labor.

"Death and birth. The great circle." Bitsy doesn't usually wax philosophical. I looked at her. She was watching the young woman struggle with her seat belt. "I'd better go pick up the ham I'm taking to Diane's."

"Bitsy, you know I'm kind of tied down

here but if you think there's anything I can do, this evening or something . . ."

She turned to me and I took an involuntary hop backwards. The light now shining in her eyes was one I'd learned to mistrust years ago.

"Margaret, there certainly is. I'd been wondering what we were going to do, you know, because we can't meet in the town hall anymore. I mean, what with the hostile atmosphere down there and no telling if there's a spy, who knows but the room is probably bugged. And we don't want to start meeting in our own homes because, after all, these are supposed to be public meetings. But I've had the most marvelous brainstorm."

"Bitsy, I was talking about Diane. What are you talking about?"

"But this will help all the way around," she marched on, heedless of any questions in her path. "It's the perfect solution."

Ignoring Bitsy's brainstorms is always an attractive and usually a healthy option. But as this brainstorm seemed to be involving me in its solution, knowing more appeared to be the safest alternative. Forewarned, and all that. "What's the perfect solution to what, Bitsy? What meetings?"

"The Townscape Committee. We're going rogue."

Now there was an image. The Townscape Committee is made up of mostly mild mannered, retired gardening types appointed by the mayor, along with a few younger souls like Bitsy thrown in to do any heavy labor. As far as I know, their usual purview is making recommendations about what color petunias to plant in front of the courthouse each spring.

"Rogue? How?" I asked. Wandering the streets after dark with secateurs and trowels? "And why?"

"You haven't forgotten the Pigeon Episode have you? Or the welcome sign? Or Harriet's garden? Or what about Diane and Doug's fishpond, did you hear about that? And now with the fire we need to divorce ourselves from the town altogether. Why are you looking at me like that?"

I couldn't even begin to answer.

"You do see there's some connection between all these things don't you? Well, it doesn't matter whether you do or not. Because we do." Her every quivering muscle dared me to challenge that conclusion.

I coughed. "So, uh, where are you roguing off to?" And why did I feel the cold hand of unavoidable entanglement settling on the scruff of my neck?

"Don't you see? Here. The bookstore. We'll have the meetings here."

"Tell me again," I said slowly, in as unaccommodating a voice as I could muster, "why you aren't meeting at town hall anymore."

"Hostile environment."

"Mm. So why here?"

"Because, Margaret. Bertie's is gone. We'd already been toying with the idea of moving the meetings away from town hall to Bertie's, anyway. That was a good place for all kinds of reasons. A 'great good place.' Do you know what that means? You should be familiar with that term, you of all people. And now that Bertie's is gone, and especially considering everything else that's happened, a bookstore is one of the last great good places you can find in any town. Your bookstore, Margaret. It's a good place and people like to come here."

I didn't know what to say.

"So the meeting's tomorrow night at seven. And you don't need to do a thing. I'll bring the coffee and nibbles."

Nibbles. I still didn't know what to say so I said nibbles quietly to myself several times as she headed for the door. She stopped with her hand on the knob.

"Margaret, I forgot to tell you, your kitchen really does look fabulous. And there is one thing you can do."

I raised my eyebrows.

"Stay out of the kitchen until after the meeting."

CHAPTER 17

The greening of Bitsy was probably my fault. Not her green thumb, or her lifetime membership in the Garden Club, or the unhealthy interest she takes in the state of my backyard. The mystery of those gifts was bestowed upon her by the same slaphappy fate that has me fondling books day in and day out. But this activism of hers was something new. And thinking back, now, I could pinpoint when this particular bee landed in her bonnet.

When the town was all abuzz over passing the Historic Zoning Ordinance, with endless public input meetings and fraught question-and-answer sessions, I ordered in some books for a window display about communities, neighborhoods, and town planning. I may not run out and join clubs and societies the way Bitsy does, but I do have my moments of community involvement. I just tend to have them from behind stacks of books. One of the books I ordered was *The Great Good Place,* a title that caught my eye in a magazine article about vanishing downtowns.

Bitsy bought that book. I'd forgotten. Then she'd ordered a copy of *The Geography of Nowhere* and started reading Wendell Berry. And feeling compassion for pigeons and "organizing" the Townscape Committee.

What else might she have been up to lately, I wondered? Not assuming anything as far as she was concerned was not turning out to be especially comforting. My roiling mind was glad when lunchtime brought a rush of business to distract it.

What lunchtime didn't bring was Eunice for her afternoon shift. She didn't answer her cell, either. I would have hoped that meant she was in the car, in a rush and on her way, and not picking up because that's the safe way to drive. But when I'd called yesterday to see if she could take Fran's shift, she'd answered while at the top of Sam's Gap on her way to Asheville. Sam's Gap is a snake-winding, two-fisted, white-knuckle pass over the mountains featuring a cascade of runaway truck ramps. Possibly she was miffed at my having asked if she were out of her mind answering the phone

179

on a road like that. But twelve-thirty came, and one o'clock, and neither brought Eunice. I was disappointed. This was so unlike her reliable ways. I called again and left a message asking if she was okay and to please call back.

But it was destined to be a lunchtime of disappointments. Gene didn't arrive with a sandwich, either. By a quarter past one I was making a reluctant decision between peanut butter in my off-limits kitchen or calling out for pizza when the bell jingled over the door.

" 'Lo, Margaret."

"Oh, George. Hi."

"At least your stomach is happy to see me." We listened as my tummy gurgled the mating call of a small pan pizza with mushrooms and green olives. "Doesn't that scare the customers?"

"It discourages shop lifters. What can I do for you?"

"I brought you lunch." He started to put a grease-stained bag down on a book. I scooped the book out of the way and the bag landed harmlessly on the counter. I looked at him more closely, wondering what had him so dithery. It's never like George to be careless around books.

"Well, thank you, from both of us," I said,

patting my stomach.

He said nothing and studied the wall behind me, his brows drawn down over his doggy brown eyes to help in the effort. I let him work at that for a few minutes to see if anything was going to develop from it. Nothing did and finding my patience for him and his quirks in unusually short supply, I finally interrupted him.

"So, uh, George, to what do I owe this unexpected pleasure?"

"Just being friendly." He coughed and cleared his throat and looked off into the other room.

"Yeah?"

"Sorry about what I said last night. About Mashburn. You know." He took a breath, squared his shoulders and turned back to me. There was a peculiar look on his face and I realized with a start that it was a smile. "By the way, speaking of Mashburn, you seen him lately?" He probably thought he sounded casual and looked carefree. I tried not to discourage him by wincing.

"I saw him this morning about ten." I thought for a minute while his face continued struggling with breezy and light-hearted. Woebegone has always come more naturally to him, though, and it was gaining the upper hand. "But why the lunch,

George? What made you think I hadn't eaten yet?" Those two questions tipped the balance and any success at Jolly George receded as his innate misery washed back over him.

"Oh, no, you haven't eaten, have you? God, I'd hate to think your stomach makes noises like that even after you've eaten. Here," he opened the bag and pulled out a handful of fries and shoved them at me, "eat these before it comes out here and attacks on its own."

I popped a fry in my mouth, still looking at him, still thinking. The fry was crispy. Still hot. "Thanks, George. Now answer my question, please."

He didn't.

"Okay, we'll walk through it together. Somehow you know that Gene was planning to bring me lunch, right? And somehow you also know that he didn't. So how do you know that? And since you know he isn't bringing me lunch, do you know where he is? Is this lunch your way of telling me that he's unavailable? That he's down at the station helping with your inquiries, as they say?"

"No, Margaret, no," he waved his hands in the whoa, whoa, whoa way I often use, usually to no effect, on Bitsy. It made me wonder how shrill my voice was getting. "All I know is I saw Bitsy and we got to talking and I guess I told her something about the Fire Marshal and the detectives still wanting to talk to Mashburn and she happened to mention that he'd been planning to bring you lunch."

"He didn't go down to the station this morning?"

"No, no one's seen him. Except you. And of course Bitsy when he left here," he paused to clear his throat again, "this morning."

"So, if you thought he'd already brought me lunch, why did *you* bring me lunch?" I picked up the bag and shook it at him. "You couldn't just ask me if he'd been here, you had to bring this and ask my stomach? Since when don't you trust me, George? Boy, talk about low down. I'm disgusted with you and with my stomach for falling for it."

He looked as though I'd beaten him over the head with the lunch. He sighed and took the bag.

"Hey, where are you going with that?"

"Giving it to Lambert."

"No way, buster." I snatched it back. "I'm eating the evidence." I reached in and pulled out what turned out to be a cheeseburger with the works. I unwrapped it and took a bite.

"Sorry, Margaret. I'm a doofus."

"At least you got that right." Juice dribbled down my chin and made inroads into restoring my temper. "So, you want to make up for it?"

"Being a doofus?" he asked. "Sort of my natural state, don't you think?"

"No, for playing a rotten trick. That's not like you, George."

"You got the lunch. What more do you want?"

"Tell me what happened. How come Doug didn't make it out with Claire?"

"While you're eating?"

"Oh." I looked at the hamburger and put it down. "Why don't you go browse the dead and depressing while I try to finish?"

"I can't tell you everything, Margaret."

"Then tell me what you can."

He shrugged and lumbered off toward the philosophy section. I ate a few fries and wondered how far I could press him. Would he tell me if they suspected arson? Would he tell me why they were so anxious to talk to Gene? Did I want to know why? And, if I didn't want to know why, what did that tell me about myself? I picked up a pen and one of the napkins that came with the lunch. While absently finishing the burger, I at last

184

gave free reign to the questions disturbing my mind.

"You finished eating yet, Margaret? I got to get back before too long."

I looked up from the napkin where I'd ended up making a ghastly sort of list. Seeing words like "Duckie dead. How?" jotted so slap-dashedly on a fast food napkin unnerved me more than I would have thought.

"Geez, was the burger that bad? Because, you know, you're going to have to take your hand away from your mouth if you're going to ask me any questions. You going to puke or something?"

I crumpled the napkin and shoved it in a pocket, took a deep breath and let it out again. "No, I'm fine, George. Thanks. Ready?" He shrugged one shoulder. "Was it arson?"

"It looks . . . ," he hesitated before continuing. "It looks suspicious."

"Suspicious like on purpose? Couldn't it have been an accident? Maybe Claire and Doug lit some candles and left them burning? Maybe a deep-fat fryer got left on?"

"Doesn't look that way."

"What does Claire say?"

He shook his head. "Can't go there without compromising the investigation."

"Oh. So, what about Duckie? Why didn't

he get out?"

George thought about that, maybe struggled with something, then said, "Doug wasn't in any shape to make it out."

"What, he was overcome with smoke? He was plastered? He panicked and had a heart attack?"

"Postmortem won't be done for a few days. Look, Margaret, that's enough. I've gotta go and I've already told you too much."

"One more question, George, please." It didn't come out as smoothly as I wanted. "Why are you looking for Gene Mashburn? Is he some kind of suspect?"

"That's two questions and the second one pretty much answers the first. You know, Margaret, he's not a real savory guy." He picked up the empty lunch bag, crushing it into a tight ball. "Leona likes him, doesn't she?"

"She likes you, too, George. She's got good sense."

"Yeah, I'm a winner, all right. Mind if I get a drink of water before I head out?"

"Help yourself."

He went through to the kitchen and I pondered what he'd told me. And what he hadn't told me. What did happen to Doug? Was Claire a suspect, too? And why hadn't

I asked George exactly what he'd meant by "not real savory"? Or how it was that he knew whatever it was that he was hinting at about Gene? This business of being involved was giving me a grade A headache. I was massaging my temples when George came back out.

"You know, George," I said without looking up at him, "Gene hasn't gone anywhere. He left his bike in the kitchen . . ." Then I did look at him. "But you knew that, didn't you? Did you get a good look at it? Find the nail hole? Are you satisfied?" He didn't look terribly impressed. "And in case you're wondering, he lost his car keys in the fire."

"Ever heard of a bus or a rental car?" he asked.

"Oh."

"Margaret, look, I don't mean to worry you or upset you or whatever, but if you see him, tell him to give the station a call. Or you call. Okay? We just need to talk to him. Really. It's just questions. We're talking to everyone. Poor Bertie's been talking to people most of the day and Claire and Diane and Leona and . . ."

"Leona? What's she got to do with it?"

"We're interviewing everyone who was at the Garden Club dinner last night. Mom included. Boy did that one take awhile."

George's mother is a woman of many words.

"What about me?"

"Were you on the second floor or in Mashburn's apartment any time last night?"

"No, but I mean what about the rest of the people who were eating downstairs?"

"We'll let you know. And Margaret, you be sure and let Mashburn know that he better come see us. If you see him. Bye, Margaret."

CHAPTER 18

How lovely it would have been if the afternoon had mellowed into a pleasant haze of bookselling. But every second customer wanted to talk about the fire. Rumors were already making the rounds, which was only to be expected, and at some point I started adding the more interesting ones to the list on my crumpled napkin. I wondered, as I scribbled, if any truth also happened to be circulating. My favorite rumor had the ghost of the original bank president smiting Bertie's because the twin devils of music and alcohol were violating his memory.

Eunice didn't show up and she didn't answer her phone. I left another message and wondered if I should have mentioned her absence to George. Probably not. He would only have told me not to worry. Easy for him to say, even if only in my imagination. I gave not worrying a try, anyway.

Leona didn't totter in for her afternoon

tea. She doesn't always, so I decided not to worry about her, either. Maybe she was making a condolence call on the widow. Maybe she was helping the police with their inquiries. One of the rumors had an unnamed member of the Garden Club burning Bertie's for an unspecified transgression. The Case of the Horrible Horticulturist.

Most of the theories featured Claire in a love triangle. Some of the racier ones had her in a quadrangle. It was probably only a matter of time before someone had her sponsoring an orgy in the third floor apartment. After all, she'd been caught on film departing the building in a flaming bathrobe and no one believed that was because she'd been running herself through the restaurant's industrial dishwasher.

From what I've seen of Claire, she has a sense of humor, though, and that's good. It was going to come in handy dealing with everything being said. But, whatever part of the love geometry might be true, I couldn't believe she purposely set the fire.

Claire came to Stonewall from Asheville about a year ago, red hot and ready to be Bertie's heir to the restaurant, having earned her apron working in cafes, restaurants, and chic bars in exotic Nashville and

Atlanta.

I didn't take to her immediately. She had the idea that, being two single business-women in town, we should have a lot in common. Maybe it was a generational thing. Claire's one of these under-thirties always in a skirt and cute shoes. Maybe it was jealousy on my part. Imagine being in the restaurant business and maintaining that kind of figure. Just walking past Bertie's makes my blue jeans feel uncomfortable. But really my antipathy had more to do with Claire's suggestions for improving the bookstore. I have a hard time accepting advice from people who wouldn't know a book from a doorstop.

"Margaret, this place is so quaint," she'd said. "But why do some of the books look so old? Gosh, this one must be a hundred years old. Can't you afford to stock all new ones? Oh, and have you ever thought about clearing this room out and putting in a coffee bar?"

It had been hard on my onion ring habit, but I avoided Bertie's for a month or two. I'm not sure Claire even noticed. She's never appeared to hold my lack of enthusiasm for her advice and pep against me, anyway. And then she got more involved in running the restaurant and started meeting more people.

Like Duckie, apparently.

The day wound to a close and I locked the door behind the last satisfied customer. It was past my regular closing hour of six but a customer in the store is worth money in the till. As I started settling the cash register, the phone rang. It wasn't Eunice. But it was Fran calling to say she was back in town and ready to work all day tomorrow and the next if I needed her. How did that sound? Would I welcome some time off? I smooched the receiver as loudly as I could and asked what she thought.

To celebrate I stepped back to the kitchen and liberated the last beer from the refrigerator. The bike leaning against the stove tried to catch my attention, probably wanting to know when its rider was coming back. That was a question I was just as happy to ignore. I turned my back on the bike and its pathetic flat tire.

Eunice had lent me a CD I'd yet to try, so equipped with the twin devils of alcohol and music, I sashayed back out front. The CD was a double, *The Gaelic Collection* by Runrig, a Scottish rock band she thought I might appreciate. It's not necessarily something I'd play during business hours but the evening was my own. I cranked it up, popped the beer top, and did a Scottish two-step as I counted down the drawer.

The electric guitar was very jazzy. I had no idea what they were singing but they sang it so well and didn't seem to mind if I joined in. We finished reconciling the cash register, and as they were still going strong, I grabbed up the dust mop and we took a twirl around the floors.

My kitchen may defy Bitsy's powers of description from time to time, or most of the time, but that's only because the store gets the lion's share of my cleaning energy. It's an uneven distribution of a finite reserve with which the kitchen and I are both comfortable. I placate the kitchen by telling it that it exudes an enviable and sought after lived-in look. The kitchen shows its appreciation of the compliment by not turning green either with envy of the store or with mold.

Ordinarily I save store cleaning for Sunday mornings. Give me a pot of coffee, a mop, clean rags and then stand back. The place is caffeine-clean in no time. But sometimes I find myself cleaning on odd days for no apparent reason. At times like this I don't ask myself why. I follow my dust rag along and let my mind wander its own paths. Stream of conscience cleaning.

The Runrig boys took a melancholy turn. I slowed down and my thoughts turned toward supper. Which brought to mind Bitsy's admonition to stay out of the kitchen, which brought me back again to thoughts of the bike and the absent Gene Mashburn. Thoughts I'd rather not dwell upon. I tried losing myself in the always atrocious accumulation of dust on the bottom shelves. It's also a good place for losing one's appetite. I swear it's as though my place is a regular stop along the trade route for some pack of ever-shedding dogs. Though why I single out dogs, I don't know. Maybe it's an infestation of sheep in the wainscoting.

Far from losing my appetite this time, though, I realized I was beginning to salivate. I stood upright and took a sniff. Something lovely was in the air. Hard to say exactly what. Something tastier than Endust, anyway. I must be hallucinating. I pulled a tissue from my pocket and carefully blew my nose. Too much dust, obviously. But it was still there. Was it meat? Cheese? The musicians had livened up again. Maybe they could smell it, too. What did haggis smell like?

Armed with my trusty, dusty rag, I followed my nose and we found ourselves at the kitchen door. I paused there, contemplating my next move. If the music weren't so loud, I could probably hear sizzling to complement the delectable aromas working their way between the door and the frame. I might also have heard the intruder in the kitchen in the first place. Rather than turn the music down, now, though, I kept it cranked up to cover my movements. If someone wanted to surprise me with invasive cooking, I planned to surprise that person with a stealthy approach. I eased the door open.

"Hi. I was about to come get you. Supper'll be ready in a tick."

I beheld this vision through narrowed eyes. Mr. Domestic. Lacking only an apron. Gene Mashburn at the stove, spatula in hand. The table was set. Candles lit. I owned candlesticks? A bag of potato chips and a six-pack of Coke lent casual grace notes as the centerpiece.

"Good thing I don't keep the back door locked."

"Kind of surprises me you don't."

"And keep out wandering cooks? What a notion." I leaned against the doorjamb, arms crossed, watching him as he collected plates and slid sandwiches onto them from the frying pan.

"Smells delicious."

"Thanks."

"I'll be right back." He raised his eyebrows. "Get rid of this." I held up the dust rag. "And I'll tell the boys out front to cool it." I slipped back out front, put the dust rag in my dirty rag bag, turned off the music. Wondered if I should call George. My stomach counseled that we eat first and make decisions or phone calls later.

"I was telling Bitsy this afternoon that you're a domestic soul. This is nice," I said, sitting down.

"Man's gotta eat."

"So you said."

"Sorry about lunch. But I'm hoping this will make up for it." He was watching me anxiously so I picked up my sandwich and cast an appraising eye over it.

"A Reuben?" I took an exploratory bite. Not quite a Reuben. A Reuben with a difference. "Wow."

"You like it?"

For answer I took another bite.

"Made with kimchi instead of sauerkraut. I call it a Seoul Food Reuben."

I tried not to aspirate kimchi. "Your own recipe?"

"If you can call it a recipe."

"It's good," I said, nodding and munching. "It's surprising, too, and I like that."

He sat back, looking happy and relieved, then leaped forward again and opened the potato chip bag and popped the tops on two of the cans. He handed one across to me then offered his can for a toast. "Here's to your bonny blue eyes," he said, and my cheeks grew warm. "May they never meet."

"You're a very strange person, Gene Mashburn."

"I aim to please."

We settled into eating the sandwiches, crunching chips, and smiling tentatively across at each other. Then he said, in what was probably meant to be an offhand way, "You didn't ask why I didn't make it for lunch." But I saw the slight twitch in his left eye as he waited for my answer.

I chewed another bite, making him wait a bit longer. And then I wasn't entirely honest. "I didn't want to be nosy."

"Ah," he said, nodding as though I were somehow profoundly wise. That made me feel guilty, something I *am* profoundly good at. So I opened my mouth and my day spilled out, from Bitsy's insinuations, to the absent Eunice, to the plethora of rumors running around town, to the visitation of doleful Officer Buckles.

197

"So, you see," I summed up, "I'm not entirely sure I want to know why you didn't make it for lunch." I concentrated on the last bites of my sandwich, admiring the caraway seeds in the rye and the perfect, overall crisp browning. None of it as fascinating as I made it look.

"I saw George before I came over here," Gene said.

"Oh. And you're not in the slammer. That's encouraging."

"Were you worried about that?"

"I didn't know what to worry about. So many choices."

"George said you were worried about something."

"George isn't happy unless everyone is worried about something."

"George is worried," Gene said. "About you."

"What, has he been comparing notes with Leona? Does he all of a sudden think I'm a, what was it? A sensitive screecher?"

"No, screecher is what your sister is. Little creature is what your cousin called you. I think that's kind of sweet. Anyway, he was more worried about you in terms of me. Of whom he hasn't got a very high opinion."

"George has a hard time letting go."

George hasn't really got any illusions

about the two of us ever getting back together, so that was an automatic and pretty meaningless remark. But I'm not always good about asking the questions that are obvious and probably should be asked. Like, did George have a valid reason for his root-cellar-level opinion of Gene? It's not that I wasn't wondering. It's that there's a disconnect between the questions like that moseying around in my brain and my willingness to utter them out loud.

Maybe that has something to do with my not liking confrontations. Or with a preference for the path of least resistance. Or with my general lack of interest in getting involved.

I could hear Bitsy clearing her throat in my head. If I let my imagination go any further I'd be feeling her bony elbow poking me in the ribs.

"Are you all right?" Gene asked.

"Hm? Oh, yeah. Sorry," I said. "So, did you find out if you can salvage anything from the fire?"

"Can't go in yet."

"How's the place structurally?"

"My guess is fine. It's a solid old building and the fire department got things under control pretty quickly."

"George didn't happen to let loose any

more details, did he? Like who started the fire? I take it they don't really think you did or you wouldn't be sitting here."

"Notice the change in clothes?" I noticed the change in subject. But he spread his arms wide and I realized I hadn't paid any attention to what he had on. Except that the colors in the plaid shirt were a lovely compliment to his blue eyes. I peeked under the table. Chinos instead of blue jeans. New shoes, too.

"Been shopping? I guess that makes sense. Man's gotta be dressed."

He wiggled his eyebrows at that and I tried to ignore them.

"I did some shopping after I saw George and talked to his friends down at the station. They wanted what I was wearing last night." I stared at him. "So, I guess the jury is still out on what they think. But don't worry. They've got Claire's bathrobe, too. They're just being thorough."

"But couldn't it have been Duckie?" I managed to splutter. "Maybe he was despondent over his problems with Diane. George said he wasn't in any shape to make it out. Maybe he committed suicide and started the fire to cover it up, you know, so Diane could still collect insurance or something." He looked at me with his pseudo-mental health look. "What? What's wrong with that idea? It makes more sense than Bitsy's idea that the Mafia did it."

His eyes dropped and he started fiddling with the pop-top on his can. It broke off. "George didn't tell you?"

"Tell me what?"

"Doug was murdered."

"My god." My god. And the police weren't entirely sure this man hadn't done it.

CHAPTER 19

"No one who could invent the Seoul Food Reuben could be a murderer, dear," Leona said.

"I'd like to believe that."

"Don't you?"

"I don't know. I've never met one before. Either a murderer or a sandwich inventor."

Leona and I were sitting in her kitchen the next morning drinking coffee. I was up and looking halfway presentable at an unnecessary hour considering Fran would be opening the store. But only halfway presentable because the other half of me was suffering the effects of two nights, now, without enough sleep. Leona had at first complimented me on my bright and early rising. Then she'd taken a second look and hurried to plug in the coffeepot.

"Leona, how is it that you're so sure he didn't do it?"

"He told me he didn't."

That simple. He'd told me that, too. After I'd come close to throwing up that lovely sandwich at the news Doug was murdered. I'd controlled myself for the sake of his new shoes. Instead I chugged another can of soda, a contributing factor to my sleepless night. He let me sit there and had quietly gone about doing the dishes and wiping the table and putting away the potato chips and blowing out the candles.

"I had an idea for dessert," he'd said when the kitchen was again spotless and alien looking. "But we should probably save that for another time. Do you ever get away from here during the day?" I just looked at him. "You know, time off for good behavior?"

"Oh, there's an apt turn of phrase. Yeah. I'm taking the next couple of days off."

"I was thinking, if you want to, you could stop by the old school building and I'll show you the plans. I think you'd like them. If you want to. No big deal."

"Thanks. I'll let you know. Oh, I didn't even ask. Did you find a place to stay?"

"Yeah, I did."

"That's good."

"Yeah."

We didn't seem to have anything else to say. I could have asked him where he was staying but I didn't. Finally he coughed in a leave-taking way and opened the back door.

"Good night, Margaret."

"Good night. Thanks for supper."

"It was my pleasure." He pulled the door shut behind him and I put my head down on the table. "Oh, Margaret?"

I jerked upright. "What?"

"Lock the back door, okay?"

And I did. And I'd gone to bed and not slept. And now found myself sitting here surrounded by Leona's faithful multitude of African violets.

One thing Bitsy and I agree on without equivocation is that we both despise Leona's African violets. Not a sentiment either of us is proud of. But they are the doted upon small dogs of her life, the spoiled grandchildren she never had, about whom she runs on with uncharacteristic saccharin maunderings. It showed the depths of my despond that I was sitting there now, stroking the leaves of one.

"You know, dear," Leona said, moving the violet out of my reach, "knowing that your mind is uneasy with suspicions, as he surely does, don't you think that if he were guilty he wouldn't be interested in seeing you again?"

"That's an interesting bit of convoluted comfort."

"And that's your trouble, dear. Over-analyzing." She patted my hand and offered me another cup of coffee.

"No, thanks. Maybe I'll see if I can take a nap later and more coffee now won't help that. You're going to miss your morning cup at Bertie's aren't you?"

"It gave me a reason to get up and stirring. I'll just have to find another reason."

"You're always welcome over at my place. You know that."

"I do know, dear. The trouble is that you so often barely make it up in time to open the store and when you do you aren't the most pleasant of conversationalists. First thing in the morning, that is."

I grunted something unintelligible to give her the satisfaction of being right. "You could always come over early and prod me awake."

"Not without danger pay, dear. But don't worry about me. Something will work out and in the meantime I'll be happy to come over for afternoon tea. You're much more civilized when you've been around your books for several hours."

She got up and poured another cup of coffee. Not for either one of us, but in a third, violet-decorated mug. My sleep deprived brain found this confusing but sorted it out

205

without too much pain.

"Bitsy appearing any minute?" I thought maybe I'd disappear before she did.

"No, dear."

Then I caught the unmistakable sound of stocking feet padding down her hallway and looked up to see Gene Mashburn, covering a yawn with the hand not dangling his shoes, hair tousled and damp from a shower. An uncanny knack, this guy had, popping up this way. The yawn turned into a crooked smile when he saw me. He looked so good.

"You taking in boarders, Cousin Leona?"

"A friend in need, Margaret."

And whether it was logical or not, that statement of her faith in him was enough for me. I sat back and watched him stir sugar and cream into his coffee and thought about the evening they must have spent together. Leona nattering on about her African violets, Gene taking an interest and maybe offering to repot one or two for her. Or the two of them comfortable in the twin, chintz-covered overstuffed armchairs in her living room, surrounded by and at risk of being smothered by crochet, with more violets looking over their shoulders as they watched something companionably on PBS or The Learning Channel.

"That's her trouble, you know," Leona

said through a fog, "letting her attention wander like that."

"I think she dozed off," Gene said.

"I did not," I lied.

"You'll have noticed she's not at her most charming first thing in the morning," Leona said.

He was either kind enough not to comment or he'd seen the brief, uncharming look I'd given Leona and he had a healthy sense of self-preservation. "I was asking if you'd given any more thought to stopping by the school."

Had I? Yeah, that had probably contributed to some of the tossing and turning last night. Not as much as the memory of him wobbling down the street with a can of gasoline the night before the fire. Or the stirrings of unease that crept around when I wondered what exactly George knew. Or thoughts of that curious midnight hike with the flat tire. Probably he'd vacated the apartment for Doug and Claire's convenience . . .

"You go on. When she wakes up I'll send her over. Best to let sleeping Margarets be."

How kind, I thought, and went back to softly snoring on Leona's kitchen table.

"I'm not asleep," I said a few minutes later.

207

"No, dear, you've just been resting your eyes for the last half hour."

"Whoa, that long?" I sat up and was glad to see I hadn't drooled all over her table. "Well, thanks for the nap, anyway. You want to walk over to the school with me later?"

"You're not going now?" she asked.

"No, Fran's been gone awhile. I should fill her in on what's what."

"On the fire? On the fellow who's put that sparkle in your eye?"

"On business, Cousin Leona. The store. Continuity keeps us sane and the customers happy."

What she had in her eye was that complacent, all-knowing, elderly cousin look she has down pat. There's no arguing with that look. She'll believe what she wants to believe. But it did make me try to catch my reflection as I gave my coffee cup a rinse. Sparkle in my eye, eh?

"Don't make yourself cross-eyed looking in the faucet, dear. Go home and look in a mirror. It's there. That's your trouble, you know, not believing what you're told."

"And if I believed everything I'm told what would you say?"

"Hmph."

"That's what I thought. Thanks for the coffee, Leona. Thanks for putting up Gene.

Thanks for putting up with me." I gave her a kiss on the way past. "See you later." I left her trying to look fierce, but the flustered pink in her cheeks gave her away.

As I crossed our backyards to my kitchen door, I sniffed the air for any lingering smoke. None, at least not this many blocks away. Maybe if the wind were blowing directly from Bertie's, but as it turned out the day was calm and sunny. I hadn't noticed that when stumbling over to Leona's first thing.

Starlings were fussing overhead in the old silver maple between our yards. They're Leona's least favorite birds and she fusses at them as much as they fuss at each other. According to one of the bird books in the store, starlings are great mimickers. After reading that, I told Leona that if she would only speak more sweetly to them or maybe sing to them they might sound less like cranky old ladies. This morning the starlings were saying things much like what she'd said in reply.

I blew a raspberry to them and tried to open the back door. It was locked. Not being used to keeping it locked during the day, I hadn't thought to bring my keys with me. The starlings were now busy taking notes on how to sound like a ticked-off not-so-old lady and I went around to the front and met Fran opening up.

Fran is in her mid sixties, roundish, grayish, an insatiable reader. She was a good customer before coming to work for me. Now she's that person all small bookstores hope the bookselling gods will send them and let them keep — an intelligent, capable, available person who can afford to work for an embarrassingly low wage and no benefits other than an employee discount and the privilege of spending time with books.

Fran gives me four days a week and spreads the rest of her time between volunteering for Meals on Wheels and dreaming of the traveling she and her husband, Jim, plan to do when he retires. I selfishly encourage him to put that time off as long as possible. He must have at least ten good years left in him, fifteen if he takes care of himself. I gave him a copy of *Fit for Life* last Christmas.

"You're out and about early," Fran greeted me. "I thought you might be sleeping in."

"Nope, been communing with nature. How's your mother?"

Fran walked around behind the counter and perched on the stool. "We'll either be moving her in with us or looking for a nursing home soon."

"Oh. Wow. Which would you rather do?" I knew immediately which I'd rather she did. I wondered if her mother was open to bribes.

"Not sure." She shook her head. "I'd rather not deal with it at all. So what's been going on around here?"

"Sophomores are reading *A Separate Peace* and we're out until the order comes in but by now all the darlings should have their copies anyway. Let's see, I sold that set of Waverley novels that's been sponging off us for the last two years. The woman is coming by today or tomorrow to pick them up. They're in two boxes on the bottom shelf there. And . . ."

"And Bertie's burned down and Doug Everett died in the fire."

"I forgot to tell you that last night, didn't I?"

"Oh, no need," she said. "Jim called and told me yesterday morning. It's the talk of the town, though. That's for sure."

"Rumors are flying."

"Isn't that the truth. You know, I can't remember the last time someone died in a fire around here. My heart aches for Diane and the girls. 'My *three* beautiful girls' Doug called them. Well, it's just sad." Fran shook her head, as though disbelief and sorrow might bring Doug back to his family. "He owned that building, didn't he?"

"Did he?"

"Oh, I'm pretty sure he did," she said. "Bertie's been after him for years to sell it."

"Huh."

"And then there's Bertie's. When I think of all the good times we had there. Whoosh. Up in smoke. Well, not the memories. Memories can't go up in smoke, can they? But the whole thing is almost too much to take in. Any official word on the cause yet? Margaret?"

But I was busy adding to the paper napkin list I'd started yesterday and transferred to today's pocket. "Duckie owned BT building?" went on it and then "Bertie wanted building?"

"What's that?" Fran asked.

"Note to myself." I jammed the list back in my pocket, at the same time choking down the words "Doug was murdered." For some reason I couldn't say them. Too shocking? Too raw yet? I didn't know so I rushed on. "There's something else, Fran. Eunice has flaked out on us. She didn't show up for work yesterday and isn't answering her phone. Or returning messages."

"She's gone Amish," Fran said.

"Really? Can you just do that?" I tried

picturing six-foot Eunice in a plain dress and apron. Her tattoos didn't fit in. "The other day she was talking about joining a monastery in Minnesota. I didn't realize she had such exotic religious tendencies."

By now Fran was laughing. "No, no, sorry. Going Amish is was what my great niece calls it when she decides to rough it by leaving her phone at home."

"Oh, well Eunice had her phone with her on the way to Asheville day before yesterday."

"Low battery, no reception, she lost it," Fran ticked off the reasons Eunice might not have received or returned my messages. "Or she really did flake out. But you're right. It isn't like her to miss work. Did you go knock on her door?"

"No, I didn't. I don't know whether I'm more worried or aggravated. But I guess if I haven't gone over there, I'm more aggravated. I'll stop by today. You never know, maybe Archie pounced once too often. So. . . ."

"And so, Margaret, what else is new? Anything less tragic or aggravating going on?" Fran could use lessons from Leona on looking innocent.

"Nothing much," I said sweetly.

"Oh, oh, but wait, let me get a better look

213

at you." She leaned over the counter, eyes wide. "I thought so. Why, I can tell just by looking at you."

"Oh, for heaven's sake."

"So what's he like?" She settled back down on the stool like a broody hen. Her unmarried daughter lives off in California so she makes do with vicarious mother thrills where she can get them. "Is he as cute as Claire says? She was in line behind me at Kroger's last night. Wouldn't you know Jim didn't do any shopping the whole time I was gone? And wasn't that awful about Claire? And wasn't she lucky? Oh, and then I saw Bitsy this morning when I was getting gas. So, is he as shifty as Bitsy claims?"

I pulled one of the rocking chairs around to face the counter and sat, legs crossed, gently rocking.

"Now you look like the cat who swallowed the canary."

"Go check out the kitchen."

She did and came back suitably stunned. "You're nesting? He's that impressive? *I'm* certainly impressed."

"Not me. He did that."

"Holy cow."

"And he cooks."

"And you haven't dragged him off to the

wedding chapel yet?"

"Is that what you would recommend to your daughter after knowing the man for approximately three days?"

The bell over the door jingled and Fran immediately turned her smiling attention there. The hallmark of good customer service. Also a handy way to avoid answering my question. As she and the customer headed over to the cookbooks discussing various Mediterranean recipes, I headed upstairs. There I brushed my teeth, also avoiding answering a question by not looking at my reflection from the nose up. Whether there was a sparkle in my baby blues or not would have to wait until later. Contemplating whatever that sparkle might entail would have to wait, too.

I clattered back down the stairs, told Fran I'd spell her over lunch, and waved goodbye.

My car hacked its requisite number of times. I should get that checked out, but it always purrs to life afterwards so that probably won't happen anytime soon. I caught a glimpse of Leona waving from her back porch but ignored her the same way I'd ignored the alleged sparkle in my eye and my feet trying to hijack me and walk me in the direction of the old school. I backed out and headed down the alley, on my way somewhere else instead.

First stop was the bakery over on Market. They bake the most wonderful breads and the best muffins in town. Actually, Bitsy turns out a mean muffin, too. And she can blow you away with things like strudel. Her apple strudel is my favorite. The smell in her kitchen when strudel is in the oven is beyond compare. Cinnamon, cloves, nutmeg . . . I suddenly realized I should have eaten breakfast before coming here, but I parked at the curb, composed myself, and went inside.

It was like stepping through a curtain of warm yeast and spices. In order not to disgrace myself by slobbering all over the display case, I quickly bought a cup of tea and an order of hot buttered walnut raisin rosemary toast. Heaven. I sat at one of the tables near the door and watched while other people gamely attempted to place coherent orders in that heady atmosphere. Most of them probably bought twice as much of anything as they'd intended to.

After inhaling the first piece of toast, I was able to concentrate better and started catching bits of passing conversations. Not surprisingly, many of them included speculations on the fire and Doug's death.

Claire's name came up, of course, but not in any ways more unusual than I'd heard yesterday. I even heard Mafia once, bless Bitsy and her gullibility. One woman said she'd heard it was Eleanor DeAngelis who reported the fire. Considering what odd hour of the middle of the night that must have been, it seemed unlikely, but who knew? There were head shakings and mostly genuine sounding murmurs of sorrow for Diane and the children. The interesting thing was that no one mentioned the word murder. No hints even.

I played around with the toast crumbs on my plate while pondering the significance of that. Why, when rumors as ridiculous as my forty-year-old Mafia number were playing the field, was no one avidly reporting the choicest bit? Was the murder a piece of information only a few key people other than the police were privy to? Key people like suspects? Should Gene have told me about it? Or, for that matter, was it even true? There was a stumper.

"Reduced to writing grocery lists on grease-stained napkins?" William DeAngelis asked, startling me.

"Sad, isn't it?" I said, refolding my poor old napkin list and returning it to its home in the depths of my pocket. I wondered if he'd been able to read anything on it. An embarrassing sort of list with which to be seen. The next rumors to circulate would include Margaret Welch, deluded detective.

"Surely you haven't left your shop unattended?" he asked.

"Fran's there, William. Did you want to stop in and pay your bill?"

"No, but it's strange seeing you out from behind your books, you know, and it's happened twice now in one week. It's disconcerting. I hardly recognize you."

"It makes me light-headed, too," I said, standing up and moving toward the counter. I thought about telling him he didn't look the same, either, without a corpse or two in tow but decided to save that line for a more appropriate occasion. "Any word yet on when the funeral will be?"

"Which funeral?"

Which funeral? I suddenly felt panicked. "Why? Who else has died?"

218

CHAPTER 20

"Tut, tut, people die all the time, Margaret," William said. "If I asked you if 'the book' was out, would it make any more sense than you asking me about 'the funeral'?"

Oh, swell, nothing like asking William a supposedly simple question in a public place for attracting attention. All ears were now attending.

"Or does the bake staff here speak of 'the doughnut'?"

"Yeah, okay, I get it. Sorry, William." I turned my back on him, hoping he'd stay with the majority of his audience. I'd come in here for something to take to Diane. Time to be about my business.

"Of course you were probably referring to services for my poor dear cousin-in-law, Douglas, *n'est-ce pas?*"

What a fruit. "Yes, I was William. Do you know when it is?" I edged further along the display case. He has no sense of personal space.

"Tomorrow. Ten thirty. And if you were thinking of taking dear Diane that tunnel of fudge cake, she already has more cakes than any grieving widow should be asked to cope with. Why don't you be original and take her bagels or some sort of sandwich rolls?"

He had a point. I bought the tunnel of fudge cake, anyway, and a crusty round loaf of the walnut raisin rosemary bread, William tsk-tsking closely over my shoulder. I rolled my eyes for the benefit of the young woman at the cash register, which wasn't nice of me because then she nearly choked trying not to laugh. On the way out, I heard William asking quietly if that had been the last tunnel of fudge cake.

He'd guessed right, though, and my next stop was the Everetts. Not a visit I looked forward to. It's not as though Diane and I were ever particular friends. But I'd known her and Doug since we were kids. And Doug had been a neighborhood pal way back when, playing kick the can with Bitsy and me into the summer twilights, hawking lemonade from homemade stands, running days-long, sweaty, Monopoly marathons. He gave me a kiss at the top of the jungle gym when I was in third grade and he was in fourth. I hit him right between the eyes with a slush ball.

I sighed at the memories and made my way across town.

Diane and Doug lived in an area called the Grundy Addition. It's another neighborhood that's prone to large marsupial perambulations. You have to say it like that, though, because possum, as a word, is too common. Picture the possum with a top hat, a gold-tipped cane, and keys to a Jaguar or a BMW Z-3 and you get the idea. It's a picture I'm especially fond of because the grown-up Duckie had a sly look about him. If he'd ever grown a mustache, it couldn't have helped but look like whiskers sprouting on either side of his pointy nose.

I parked at the curb behind a familiar car, then tucked the loaf of bread under my arm and headed up Diane's walk. The tunnel of fudge cake stayed behind on the front seat. That was an impulse purchase for someone else.

The houses along these streets were all built in the 1940s and 50s. But no post-war ticky-tacky boxes these. They are substantial and comfortable and surrounded by deep, green lawns. It's the kind of neighborhood where black jockey statues used to meet you at the end of the front walk or outside the front door, lanterns held aloft in perpetual welcome.

I didn't see any jockeys as I glanced around on my way up Diane's flagstone walk. Maybe there's a quiet corner of the county landfill set aside as a graveyard for politically incorrect lawn ornaments. That thought gave me a moment of warm pleasure that must have lingered somewhere on my face after I rang the doorbell.

Bitsy opened the door.

"What? What's so funny?" she asked. "Have I got something stuck in my teeth?" She zipped a fingernail between her front teeth. "Gone?" She bared them at me. I opted for nodding rather than explaining. "Good. Oh, and thank god you're here, Margaret." For some reason she was whispering. Then she stuck her head out the door, looked left, looked right, and pulled me inside. "You got here just in time."

Once inside, we had a brief skirmish over who was going to propel me down the hall. I won, probably because the better part of her mind was taken up with whatever circumstances had her yapping *sotto voce*. I took advantage of her preoccupation and put the brakes on any further progress.

"Bitsy, I only came to drop off a loaf of bread. She doesn't need me hanging around."

"Bread?" Her mind flipped channels. "You haven't been messing around in your kitchen, baking, have you?" I flashed the loaf at her, still in its bakery bag. "That's all right, then." And she was back to the previous channel of desperation, "but Margaret, you've got to help me."

"With what?" I hated sounding unfeeling or un-neighborly or at least un-near neighborly, but given the present situation what could possibly need doing that Bitsy wouldn't handle far more gracefully than I?

"Bitshy? Whoizhit? Bring'em on in an' we'll have a lil drink."

"Is that Diane?" I asked. Bitsy could only nod. "She's plowed?" Here indeed was a situation that Bitsy might have trouble with. The only thing that would make it more uncomfortable for her would be if Diane also happened to be puffing on a fat cigar. "Well, Bitsy, you know, people react to grief in strange ways sometimes. Where are the girls?"

"Doug's mother took them," she said.

"And Diane's mother?"

"Lying down with a sick headache. She just wandered off and left me to cope. Tears, I can cope with. Shock. Maybe some ranting and raving, but this . . ."

"No one else is here?"

223

She shook her head.

"C'mon an' join the party," Diane hiccupped from wherever she was letting her hair down.

"Margaret," Bitsy pleaded, "help me out with her, please, just for a while."

"Surely she's got friends you can call."

"And let the rumor mill run wild? You know what this town is like. The least I can do is protect her from that."

Sometimes I find myself looking at my sister through eyes suddenly emptied of all the old sibling baggage. She is a decent human being. "Okay, Bitsy. I'll stay for a while. Why don't you go make some coffee."

"Margaret, Margaret, Margaret," Diane greeted me. "You like margaritas, Margaret?"

"No, I've never gotten the hang of tequila. Is that what you're drinking?"

"No, too much trouble to mix 'em. Give me a lil whisky, though, and I'm happy as a lil ol' clam." She seemed happy enough for a bushel of clams.

I'd found her in the living room, sunk deep and slightly cockeyed into an overstuffed sofa and maybe a bit deeper and more cockeyed into the whisky. She looked safe enough, though. At this point she probably couldn't get up out of the sofa without help. Maybe with a bit of encouragement she'd sink the rest of the way into the sofa and sleep it off.

I sat opposite her, in a chair so soft and large that I was tempted to take up residence in it. There wasn't quite room for a pony but a good-sized cat would find adequate space to stretch out next to me. About two yards of highly polished coffee table separated the Diane-engulfing sofa from my chair and I put my big blue canvas purse down on it. I call it a purse. Bitsy calls it my mobile bookstore. She doesn't mean that as a compliment but I'm fond of both the bag and the description anyway. And now I was happy to discover another point in its favor. Strategically placed, my purse turns out to be the perfect size for a bottle of Scotland's best to hide behind. It might not be a lasting solution, but at least it might give Bitsy and me time to distract Diane into some other form of grief therapy. I did find it interesting, and somehow typical, that even in her dissolute grief Diane was maintaining her standards. Crawling into a sofa and a bottle of single malt must be class.

"Diane, I'm so sorry about Doug."

"About which part? That the ungrateful sonofabitch was unfaithful, which kind of rhymes, or that he only escaped becoming a crispy critter by cheating because he was already dead? That's cheating twice, yashk me."

"Pretty much the whole thing, I guess." No wonder Bitsy was at a loss. She would definitely have trouble fitting this behavior into any of the handy compartments she uses for organizing daily life as she likes to know it.

"That's sweet of you to say, Margaret, Margaret, Margaret, how come no one ever calls you Margie?"

"Because I'd kill anyone who tried." Oops.

"Good thinking. I like a woman who knows how to stand up for herself." She struggled briefly to rise and be counted among that number but thank goodness the sofa defeated her.

"Here we are," chirruped Bitsy, arriving with a laden tray and beaming too brightly. "Margaret, why don't you take your mobile bookstore off the table so I can put the tray down."

"Oh, there's plenty of room, Bitsy. See? I'll move it down to this end."

She was about to argue but caught on with an appreciative widening of her eyes as I slid my purse and its furtive companion down to the other end. She arranged the tray then sat carefully on the edge of the sofa. She must have experienced its clutching depths some time in the past and wasn't taking any chances.

"Coffee, Margaret?" she asked. "It's freshly ground and freshly brewed. I used some heavenly smelling gourmet beans I found in the kitchen. I know I'm dying to try some." She faltered there, then floundered gamely on. "Diane? Coffee? And how about something to eat?"

Bitsy relaxed into her element. She'd always loved playing tea party with her dolls, too. Getting into the spirit of things myself, and to encourage Diane to eat something, I politely took slices from several of the goodies Bitsy had arranged so pleasingly on the tray. Then, while Bitsy fixed a plate for Diane, I took the opportunity to look around the room.

It's one of those living rooms that doesn't look as though a lot of living goes on in it. Bitsy has one that looks that way, but I know it's an illusion. She and Rodney use the room; they just live careful lives. But the way this room looked, and considering that two teenage girls and all their paraphernalia live in the house, it was hard to believe any of them spent much time there. If I were to get up and walk across to the French windows, I'd probably leave a trail of footprints in the lush pile of the carpet.

Glancing out those windows, now, I caught sight of the remains of the fishpond. The scaly victims must have been removed but scattered shards of cracked, glazed tiles still glinted in the sun. They looked abandoned and hopeless.

What with the shock of the fire and Doug's death, I'd forgotten about my plans to play detective at the Garden Club dinner. How naïve and innocent we were two nights ago. If I could whistle, now might be the right time to break into "What Kind of Fool Am I."

So, I asked myself while munching a second slice of something delicious with dates and chocolate chips in it, was there a connection between any of the acts of vandalism? Was Doug's fishpond explosion in answer to the downtown pigeon massacre? Or Harriet's melted garden? For that matter, was the fire an escalation of those activities? Except, if Doug's murder were an escalation from manure in a dumpster or goats terrorizing a bulldozer driver, someone had skipped a few steps. If it were murder. I sipped Diane's gourmet coffee, hoping it was loaded with gourmet caffeine that would nip my blossoming headache in the bud.

"Margaret, you're always so quiet," Diane slurred. "One of the things I've always liked about you. You too, Bitsy, 'cept you're noisier."

"Margaret," Bitsy grated between long-suffering teeth, "I was telling Diane that we know what her girls must be going through, having lost our own father when we were young."

" 'Cept your father probably wasn't a cheating sonofabitch," Diane said. "Probably wasn't murdered either."

Bitsy dropped her coffee cup.

CHAPTER 21

Luckily Bitsy's cup was almost empty. Between the two of us and a handful of Diane's beautiful and obviously expensive paper napkins, we got things mopped up and tidy again. I took a deep breath and was about to be crass and ask Diane what exactly had happened when Bitsy leapt in.

"Oh, surely not. You're just distraught, Diane, and no wonder. I mean this whole situation has been a nightmare for you. But you need to think about the girls, now. You can't be saying things like that. Really, you mustn't."

Diane shook her head enthusiastically, stopped to let her eyes quit jiggling, then started nodding. "Oh, but it's true. Died with his pants off in the sofa bed."

"But surely he was overcome with smoke. Margaret, you tell her. You said it yourself, it was a horrible, terrible accident."

"Oh, but Bitsy," Diane said, "it is so hard

to accidentally fold yourself up like that in a sofa bed with just one foot sticking out." Bitsy snapped her mouth shut and Diane grinned wickedly, albeit crookedly, at her shock. Then she turned to me. "You knew the sonofabitch was murdered, din't you, Margaret."

"I heard something about it," I said quietly. I waited a minute then went ahead and asked. "How was he killed? Do you know?"

"Margaret!" Bitsy shrilled.

" 'S'all right, Bitsy, no secrets 'mong friends. He was strangled." Diane put her hands around her throat and made a ghastly face. Bitsy turned away and tried not to retch. I studied my knees.

When I looked up again Diane had sunk further into the sofa. Her eyes were closed and tears ran down her cheeks. By the time Bitsy regained her composure, Diane was asleep.

Not knowing what else to do, I started clearing away our tea party. I heard an exhalation from Bitsy's side of the coffee table and flicked a glance at her. She was sighing and shaking her head, two things she does that signal an imminent pro-nouncement, usually of a conclusion she's reached by way of a snap judgment. Worse, she was regarding me with what I've tried telling her is an unattractive, slitty-eyed look. My view of that look might be jaundiced, though, because it's usually a further signal that her pronouncement involves me.

But she didn't say anything. She took a throw from the back of the sofa and gently covered Diane with it. Then she followed me, like my own personal shroud of gloom, when I carried the tray out to the kitchen.

She brought the bottle of Scotch.

"I can't believe you knew he was murdered and you didn't tell me. I can't believe you asked her for details. I can't believe you're actually going to go see that Mashburn character. He's so obviously the murderer. Did you even think of that? I can't believe you didn't."

Bitsy paced up and down on Diane's Italian tile kitchen floor after pouring the Scotch down the drain. I'd made the mistake of trying to make inconsequential, soothing small talk, telling her that Leona and I were taking a walk later to look at the plans for the old school.

Now I weathered her storm by estimating how many of the beautifully patterned blue, green, yellow, and white tiles had sacrificed their lives for this floor. The kitchen is about

232

half a basketball court larger than mine. Had the floor cost as much as I make in six months? More? While Bitsy catalogued the things she couldn't believe, I let my mind be boggled by the unbelievable wealth she was working so hard to wear out under her pointy shoes.

"And poor Claire. My god, she probably didn't even know Doug was there stuffed in that sofa like that. And that goes right back to that Mashburn again. Claire was probably there to meet him and now poor Diane is convinced that Doug was cheating and this is all too much."

The counters were tiled, too, with a complimentary pattern of a lighter blue and white. I was admiring the dishes in one of the cupboards, turning over a dinner plate to see who made it, when I realized Bitsy's list had petered out.

"I can't believe you." Good to the last drop.

"Bitsy, you're right," I said, carefully returning the plate to its stack of compatriots, "The whole situation is horrible. It is." I looked around and shivered, wondering what comfort this cold expanse of kitchen could be to Diane or the girls. "When I heard last night that it was murder, calling anyone to talk about it was the absolute last thing on my mind. Then, when I didn't hear anyone else talking about it this morning, I wasn't even sure that I was supposed to know about it. To tell you the truth, I wasn't even sure it was true. But now that we know it is, I'll tell you what I don't believe. I don't believe Gene had anything to do with it."

"Of course not. You've let him sweet talk you."

"He's the one who told me it was murder, that's hardly sweet talk."

She studied my face until I got annoyed and looked away. "He told you and yet you thought it might not be true. That's interesting."

"Why?"

"Why did you think he'd lie about it?"

"I don't know. Look, I've got things to do."

"You've got places not to go," she said.

"What?"

"Your kitchen."

"Yeah, yeah, yeah." I retrieved my purse from the living room. Diane was still asleep and likely to stay that way for a while. Bitsy trailed after me to the door.

"Well, thank you, Margaret."

"For what?"

"For staying, of course. And for agreeing to have the meeting tonight at your place.

People will start showing up shortly before seven. I've asked them all to please be prompt."

"Swell."

"Oh, and you know, Margaret, you might look on dealing with Diane this morning as good practice. You know, for when your new friend, what's-his-name, reverts to his true nature."

Occasionally I surprise myself. I walked back down Diane's front walk, admiring her herbaceous borders, hopped nimbly into my car, and purred off up the street. All without having added to our fair city's newly revised homicide rate with a spot of almost surely necessary sororicide.

CHAPTER 22

We wended our way back to our own side of town, the tunnel of fudge cake, my car, and I, leaving behind sister and sorrow. It was tempting to close my eyes as we rolled past the broiled Bank Tavern but common sense won out. Curiosity, too. I slowed to get a better look and was surprised by how nearly normal the exterior looked. In fact, the eye of an unobservant passerby might be caught by the yellow crime scene tape but miss the blackened and broken upper windows altogether. The driver behind me honked and I moved on, turning right at the end of the block.

Another right put me on Depot Street where Eunice rents an efficiency above a florist. Flowers by Anna Marie occupies the ground floor of a two story red brick building in a block of mixed modern and turn-of-the-century storefronts. Anna Marie's large windows are crowded with lush plants and bright flowers. The shop next door is Ledford's Vac and Gun, whose window display features a frilly-aproned mannequin pushing a Hoover beside a rack of Remington shotguns. The mannequin has been smiling at customers for as long as I can remember, perpetually happy with her vigilante domesticity. In the narrow space between Ledford's and Anna Marie's is a recessed stoop and a door with cracked, white paint, behind which rises a dusty stairway to three pokey apartments.

Before getting out of the car, I tried Eunice's phone one more time. Still no answer. For some reason I hesitated knocking on her door. It felt like intruding. But I managed to argue myself out of that notion successfully when I remembered how annoying it was that she hadn't shown up for work and how irritating it was going to be if I had to advertise for someone and replace her.

The street door was locked. I gave the knob a good rattle, anyway. There were three mailboxes, each neatly labeled. Eunice's was the third, Two C. There was no buzzer or intercom, no door bell. I rattled the knob again to relieve some frustration then went next door on the off chance Anna Marie keeps tabs on the upstairs tenants. A tidal wave of eucalyptus almost washed me back outside, but a cheerful young man doing something with carnations invited me further in.

"Yes ma'am, and what can I do for you today?"

"Hi, is Anna Marie in?"

"Not until after three. But maybe I can help?"

"Maybe. Do you know Eunice Buchanan? She's probably about your age, lives upstairs?"

"Here?"

"The back apartment. Two C."

"There's apartments up there?" He looked at the ceiling then back at me. "Cool."

After establishing that he'd never even wondered what was upstairs, he followed me outside, still holding a carnation. We stood on the sidewalk together, looking up at the second floor windows.

"That is so cool," he marveled. "How do they get in?"

I pointed to the recessed door.

"And your friend lives in back? You want to see her windows? Come on."

"Cool." We went back through the shop and on through a room crowded with work tables, rolls of wire, papers, ribbons, shelves of vases, and several industrial coolers. "You don't need to keep an eye on the shop?"

"This won't take a minute." He was already unlocking the back door. "There now, see? And look, there's a back stair, too. We can go on up and knock on her door."

While he bounded up the stairs I looked around at ground level. We were in a service alley similar to the one behind my house. This alley was wider, though, and bordered by the Little Embree, a creek that struggles through most of town. A block over, behind the courthouse, the alley and the creek have been incorporated into a city park. There the Little Embree stretches and breathes and gurgles contentedly. Here it skulks through brambles and scrubby trees. On the other side of the creek, rising beyond a long low building housing a tire service center, is Bertie's Bank Tavern.

"Door's locked." My eager guide was back on earth. "No one answered when I knocked. Do you see her car? You want to leave a message for her with me?"

I hadn't thought to look for her car but didn't see it and that reminded me. "Did you see or hear a cat up there?"

"A cat? Cool. No. Probably taking a cat nap." He grinned.

"What's your name?"

"Kevin."

"Kevin, I'm Margaret. Thanks for all your help."

Kevin waved and went back to his carnations, whistling "The Yellow Rose of Texas." To cover all bases, I poked my head in at Ledford's next door. Mr. Ledford recognized my description of Eunice but couldn't remember when he'd last seen her.

"These young things come and go," he said. "Can't keep track of them. Don't try to."

I scribbled a note and dropped it in her mailbox, hesitated, then scribbled two more and dropped them in her neighbors' boxes.

When I pulled into Leona's driveway a few minutes later, the tunnel of fudge cake still looked comfortable so I left it once again to its own devices and knocked on Leona's door.

"There you are," she said upon opening it. "I tried flagging you down when you drove away earlier. The sun must have been in your eyes or I'm sure you would have seen me."

I'd been facing west but never mind. "I'm sorry, Cousin Leona. Was there something you wanted?"

"It mustn't have been terribly important, dear. I seem to have forgotten."

"Oh well. Feel like walking down to the school, now?"

"Let me just get my pocketbook."

"You'll hardly need it." But she'd already disappeared back inside. She has probably never gone anywhere without one, anyway. I think she mourns the day gloves and hats went out of style. I decided not to schlep my own gargantuan bag down the street and locked it in my trunk. "How did he win the bid for redesigning the school without already having plans worked out?" I asked when we were finally underway.

"I don't know how these things work, dear. Perhaps he came highly recommended and was hired on the basis of previous work. It's not a government job, after all. The consortium, whoever they are, can hire whomever they please."

"Who are they?"

"These are all questions you can ask Gene, aren't they? Now, where were you off to in such a hurry this morning?"

I creep down the back alley at five miles-per-hour and this woman who's itching to get her hands on the steering wheel of Gene's supersonic car calls that being in a hurry. "I went to make a condolence call on Diane."

"Ah. That's what I was going to tell you

when you raced past, ignoring me."

"I wasn't ignoring you. The sun was in my eyes, remember?"

"You should know I was being sarcastic about that, dear. My sense of direction isn't that confused. And what I was going to tell you might have come in handy for your visit. I was going to suggest you not say anything to anyone about Douglas being murdered, as I am not sure it's public knowledge, yet. I hope you used the good sense with which you were born."

"Just barely." I filled her in on the details of my condolence call, leaving out the role played by the whisky and the exuberance it lent to Diane's revelations.

"Good heavens," Leona said faintly, "she must be in shock. And of course Bitsy's right, Claire might have been completely unaware he was there. Only his foot, you say, was sticking out? Good heavens."

My steps slowed down and I'd dropped behind Leona before she noticed.

"Come along, Margaret, don't drag your feet. There, I haven't said that to you since your were five years old. You'll notice I'm still on my way to the school. Just because that wretched man got himself strangled and tucked away in the sofa bed in Gene's apartment still doesn't mean Gene had any thing at all to do with it. I'm surprised at you," she tsked.

And so we proceeded up the familiar wide concrete stairs to the front door of the school, Leona clucking and shaking her head and perfectly content holding my arm.

Gene had left the front door unlocked for us. I pulled it open with a strong sense of the once familiar washing over me. It clanged shut behind us, leaving us in a stale, still twilight. So different from the day the last end-of-school bell had rung in these halls. Then, the bright air had echoed with the shouts and laughter of children, pushing and jostling each other, so anxious to rush out through the doors into their sunburned summer vacations they already felt late getting started. Leona and I stood for a minute, letting our eyes and our memories adjust.

"He's working upstairs, dear, in the old art room."

We disturbed at least a decade's worth of dust as we climbed to the second floor. I imagined it was all the chalk dust ever generated within these walls, finally settled out of the air and well on its way to forming a new class of sedimentary rock.

Only the first floor windows were boarded up to discourage vandals and intruders, so as we climbed the stairs the light grew.

When we reached the top I also thought I felt the movement of fresher air. Or maybe that was an illusion created by the strains of music wafting down the hallway toward us. It was something instrumental that I couldn't identify but it was lively enough to send whatever ghosts had followed us up the stairs back into the shadows down below.

The art room had been at the end of the hallway in a corner room with large windows on two sides. Certainly a logical place for an architect to set up shop. A singing architect, as it turns out.

"He must be better at designing buildings than he is at singing," Leona said, patting me comfortingly.

"Unless that's why he ends up moving around the way he does."

I was half disappointed not to find him surrounded by large pots of tempera paint and coffee cans full of fat brushes. Instead he was sitting on a stool leaning over a drafting table. A laptop computer was set up on another table that was surrounded by four comfortable looking office chairs on wheels, one positioned in front of the computer. Not so much as an abandoned art smock haunted the furthest corner of the room. The smells of paste and clay and construction paper had drifted out long ago.

"Hey, great, you made it," he broke off a particularly anguished note to greet us. He reached over and turned down the volume of the portable CD player sitting on the windowsill at his elbow then crossed his arms and smiled at us. How could I have ever entertained doubts about those eyes? "Place bring back memories?" he asked.

"Enough so I have trouble picturing how you're going to transform it," I said. "Don't you think people will expect to find knee-high furniture in the condo you make out of the first grade room?"

"Furnishing's not my responsibility. How about you, Leona?"

"I'm not as sentimental as Margaret. I think this is a splendid idea. I hate to see a perfectly good building going to waste."

"Whose is it, by the way?" I asked.

"It belongs to a group."

"I knew that much."

"A consortium of four. Ed McKinney's one, the bank manager Nancy Umphrey, and then there was Doug Everett."

"And the fourth?" I asked.

"Well, now Margaret," Leona said on top of me, "there you have it. Wouldn't you say it's entirely unlikely Gene would murder Douglas and then stuff him in that unfortu-

245

nate sofa when Douglas was one of his employers?"

Some look made a fleeting appearance on Gene's face at that statement. Was he taken aback? Ill at ease? Maybe it was his conscience goading him to remember his manners. "Would you like to sit down?" he asked, hopping from the stool.

"Thank you, dear, but no. I'd like to go visit my old classroom," Leona said. "No, no, you two stay here, I can find my way." She fluttered an uncharacteristic pink wave at Gene and left.

I listened to her receding footsteps then, to be sure, I stuck my head out the door. The hallway was empty. "So what happens to the consortium now that Doug's gone?" I asked, turning back into the room.

"Hm?" He'd sat in the chair in front of the laptop, leaning back, elbows propped on the chair's arms, fingers knitted across his chest. He looked at home, very comfortable.

I took the chair opposite him. Very comfortable indeed. I swiveled it back and forth a time or two. "Does Diane inherit Doug's share or whatever you call it?"

"From what I know of how the consortium is organized, not automatically."

"The other members stand to benefit from

246

his death, then?"

"Possibly."

"Motive for murder?"

He tipped one hand back and forth in a maybe, maybe not gesture. "Depends on how successful the project is. Whether or not the condos sell, how much they sell for. The members are obviously hoping for success. They have the option to leave Doug's share with Diane or they can buy it from her."

"And Nancy's one of the members. I guess I've been more out of touch than even *I* thought." And now Nancy was retiring and leaving town. Leaving this whole half of the country. But I'd promised not to say anything. Hm. "So who's the other?"

"Hm?"

"The fourth member of the consortium."

"That would be me."

I was afraid of that.

"I didn't kill him, though, you know."

"That's what they all say."

"And some of us are right."

We sat eyeing each other. He'd shown all along he was at least superficially concerned about what I thought of him. And if I needed further proof of that, during the last few minutes he'd run an agitated hand through his hair enough times to make most of it stand on end. Not a pacifying look but charming in an alarming sort of way.

"You don't really think I did kill him, do you?" he finally asked.

"Put it like this, I'll be really pissed off if it turns out you did."

That smile. "Want to see the plans for the renovation?"

He spent the next fifteen or twenty minutes unrolling drawings and plans and bringing renderings to life on the laptop. If his hair hadn't already been standing on end, the energy he used to pantomime the details and the touches still waiting to leap from the inside of his head onto paper or screen would have animated his curls with sparks and fizz. I got lost in a world of knocked down walls and rooms with views.

"This is fantastic. Leona needs to see these," I said, smoothing my hand across a rough sketch of the reconfigured gymnasium. "Oh my gosh, how long have we been here? She never came back."

We exchanged not-quite-worried looks, abandoned the plans, and headed out the door.

CHAPTER 23

The fifth grade classroom was at the other end of the hall from the art room. The door to the room was closed so Leona might not have heard us coming. But neither did she look around when I opened the door. She was sitting primly on an upturned box at the back of the classroom, eyes on the front of the room, intent on whatever she was seeing or remembering, maybe observing a ghostly student teacher struggling for domination of her captive ten-year-olds.

"Maybe I'll sell my house," we heard her say.

"What?" I stepped inside the room.

"Oh there you are, dear. I said maybe I'll sell my house, when Gene has finished with all this, and I'll come live here in whatever arrangement he makes out of this old room. I always felt as though I lived here, anyway. And I often wondered if the children wouldn't possibly be the death of me, so why not finally move in and then, when I'm ready to, I can just expire in some quiet corner. Provided there are quiet corners. I wouldn't want to move here unless the acoustics are improved. All those clattering feet out in the hallway will haunt me forever. Besides, if I sell my house, then I won't have to worry about the drains, anymore."

"Do you worry about your drains?"

"No, but I always worry that I should."

"But what would I do without you right next door?"

"We'd each get more exercise and I will leave some of my African violets behind with you."

I thought about Leona's half-serious idea later as I drove the tunnel of fudge cake over to its final destination. Not about being the beneficiary of sudden violets, that didn't bear thinking about at all, but she'd looked so wistful thinking about going home to the place where she'd felt most alive. And why not? I'm mostly content living in my book-store. Going to live in the school might be the connection she needs to keep her going for another decade or two.

And maybe it would start a trend. People seeking out the places where they've felt particularly comfortable or happy or useful or whole and moving in. Bitsy's husband, Rodney, for instance. If anyone ever took a notion to turn his bland insurance office into living space would he yearn to pull up stakes and move in there? Probably only over Bitsy's dead body.

Which image brought my thoughts crashing back down to the task at hand. I was on my way to Bertie's house with my offering of chocolate, fat, and calories. I'd had to look her up in the phone book, though, because Bertie, in my mind, doesn't come separate from the Bank Tavern. That she ever went home at night to a house with her own non-industrial-size stove and refrigerator shouldn't have come as a revelation, but there it was. Perhaps somewhere in my onion ring—obsessed mind I'd pictured her hanging herself up each night on the row of pegs with the clean white aprons and each morning shaking herself awake, hopping down, and turning on the deep-fat fryers.

So now I wondered, as I rolled to a stop in front of her 1920s bungalow, was she having separation pangs? Could she or would she start over? Or was the building forever tainted by Doug's murder? Ringing her doorbell, I hoped my tunnel of fudge offering would sweeten these nosy questions and several more I planned to ask.

An amazing vision opened Bertie's front door.

"Margaret? Hello? Is that for me?"

"What? Oh yes, Bertie, sorry. Here." Bertie liberated the tunnel of fudge cake from my hands. I hadn't even recognized her and must have presented quite a photo op for the deer-in-the headlight look. "You look so . . . ."

"Pink? It's my private passion. I don't wear it much at the restaurant. Clashes with the spaghetti sauce and chili." She was certainly making up for it at home. She had on a floor-length, hot pink caftan. "This is new. Do you like it? I ran out and bought it yesterday. After the fire and all, you know. My way of dealing with shock, I guess. Would you like to come in?"

"Where?"

"Here."

"I mean, where did you buy it? I've never seen anything like it."

"Marvelous, isn't it? Never know what you'll find down there at the Town Shop. Can you believe this was marked down? Seventy-five percent off. But come on in. Turns out it attracts hummingbirds and they're feisty little turkeys."

Bertie must be something north of seventy. She and her husband, Vern, ran the

Bank Tavern together, he keeping bar, she tending the grill, until he died of a heart attack ten or so years ago. That wasn't a good advertisement for the artery-clogging effects of Bertie's onion rings but hasn't seemed to make any difference in business.

I don't have a clear picture in my mind of Vern, anymore, not having spent much time hanging out in the bar as a child or as an adult. But I've always thought of Bertie as monochromatic. She has white, fluffy hair, wears a white uniform and apron at work, and always appears to be lightly dusted in flour, whether she's been baking or not.

Her house, it turns out, is a riot. From the outside, with its sedate brickwork and unassuming trim, I expected nothing more than a staid, slightly dated interior. A lot of beige, maybe, with some understated avocado. Her electric caftan should have clued me in, though. Stepping over her threshold, I entered into the most amazing jungle of sensations. Colors leapt off the wallpaper and the upholstery, met up with more colors dancing off a scattering of rugs, and together with the pictures vibrating on the walls they all grew and twined together. I could hear exotic birds calling and expected elephants to trumpet any minute. Why this woman worried about a splash of pink clashing with spaghetti sauce, I can't imagine. Maybe that's an excuse to keep her personal color scheme private.

Actually, I did hear birds.

"Hiya toots."

"Bail out! Bail out!"

"Hush, you two. Don't pay any attention to them, Margaret, or they'll never shut up." She was referring to two military macaws in a large cage at one end of her living room. I hadn't seen them at first because their own gaudy colors couldn't hope to compete with the rest of the room. "I'd let them out but I don't like them eating chocolate. Would you like a piece?" She held out the cake.

"Yes." All I'd ingested so far today was coffee and various forms of cake and bread. Why stop now? "I'd love a piece."

We ended up sitting in a sunroom, appropriately decorated in blistering shades of yellow and orange, just off her kitchen. I could have slipped and splattered an entire gallon jar of pickled beets in her kitchen and never noticed. Not because it wasn't sparkling clean.

The longest conversation I'd ever had with Bertie occurred when I was in high school and working for the student newspaper. The paper was doing an issue on careers and I thought it would be a great idea to interview

Bertie, her food figuring so largely in the nutritional requirements of most teenagers in town. The interview went about like this:

Me: "How long have you been in the restaurant business?"

Bertie: "What? You'll have to talk louder than that."

M: "Um, how long have you been in the restaurant business?"

B: "Since Vern got out of the Navy."

M: "How long have you owned this restaurant?"

B: "Since Vern got out of the Navy."

M: "What's your favorite part of the restaurant business?"

B: "Cooking."

M: "What's your favorite thing to cook?"

B: "Honey, you're going to have move on out now because I've got work to do."

I quit the paper soon after that but somehow Bertie and I bonded. Maybe it was the picture I managed to snap of her brandishing a spatula just before she tried to swat me with it. The interview, such as it was, never made it into the paper but the photo was on the front page and Bertie was so tickled with it she had a copy framed.

Now, squinting across from her in her blindingly cheerful room, I wasn't any surer how to proceed than I had been way back then. Although the offerings of cake and my condolences were heartfelt, my ulterior motives rested as uneasily in my mind as the paper napkin list of questions in my pocket. How could I sit here and ask her nosy questions about fire and murder?

Well, as I often find it convenient to say, "when in doubt, chicken out." Come to think of it, Bertie's birds had recommended much the same thing. So I settled more comfortably into one of the wicker armchairs and took a melting bite of tunnel of fudge.

"Your whole house is a feast, Bertie."

"Why, thank you, honey. I've never thought of it that way. A feast? Yeah, I like that. I've gone a little wild with the colors, haven't I? That happened after Vern died. Those damn birds in there were his babies and I ended up spending so much time moping and staring at them after he passed that I missed him almost more than I could bear. My daughter said I should get rid of them. They're noisy and dirty and they swear like sailors and she said I should clear them out if they made me so melancholy. That's exactly what she said, melancholy. Like I was some delicate thing swooning on a settee in the corner. Hell. I just missed him is all. So I started painting. And by god, now my whole house looks like Vern's damn birds and it makes me smile just to wake up of a morning." To what exotic dawn of colors in her bedroom, I wondered?

"How else are you bearing up after the fire, other than cornering the market on pink caftans at the Town Shop?"

Bertie seemed to deflate before my eyes. Even the pink glow from her caftan couldn't disguise how tired and old she suddenly looked. "I don't know, Margaret. I tell you, I loved that place and most of me wants to jump right back in and get it going again. I don't take too well to sitting still. Haven't ever really had that luxury. I don't know what to do with myself without biscuits to make at five A.M." She laughed and added, "Unless I start on the outside of the house and frankly I'd be afraid my daughter would have me committed if I did that."

"You know, I always thought you owned the building."

"No, Vern never wanted to be tied down like that. Must've been his years in the Navy. His daddy was in the Navy, too. Vern liked to think of himself as a vagabond but I tell you, once we opened up the Bank Tavern it was like he put down a hundred-foot taproot. Only you'd never get him to admit it. Now, I wouldn't have minded owning that building. And I talked a time or two to Doug about it. Should've saved my breath. He was damned stinky about it and that's me being as pleasant as I can towards that particular dead."

"You didn't like him?"

"Did you?"

I took several more bites and thought about that. "I did. I used to, anyway. In passing. But we didn't socialize, which I suppose says something. And from my own impression of him a few days ago, and from what I've heard, he'd turned into a bit of a jerk. So what changed? He wasn't hard to like when we were kids."

"There's no mystery in that." Bertie rubbed her thumb and forefinger together. "It does things to some people. And I could've told you it was doing it to him just by the choice of suits and ties he wore. Doesn't anybody wear suits and ties like that unless they like money, make lots of it, and want a whole lot more."

"His suits?" I tried to picture what he'd been wearing when he came in the bookstore. "You're right, I couldn't put my finger on it, but you're right. He'd adopted that, that . . ."

"Young G.Q. Gipper look?"

I snorted a piece of cake and she smiled

with an interesting mix of smug and wicked pleasure. I always knew I liked Bertie. "You know the guy who rented the apartment upstairs, Gene Mashburn?" I asked.

"Now *he's* got great bedroom eyes."

I lost my train of thought and had to administer another bite of tunnel of fudge to recover. "He thinks the building is still structurally sound. They'll need to get an engineer or something in there to check it out, but there's probably no reason why you can't reopen. And maybe Diane will want to get rid of the building and be happy to sell it to you."

"You think? I didn't tell you about the other part of me. That part says turn the business over to Claire. It's what I planned to do eventually anyway."

"And then you could still go in and make biscuits for her."

"Oh, probably not. What I always said was, when it comes time, I'll just go. A kitchen doesn't need two cooks." She stopped and waited expectantly.

"Did I miss something?"

"Never mind, it's an old joke of Vern's. My maiden name is Cook. When we were first married and I was just finding my way around a kitchen, back when he was in the Navy, he used to aggravate me by saying I

should've been named after my other grandmother, Bernice. Bernie Cook. Lord, I still
miss him," she said. "So maybe this was a
sign."

"You don't believe that, do you?"

"If it was a sign, it was about as subtle as
a billboard, wasn't it? Well, Claire's been
after me to remodel, upgrade, change the
menu, move on." She stopped, shaking her
head. "I don't know. Moving on is what's
hard."

"How is Claire?"

"Honey, you don't need to worry about
that one. Not much can get her down and
keep her down. Now, she would love to own
that building. I'd given up on it but she
asked Doug about it near every time he
came in. The way she was all over him I'm
surprised he kept coming in." She closed
her eyes and shook her head. "Or I guess
I'm not, after seeing what was really going
on." Her eyes popped open again. "And
how happy do you think Diane would be to
sell the building to Claire?"

We both chewed that over with the last
few bites on our plates.

"It was awfully kind of you to come by
with this cake, Margaret. There's not much
can go wrong, but what chocolate can't fix
it. I've always said I'd like to have one of

those medic alert bracelets, only mine would say 'Needs chocolate. Now.' You know, you're the only one's been by."

"What?"

"It's a fact. And it's only to be expected. There's been a death and people are going to behave the way people do. They either want to show their respect for the dead or gawk at the misery of the widow. That sounds hard, I know, but it's the truth."

"But you've had a loss, too. The whole town has, with the Bank Tavern gone."

"I know it. And the town will know it, too, after everything else settles down. For now, I think they're showing their respect for me by not coming around. On account of Claire and whatever she had to do with what went on."

"You don't think Claire had anything to do with the fire, do you?"

"Fire down below! Fire down below!" A shrieking, feathered missile rocketed overhead, circled the room and streaked out again.

"Mary Lou," Bertie yelled. "That was Mary Lou," she said to me in an aside. "I thought I latched that damn cage."

Mary Lou, unless it was her partner, came through on another fast circuit of the sunroom, this time without the raucous sound

261

effects. I took a couple of steadying breaths then picked my plate up off the floor and hunted for the fork that had gone over my shoulder.

"Sorry about that, Grandma, I didn't know we had company. Hi, Margaret." Claire stood grinning in the doorway, a leering parrot on her shoulder.

CHAPTER 24

"I don't think parrots are capable of leering, are they?" That was Bitsy on the phone, waking me too soon from a sound nap. I'd made the mistake of telling her about the dream I'd been having with Claire in her flaming bathrobe being chased by a parrot.

"Believe me, Bitsy, I've seen it with my own eyes."

After saying goodbye to Bertie and edging past Claire with leering parrot rampant, I'd headed home for what I figured was a well-deserved collapse. I'd completely forgotten to spell Fran over lunch, which goes to show how necessary sleep was. She, bless her, took one look at me, forgave me, and sent me upstairs with a kiss on the forehead. Of course I also forgot to unplug my bedside phone. Bitsy's call shattered my deep and untroubled sleep. She, as it turned out, was neither of those. Though thinking of her as less than deep is probably only another way that I malign my sister.

"It sounds more like a nightmare than a dream."

"I guess you had to be there," I said, wishing I were still there. For some strange reason it had been a perfectly pleasant and untroubling dream until I woke up and realized the parrot had been screeching something important. Now the thought kept niggling in the back of my mind, that if only I'd understood the parrot or could hear it again I'd know who started the fire and who killed Duckie. I stopped and thought about that a minute. If only I could hear a parrot in a dream, I'd know who killed Duckie? How much sense did that make?

"Margaret!" Bitsy shouted into the phone.

I switched ears.

"I thought maybe you'd fallen back asleep."

"Thanks for checking. So, what's your problem, Bitsy?"

"My problem is with security for the meeting tonight."

"Maybe you'd better yell into my ear again. Security?"

"Yes, it suddenly occurred to me this meeting could be dangerous. Think about it, Margaret. First we were talking about pigeons and plants. Now we're talking about murder."

"What does Duckie's murder have to do with the Townscape Committee? You don't really think someone's going to target them, do you? Are you expecting all of you to be taken out at once or are you going to be picked off one by one?"

"Don't laugh, Margaret. Someone burned down Bertie's. Someone could just as easily burn down your bookstore."

"I hope you're not serious." Of course she was serious. But seriously on the right track, or seriously whacko?

"But don't worry, Margaret, I've got a plan. I've asked George to come to the meeting tonight. And Claire and that Mashburn character. That way the two prime suspects will be right under George's nose the whole time. No surprises."

I trailed downstairs in time to help Fran close up for the day and found her chatting with that man of mystery and unexpected appearances, Gene. He was chuckling softly at something and she was in danger of drowning in his eyes. I stopped short of the squeaky third step from the bottom but it turns out those eyes are functional as well as decorative. Or maybe I'm less sylph-like on the stairs than I imagine.

"Hi," he said. "I got a strange invitation this afternoon."

"I'm glad you recognized it as strange. That's a good sign."

"Have you had dinner yet?"

"No." I joined them at the counter and stifled a yawn. "And something tells me I'd better fortify myself before this meeting."

"You've got some eggs in there. How about I go make a couple of omelets?"

I glanced at Fran. Any minute she was going to break into some mushy serenade. "What do you think, Fran? Should I let him?" She just gazed at him, looking pink. Good thing she's a cracker jack bookseller because she was falling apart on me over a simple thing like my love life. "Sounds great, Gene, thanks. I'll just help Miss Lonely Heart, here, close up. Won't be fifteen minutes."

"Oh, Margaret," she said when the kitchen door closed behind him. "Never mind his omelets, don't you want to eat him up?"

"Mm," I said and went to lock the door and flip the open sign to closed. "Bitsy, on the other hand, wants to chew him up and spit him out."

"Why?"

"She thinks he had something to do with the fire."

"Wouldn't that be a shame? I don't believe it, though, do you?" Returning to her competent business mode, she'd started running the register through its paces and was counting the money, something she's able to do accurately while talking. One of the things I love her for. "And does Bitsy's worry extend to the rumor I caught running around today that Doug was murdered?"

"So that's finally making the rounds, is it? Unfortunately, it's more than rumor."

"You're kidding." She stopped in the middle of counting the nickels to stare at me. I could see her fingers itching to get started again, so I told her briefly what I knew, again leaving out the more lurid details. "Oh my," Fran said. "Oh my." And she had to start over with the nickels. It was heartening to see she didn't cast any uneasy glances over her shoulder toward the kitchen door, though.

"You know what one of the worst things about this is, Margaret?" she asked after we'd silently finished balancing the register. "It's ruined all those bad jokes I used to make about people who really probably need to be killed."

"Doug was on your list? Well, there you go, that makes you a suspect, too."

"Hush."

"Sorry, so why was he?"

"Because he played games. We served on a couple of committees together at church and he couldn't let money go for a project or a program or even a leaky roof without arguing. Even if the money had already been raised or appropriated. And as far as I could tell, it was just a game he made everyone play until someone was mad enough to . . ." She stopped there and shook her head.

"Have you been in their house?"

"The place is like a glossy magazine advertisement. And that gorgeous kitchen? I wonder if Doug played that game with Diane? Of course, she makes plenty of her own money."

"Interesting, though." I drummed my fingers on the counter, wondering if money had anything to do with Doug's death. Then I remembered Doug drumming his fingers on my counter and hastily crossed my arms, instead.

"And Eunice?" Fran prompted.

"Damn. I don't know. She's not there. Her car's not there."

"What about Archie?"

"Someone must be feeding him. He wasn't yowling."

"Or she took him with her." She stood for

a minute, her mouth screwed up in annoyance, probably a mirror of mine. "Well," she finally said, "I'll tell you my advice. And this is good advice because I happen to be a woman and a mother. You go eat your dinner with that man in there, and then you two go enjoy yourselves and if you know what's good for you I won't see you here again until sometime tomorrow, preferably late afternoon."

"Aye aye." I saluted her. "But first we will be part of the captive audience at the meeting of the rogue Townscape Committee."

"That should be entertaining for one and all. How I do wish I could join you. But I have a date with the washing machine."

"I'll take notes."

"See you tomorrow." She waved herself out the front door and I hot-footed it to the kitchen.

"You probably just saved my life," I said, pushing my chair back from the table, replete with fluffy omelet and crisp green salad.

"How so?" Gene asked.

"I don't think I've eaten anything else today with any nutritional value at all."

"Not a good habit."

"It's not a habit. It's just the way the day

turned out." He looked quite at home, lounging there across from me. "So what's with all the domesticity?"

He raised his eyebrows in question.

"You know, the cooking, the dish-doing afterwards. Are you going through some courting ritual like a male bird, supplying tasty tidbits in hope of winning favors?"

He straightened up, rearranged the salt and pepper shakers on the table, smoothed out his napkin, cleared his throat. "I'm sure there are those aspects to the behavior." He stopped and considered what he'd said then nodded his head in agreement with himself. "Definitely. But it's also therapeutic."

"You're talking like a mental health counselor again."

"You know what they say, spend enough time with a squirrel and pretty soon you'll be chattering like one, too."

"Are you trying to tell me you're out of your tree?"

"No, my ex-wife is a psychotherapist."

"Oh. My visions of men in long white coats weren't so far off. How long were you married?"

"Fifteen years."

"Long time."

"Longer for some than for others," he said.

"Are you some or others?"

"Bit of both. You ever been married?"

"No. Various people had hopes along those lines from time to time."

"The lugubrious Officer Buckles?"

"George," I nodded. "But it turns out I'm not into that kind of hard work." His eyebrows spoke again. "On top of the bookstore, anyway. I seem to be married to my business."

"Huh."

"Huh, indeed. Well, Bitsy'll kill me if this place isn't spic and span again before that meeting."

"Why do you let her boss you around?"

"What makes you think I do?"

"Dead pigeons, off-limit kitchen, committee meetings in your bookstore," he ticked off on his fingers. "Kind of hard to miss."

"Oh, that," I said with what I hoped sounded like derision and not craven denial, "you're mistaking my master plan for spinelessness. See, what I've been doing is playing along all these years, lulling her into thinking she's got the upper hand. But one day the tables will turn and then the joke will be on her."

"Oh, yeah? And when do you expect 'one day' to come?"

"When I'm sixty-five. She should be good

and lulled by then, never know what hit her."

"You want to know what I think?"

"No, I don't because I want to be able to concentrate on doing the dishes."

"Why don't you sit down and relax and I'll get them."

"Boss me around will you? Let's do them together."

So we did, and it was comradely and comfortable, what with washing and drying and joshing and the generally close contact. Of course, we'd only eaten omelets and salad so there weren't many dishes to do and we were done in a trice. It's probably the only time in my life I've been reluctant to hang up a damp dishtowel. As I did, he came up behind me and folded his arms around me.

"Does your aversion to the hard work of marriage include an aversion to a little canoodling?"

We were exploring the answer to that when Bitsy arrived for the meeting. She arrives in good time for whatever function she's attending because she was born to be punctual. She came bustling into the kitchen, drew in a sharp breath at the sight that met her eyes, and dropped the easel and oversized pad of paper she was carrying.

"Oh, hi Bitsy."

"Margaret. Mr. Mashburn." I expected to catch a sniff of her disdain, but for some reason she had a pleased look on her face. Looking forward to a good meeting, maybe. "No one else here yet?" she asked.

"You're the first. How many do you expect?"

"No more than ten. Six members of the committee, you, George," she slid a sidelong glance at Gene, "the two guests."

"Need help bringing anything else in?"

"No, thank you. Have you got something I can use as a pointer?"

"A yardstick. I thought you were bringing nibbles and coffee?"

"There's been a change of plans, Margaret. I needed to offer Claire a reason for coming tonight so I asked her to cater the meeting. I told her it would be a great way to show that Bertie's has only had a set back but isn't bowing out."

"Kind of a major set back," Gene said. This time Bitsy looked straight at him. Gene took an involuntary step backwards and bumped into the dish drainer.

"So you didn't invite Claire to the meeting so much as you lured her here?" I turned from Bitsy to Gene. "How did she lure you here?" He reddened in a charmingly sheepish way.

Bitsy glowed with the full wattage of smug triumph. "It was like offering candy to a baby, Margaret. I told him the meeting was here and you would be here and voila." She beamed in self-congratulation, turned on her heel, and exited the kitchen.

"Nibbles?" Gene said.

"Her word, not mine. These are what I call nibbles." I nuzzled his earlobe. He returned the favor.

"She's a bit of a witch, isn't she?" he asked when he came up for air.

"Don't worry." I patted his nice shoulder reassuringly. "Very few people are able to withstand her manipulative spell. I've had years of practice and look at me."

He did look at me and I blushed. Then we followed Bitsy out front and waited for the meeting to begin.

CHAPTER 25

Claire outdid herself. On a pretty blue and white tray she arranged miniature cheesecakes, chocolate dipped strawberries, and a round of herbed goat cheese. Next to the tray was a breadboard with a still-warm, crusty loaf of pesto bread. She brought an insulated carafe of Colombian coffee and one of decaf. With a flourish, she presented hazelnut-flavored creamer and packets of brown sugar. There's just something about the smells of coffee and fresh bread that make themselves at home in a bookstore.

Bitsy had arranged chairs in three precise rows facing the easel in the space in front of the counter. I frustrated her by insisting on keeping to my stool behind the counter. I told her it was so I'd be ready in case anyone had a sudden, desperate urge to buy a book. Which was true. But I also wanted to reinforce that I am not, and do not want to be, a member of the Townscape Committee. Being more involved with my community is one thing. Getting involved with a bunch of people making a break for the edge of the lunatic fringe is another.

There were other benefits to sticking with my perch behind the counter. From there I could watch the faces of everyone else while they were busy watching Bitsy do her thing. Also, sitting at my end of the counter put me out of easy reach of Claire's tempting spread. I'd given in to plenty of temptations already today.

"The first order of business," Bitsy rapped out after thanking everyone for coming, "is . . ."

"Excuse me, Bitsy, but do I see some new members here tonight? I don't believe we all know each other." This was Harriet McKinney. I hadn't realized she was a member. Though, come to think of it, I hadn't known any of the rest of them were members, either. Harriet I at least recognized. There were two other women and two men, obviously not book buyers, though they looked pleasant enough.

Now they all craned around to look at Gene, George, and Claire who had taken seats next to each other in the third row. Maybe the three had drawn together instinctively, being the only strangers to the group.

Maybe George had arranged it with a subtle, constabulary nudge. Gene and George smiled back at the committee members uneasily. Claire was busy reading a copy of *Vogue* she'd lifted from my magazine rack.

"Forgive me, Harriet, of course. Though, these aren't new members. They're our guests tonight. You know Officer Buckles, I'm sure, and you've seen Claire at the Bank Tavern. She provided our wonderful refreshments this evening. And this is, er . . . ," Bitsy's selective memory kicked in.

"Gene Mashburn, ma'am. Pleased to meet you," Gene supplied.

Harriet fluttered a wave and turned to look at me.

"And my sister, Margaret Welch, who so kindly invited us to meet in her bookstore."

I hoped my smile came off as genuine. It might have had a hint of "I can't believe you lied like that" about it, but I tried.

"And the members of our committee," Bitsy continued. "Harriet McKinney is our treasurer; Phil Davids our secretary, and the members at large are Laura Phipps, Reba Swanson and Bill Stringer. So then, the first order of business for this meeting of the Townscape Committee is . . . ."

"We need to change the name of the committee," Phil Davids interrupted. "If we're going to secede from the town, that is, if we are going to remove this committee from the auspices of the town of Stonewall, we should change our name." Phil looked about forty, had thinning strands of hair combed across a bald dome, wore wire-rimmed glasses, a cardigan sweater, paint-spattered blue jeans and Birkenstocks. He looked "booky" but I'd never seen him before. Maybe he hung out at the library. Maybe I was judging him by his cover.

"Yes, Phil, very good. That is, in fact, the first order of business." Bitsy reasserted herself and wrote "Name" on her giant pad of paper on the easel.

"Oh, now, wait a second," George moaned. "Bitsy, I don't know if I can be a part of this if you're going to go and start rebelling against the town and all. I am a town employee, you know."

"Yes, George, I do know. And you don't have to worry because you are not a part of this. I asked you here to, you know . . ." She was probably trying to wink and covertly indicate Gene and Claire. Her efforts looked less surreptitious, though, and more like she suffers from an unattractive twitch.

"Oh, I dunno."

"Oh, come on, be a sport George," I

couldn't help saying.

Bitsy shot me a look that unfairly doubted the sincerity of my cajoling. "Shall we continue, then? Yes, Phil?"

"I have a suggestion. For a new name."

"Good."

"Actually, I have more than a suggestion. I have a contribution as well." He stopped again and everyone waited for more.

"Yes, Phil?"

"You don't happen to have a piano here in your store, do you?" he asked me.

"No, sorry."

"Oh. Hm. That's probably all right. So, you're probably all familiar with Rousseau, aren't you? Jean Jacques Rousseau. The French philosopher, 1712-1778?"

There was an impatient shuffling of feet and rattling of papers from the committee members, apparently used to Phil's ways.

"I am," George said glumly. "I bought a copy of *The Social Contract* from Margaret couple of months ago. What's he got to do with weeding and tree pruning?"

"That's what I'm getting to."

"You have five minutes, Phil, and then we move on," Bitsy said. No one jumped or looked askance at her imposed time limit. Maybe this was an agreed upon way of dealing with time hogs.

"Oh, uh, okay. I'll cut it short, then. I think we need something to unite us, the committee. And not just the committee, I mean the town. Something that will get across our message about the environment and at the same time create an upwelling of feeling for Stonewall, you know, everything that's here. The people, the landscape. And the animals. I mean, after the pigeons and Hattie's garden and well . . . Anyway, I have this anthem. I wrote it. For us. If you want."

"And what's that got to do with Rousseau?" George asked, ever the alert detective.

"Ah, oh yes, I forgot. Rousseau was interested in music as well as philosophy. In fact, he put together a well-regarded music dictionary and a book of folk songs called *The Consolation of My Life's Miseries.*" George's ears perked up at that. "And he said somewhere that one of the most powerful, and therefore one of the most dangerous, activities people can undertake is the activity of singing together in unison. You know, rise up and all that. I thought we maybe could do that with an anthem, take a stand, I mean. Against people killing pigeons and well, other, well, people. If you want."

"Rousseau said that?" George scratched his head.

"I think so. But I don't remember where. I could try to look it up. If you want."

"Phil," Bitsy interrupted, "I think that's a perfectly marvelous idea."

"You do?"

"Yes, it's terrific. Can't you all see it? Think of those shots of Olympic athletes getting teary eyed at the sound of their national anthems. Haven't you gotten caught up in that emotion yourselves? This could be extremely powerful. We wouldn't just be making a statement. We'd be creating solidarity."

At that, Phil rose to his feet, cleared his throat, and started singing in a rich, clear tenor. Pavarotti eat your heart out. He was astounding. Although the tune sounded familiar, I couldn't place it. Maybe a hymn. A Russian hymn. I could picture a choir of earnest Russian peasant men in somber, full voice. It was stately and rousing and, yes, I would have felt compelled to stand up and join in, if only I'd known the words. Definitely one of the stranger experiences I've had in my bookstore.

The members of the committee were transported by the performance, most of them nodding their heads or pumping arms in time. Bitsy stood straighter and taller, holding the yardstick proudly like a drum major's baton. Even George was enrapt, leaning forward, his mouth hanging slightly open. Gene was looking around him as though checking to see if he'd stepped off at the wrong bus stop. Only Claire was unaffected. She was still engrossed in her magazine.

When Phil's last note swept the cobwebs from the hard to reach farthest corners of the store, there was enthusiastic applause all around. During the congratulatory buzz after he sat down, Gene got up.

"Mr. Mashburn, where are you going?" Bitsy asked.

"Coffee. I need a drink."

Her eyes followed him as he stepped over several pairs of legs and proceeded to the counter, where he practically fell on the carafe of full-blooded brew and poured himself a cup before sliding along to where I sat.

"They're all insane," he whispered to me, "just like your sister."

"And I know you mean that in the nicest possible way," I whispered back.

"Oh, yeah, goes without saying."

He sucked down half the cup then looked up and realized that Bitsy's eyes were still on him and the meeting had come to a standstill. He took a few steps back toward his seat and she smiled. He stopped, moved a step back toward the counter and she frowned. He took another few steps toward his seat. She smiled again. He stopped. She glared. He gave up and sat down. She turned to Phil.

"Phil, I think I speak for all of us when I say your anthem is superb." She turned and wrote "Anthem" on the pad. "Do you have a name for it?"

"Oh, yes. And I brought copies."

He bent over and picked up a folder he'd stashed under his chair. He pulled a sheaf of papers out of it and passed them around. I was surprised to see how eagerly George took his copy. I'd never known him to be particularly interested in music. Claire tucked hers in the magazine without looking at it. Gene took a look at his and quickly downed the rest of his coffee. Phil graciously handed one across to me even though I hadn't provided a piano. Silence descended.

"The title . . . ," Harriet began then stopped.

"It's meant to be ironic," Phil explained.

"Oh."

Some heads nodded, others tilted one way and then the other as though trying to bring the irony into better focus.

"Couldn't we just call it 'Song of

Stonewall' or something?" one of the other women asked.

Lips were pursed as that suggestion was considered. Bitsy went so far as to wiggle her pursed lips from left to right and back again. That must have helped the cogitating process along because she was the first to voice a conclusion.

" 'Song of Stonewall'? No, I don't think so," she said. "No. And I'll tell you why. 'Song of Stonewall' is too expected. There's nothing about 'Song of Stonewall' that will grab anyone's attention. This will make people think."

"Yeah, but don't you think it'll make them think that we're into landscape zoning laws or something?" asked the other man. "We don't want them to think we're lawn Nazis."

George groaned. "Did you even listen to the lyrics? No one's going to think you're lawn Nazis. They'll think just the opposite. There's a clear dialectic going on here. What Phil is expressing is the need for the citizens of Stonewall to embrace the great scheme of nature as it applies to every corner of their lives. It's a philosophical anthem that distills the entire argument of thinking globally and acting locally into a moving and precise ode and that's what gives the words their basic strength and beauty."

Wow. I've always known George was a thinker but you can mostly count on his thoughts being morose and then be thankful he keeps them to himself. This stuff really turned him on. But his uncharacteristically long-winded defense of Phil had taxed him. He accepted Phil's hand in gratitude then slumped back in his chair.

"I think," Harriet quavered, dabbing her eyes, "I think it's all perfectly beautiful."

"Amen," Bitsy said and she turned and wrote the title of Phil's anthem in capital letters on her pad: "LAWN ORDER."

"T-shirts," someone said.

"What?"

"If you're talking about solidarity and you want this thing to fly, if you even know what 'this thing' is and where you're flying it to, you should get T-shirts made with a catchy logo and 'Lawn Order' printed on them." It was Claire speaking without looking up from *Vogue.*

Next to her, Gene nodded agreement. Then he whipped out a pencil and started sketching on the back of his copy of the anthem. "Here, something like this."

The sketch passed from hand to hand and finally made its way up to Bitsy. She looked it over, mild surprise and a reappraisal of Gene showing on her face.

"Not bad," she said. "What do the rest of you say? Shall we entertain the idea of T-shirts? Have a contest for a design?"

"No," George said. "You want to do this thing quickly and quietly. Hit them fast and hit them hard. You hold a contest and the whole thing drags on and on and feelings get hurt. I say you should make a motion to accept Phil's anthem and his title and Mashburn's logo, take the whole thing out to that place on the highway that prints T-shirts, and be ready to go in a day or two."

Bitsy held her chin in her left hand, stroking her cheek with her index finger in a show of serious contemplation. She turned back to the easel and tapped the finger against her lips. Turning again to her audience, she addressed the committee.

"This is a big decision. I don't want to rush any of you, but what do you think? Are we ready to commit ourselves?"

They were. To make their course of action official, Harriet made the motion. The man who'd raised the question of lawn Nazis seconded it. It carried unanimously. Bitsy was obviously born to lead. But lead where? Maybe the committee discussed that at an earlier meeting because no one asked.

"Excellent. Then on to the next order of business. Cow versus horse manure for the beds along the bypass."

Manure. I leaned my back more comfortably against the shelf behind the counter. Unless Phil had a few lines of verse on kudos for cow manure or the horrors of horse manure, it looked like the exciting part of the meeting was over. I jammed my hands in my pockets and resigned myself to a boring interval.

Something more interesting than manure tickled my fingers, though. My paper napkin list was still in my pocket. I pulled it out.

By now it was a little worse for wear because I'd accidentally used it a couple of times without thinking. But I smoothed it out and it was still mostly legible. A quick glance around showed that no one was paying me any attention. I plucked my favorite order-taking pen from the pen and pencil mug next to the cash register, turned my copy of "Lawn Order" over and rewrote my list of questions.

They turned out to be as disturbing on the back of an anthem as they were on a napkin. And now there was more to add. That whole bit about Doug ending up in the sofa bed. Which foot was sticking out, anyway? Did it matter? Did Diane hate playing Doug's money games as much as his committee mates? She told me marriage is sometimes a joke. Was she finally sick to death of games and jokes? And the way she was lubricating her grief. Was it grief? What about her saying she likes a woman who'll stand up for herself when I said I'd kill anyone who called me Margie? Was that because she's the kind of woman who would kill? What about Claire wanting to get her hands on the Bank building? How far would she go to get it? And Bertie. Was she at the fire? I'd forgotten to ask her. And why were all my suspicions about women? Couldn't I toss a man in? Oh. No. At least, not one, particular man.

So, how about William DeAngelis? It was his field full of goats, after all. And he'd been gloating over Doug's fishpond and saying unpleasant things about him. Of course, neither the gloating nor saying unpleasant things could be held against him because that's just the way he is. I put his name down anyway because that's just the way I am. Besides, didn't someone, maybe Rodney, say William got that field in a real estate deal or swap with Doug? A deal that sounded more like a swindle if the rumor was right and there was an effort to keep the field as green space. That rumor should be easy enough to run down. I put a check mark next to that question.

Gosh, this could have been a livelier and more crowded meeting if Bitsy hadn't blinkered herself into believing Claire and Gene were the prime suspects. In fact, in addition to Bertie, Diane, and William she could have invited the other members of Doug's consortium along as well. Ed and Harriet McKinney would probably be holding hands and Nancy would have gotten a last taste of Stonewall at its best and weirdest. Were Nancy and Ed plausible suspects? Maybe I was going too far.

Of course, I could always play up the resurrected forty-year-old Angel of Death Mafia Theory. Way back then, I'd really only told Bitsy the Mafia had been mentioned somewhere in the shadowy background. No names. No frills. A simple yarn meant to entertain an invalid and go no further. But somewhere along the path from Bitsy's ear to its eventual place in the canon of local juvenile lore, the story underwent refurbishing. The metamorphosis was an education for me and a minor irritation to the DeAngelis family. I jotted down Angel of Death then decided to show some evidence of having matured and crossed it out.

There was something else that should go on the list, though, something I'd heard this evening. I glanced around the room again.

They were still working out fertilizer details, apparently. Or maybe they were on to something else and it all just sounded like fertilizer to me. That was it. Manure. Could someone from the Townscape Committee be responsible for the manure in the downtown dumpster? Why? Why not? They'd certainly turned out to be a feistier bunch than I'd imagined.

I was picturing Phil singing out directions, Harriet backing a dump truck full of horse manure (or was it cow?) up to the dumpster, Bitsy standing by in hard hat, baton at attention. Then I caught sight of something waving out of the corner of my eye. Gene, casting glances Bitsyward, giving me furtive hand signals behind George's back. Oops.

"Margaret, you may not want to join the rest of us in a moment of silence in memory of Doug, but at least you could refrain from sitting there sniggering to yourself," Bitsy said.

A moment of thought would have been wise at this point, but sometimes I'm slow.

"In honor of Doug? Bitsy, you're kidding. Three days ago you were ready to roast him alive for killing the pigeons." I winced at my unfortunate choice of words but that did nothing to keep them from winging their way around the ears of our startled audience. People got whiplash looking from one to the other of us, trying to decide which of us to stare at hardest. Except George. His eyes were riveted on Bitsy.

"I think I'd like another cup of coffee," Gene said brightly. "Can I get some for anyone else while I'm up?"

CHAPTER 26

The meeting broke up pretty quickly after that. I tried laughing my words off as only so much fertilizer and the committee members kindly twittered at that and ate a bite or two. But, one by one, they made their excuses and said goodnight. Phil could be heard whistling his tune off into the dark as I locked the door after him.

Claire stayed to tuck the leftovers into her plastic containers. I thanked her for the lovely refreshments, which I'd only allowed myself to get within smelling distance of, and told her to let me know when she was ready to go so I could help her carry stuff out to her car.

George stayed behind because he had Bitsy over in a corner, tripping over herself, explaining what she'd been saying, and more importantly, doing lately. I debated going over and helping her out, then I kicked myself for even having to debate it.

"George, you know I was just blathering," I said, pulling up a chair without waiting to be asked. "You know how often people say things in the heat of the moment and how rarely they mean anything by it. Besides, Bitsy didn't say 'roast,' that was my impromptu interpretation of what she said."

"What did you say, Bitsy?"

"Honestly, George. You can't expect me to remember what I said three days ago."

"Try."

"Well, I was mildly upset about the pigeons."

"Mildly?" I murmured.

"Margaret. All right," Bitsy sniffed, "I was upset. And you would be, too, if you'd seen them flapping in their death throes all over downtown. It was horrible. It was barbaric. And I probably said something about Doug having gone too far and he wasn't going to get away with it."

"But you didn't have any contact with him?" George asked.

"No."

"What about the book?" I asked.

She swiveled her glare to me. "What book?"

"*A Walk Through Time*. You said you showed him the copy at the Historical Society."

"Just who is conducting this interrogation," she asked, "you or George?"

"Sorry."

"All right, yes, I did see him. And I spoke to him. For all of five minutes. And quite a few people, you included, saw him alive and perfectly healthy at Bertie's the day after that. And by the way, as long as you're wondering about that book, you might like to know that the Historical Society's copy is now missing. And you might ask *him* where he got his copy from." Bitsy is great at the dramatic gesture and she now performed a full-arm-extended finger point. At Gene, as it turns out, who was leaning quietly and rather handsomely against a bookshelf, hands in his pockets, observing.

"Mashburn," George groaned, "I might've known. You want to come over here and join us?" Gene kicked himself away from the shelf and strolled over. "Why don't you pull up a chair." He did. "You know, though Bitsy," George said, turning back to her, "the best use of a policeman's time isn't in chasing down lost books."

"Stolen."

He sighed.

"And anyway, before he slips away again, as he seems to be very good at doing, you might also want to ask him what he was doing with a can of gasoline the night before the fire."

This was getting complicated and definitely heading toward acrimonious but George just plowed his way forward. He'd make a good sled dog in the face of a howling blizzard. He turned mournful eyes on Gene.

"Can of gas?"

"My car was out of gas."

"Plagued with vehicle troubles, aren't you?" This gave George a moment of cheer.

"Lately. Um, may I ask a question?"

"Oh, sure, why not?"

"What book are you talking about and why do you think I have a copy?" Gene directed this to Bitsy but shied away from meeting her eyes. In any other situation this would have looked like the suspicious reaction of a guilty conscience. Except that I know what it's like to be on the receiving end of Bitsy's gimlet glare. The pain of unanesthetized laser surgery might compare.

But Bitsy's wattage suddenly dimmed. Pinkening cheeks and a small cough replaced it. I looked at her. George looked at her. Gene, noting the silence, finally looked at her.

"Ahem." We all jumped.

"Oh, Claire." I caught my breath and patted my heart back into submission with a hand on my chest. "All set?"

"Yeah, thanks. And Bitsy? Thanks again for asking me to do this. Every little bit is going to help in getting the word out that Bertie's Bank Tavern might be down for a while, but we're not out. We'll be back, bigger and better. You know, I know it was awful and all what happened to Doug, for lots of reasons if you know what I mean, but I'm beginning to think the fire was maybe the best thing that could've happened to the restaurant. Oh, and Margaret, is this yours? I found it with my stuff and thought it was something of mine but it looks like some kind of list of clues or something? Anyway, bye, George. Bye, Gene. Don't be a stranger."

I snatched my list, which had not been with her stuff, crushed it, jammed it in my pocket. Then I grabbed the two coffee carafes and headed for the door. Claire followed, chattering on, probably about her prospects and her plans. I wouldn't know because I was busy listening to myself and I won't repeat what I was hearing.

When I got back inside, the others were much as I'd left them. Bitsy's mouth was screwed up tight and she appeared to be critiquing the arrangement of titles on the top shelf across from her. Gene sat with his arms crossed defensively over his chest and his legs stretched out in front of him, contemplating the toes of his shoes. George was making crabbed notes in a worn notebook. It was tempting to leave the three of them there and go up to bed.

"Margaret, what do you know about this book that Doug was so keen to find?" George asked.

"What exactly do you want to know about it? Subject matter? Publication history? Something about the author? What size it is? What color?"

"He wants to know something useful, of course," Bitsy said. "Don't try to be funny."

"Bitsy, I haven't felt funny for days. Any of that information could be useful, George, depending on why and what you want to know."

"Let's start with subject matter."

"Wait a second, why *do* you want to know?" I asked. "What's the book got to do with anything at this point?"

"Your sister claims to have seen a copy in my apartment." Gene's toes still fascinated him. Or maybe they perplexed him. He looked unsettled. "Which it turns out she saw while you and I were eating dinner together. Actually probably while we were eating dessert with her husband and George. The night of the fire."

"The door was unlocked," Bitsy snapped. When in doubt, lash out. One of Bitsy's credos.

But she'd said she was going to do some ferreting, I remembered now. It would have been nice to assume my one and only sister wouldn't stoop so low as to invade someone's apartment. Good thing I could bolster my spirits with my new mission in life or I'd be feeling disillusioned right about now.

"If the door was unlocked, I don't suppose you can charge her with breaking and entering, can you?" I asked.

"Margaret!"

"I just like to keep these things straight, Bitsy. George, if you're really interested, I've got a copy of *A Walk Through Time.* Duckie wasn't looking specifically for that book, though. He said he wanted something that told what businesses were in which buildings around the turn of the century. He didn't say why."

"Hm. Old buildings. Right up your alley, hunh, Mashburn? But you say you don't own a copy."

"Of course he doesn't own a copy," Bitsy said. "He doesn't need to. He stole the

Historical Society's copy."

"Or Doug did." Gene straightened up, done communing with his toes. He rubbed his hands then put them in his pockets. "That's why the door was unlocked. He asked if he could spend a couple of nights. I left it unlocked so he could put some stuff up there." Bitsy regarded him suspiciously. Gene shrugged. "If the book's still there, they can fingerprint it. You won't find mine on it."

"Which proves exactly nothing," she spit.

I was getting tired of this conversation. "Knock it off, Bitsy."

"Hmph."

I was tired of the participants, too. "George, Diane might know what Doug was up to but I still don't see how anything to do with that book has anything to do with the murder."

"Probably doesn't." He closed the notebook and slapped it in his hand a few times, probably the most threatening move I've ever seen him make. No one shivered or shook. "You still staying next door, Mashburn?"

"Yup."

"And you certainly know where to find me. If you have anymore ridiculous questions," Bitsy said, standing up and arming herself with her easel and paper. "One more thing, though, George. If you're going to talk to Diane anyway, and as long as we seem to be casting aspersions so freely about, you might want to find out how grief stricken she really is. I think Margaret will at least admit that her reaction to her husband's death has been eye opening."

What could I say? Diane's name and my questions about her were burning holes through the newly amended list scrunched once again in my pocket even as we sniped.

"Margaret?"

"Oh, gosh, George."

"What was that you grabbed from Claire?"

"Nothing worthwhile."

"I hope you're not playing detective."

"The only mysteries I'd like to solve," I said, hoping to deflect George's curiosity about my list, "are why Eunice left and why she didn't give notice."

"She quit?" George asked. "Dang, she really knew her eighteenth century philosophers."

"That's just it. I don't know if she quit. I only know she didn't show up for work yesterday and hasn't returned my calls and up to now she's been completely reliable. I stopped by her apartment today and she wasn't there and neither was her car. Or possibly her cat."

"You been snooping, Margaret?" George asked.

"It's called being concerned, George. For heaven's sake. She went to Asheville on Tuesday. What if she didn't make it back? What if she went off the road in the mountains?"

"I saw her Tuesday night," Bitsy said. "At the fire. I'm surprised you didn't. She's hard enough to miss."

"Is she the tattooed Valkyrie?" Gene asked. He looked at me and shrugged. "Doug called her that. He introduced us a week or two ago. Yeah, I saw her at the fire, too."

"Really? See, George? I can't be a detective. I have no powers of observation."

"You were distracted," George said. "But, yeah she was there. Look, call me if she doesn't show up in a day or two. But missing one day of work? Not exactly earthshaking. She's young and who knows what goes through the minds of the pierced and tattooed?"

"Plenty," I said.

"And I'm plenty serious, Margaret. About playing detective. Don't."

"The only thing I'm doing is locking the door behind you guys and going to bed."

CHAPTER 27

"Are you playing detective?" Gene asked.

"No."

Bitsy and George had left but Gene and I were taking a little longer saying good night to each other on the front steps. In fact, as we were both sitting on the steps, his actual departure was at a complete standstill. I scootched closer to him. Only because it was a bit nippy out and I didn't want him catching a chill.

"What was that paper Claire had?"

"Nothing, really. You know how some people doodle while they're thinking? Or some people need to talk things out after something happens? Claire just had my version of that kind of thing."

"So what exactly is it? You were pretty quick to grab it from her."

"Small questions disturbing the fine balance of my mind. It's just a list of things I've been wondering about. So here's something else to add. That list damn well wasn't with Claire's stuff. It was on the other side of the cash register from where her stuff was."

"You think she lifted it?" he asked.

"Unless someone else moved it."

"Why?"

"Who knows? But that's the kind of thing on the list. It's nothing but a bunch of random thoughts and questions. Not even complete sentences."

"Outlining your suspicions of various people concerning Doug's murder."

"Yeah, well, when you put it like that . . ."

"I think you ought to tell George."

"Your favorite flat foot?"

"I think he's warming up to me."

"I thought Bitsy was warming up to you when she saw your sketch for the T-shirt. But now that she thinks you've stolen Historical Society property, I just don't know." I shook my head. "Dear, dear, dear."

"That's me. Two steps forward, three steps back." His arm found its way around me. "That's a bad AA joke."

"You know AA jokes?"

"I've been to a few meetings."

"Huh. That have anything to do with your divorce?"

"No, that was more the result of a judicious dose of cabin fever. Talk about an eye opener. We were living outside Colorado Springs and got snowed in one too many times one winter. Turns out we really didn't like each other a whole lot." He shivered, maybe in memory of all that snow and cold. "Kind of sad."

"So how much of a problem is your problem?"

"It will always be a problem. But these days it isn't usually much of one. Can I see your list?"

"If you'll invite me to see more of your sketchings sometime."

"Deal."

We worked out a few of the details sealing the deal and then I rather breathlessly pulled the list from my pocket. He scanned it quickly, turned it over and gave a muffled snort at Phil's handiwork on the other side. Then he read through my jottings more slowly.

"It was the right one," he said.

"Hm?"

"One of your questions, 'which foot'? He was on his stomach, head toward the wall, legs out straight. So it was his right foot sticking out."

I'd forgotten I actually wrote that down. If Claire or anyone else had read this they'd have to be wondering what kind of a nut case I was. Or worse, they might be thinking I really was playing detective. Which, I told myself firmly, I was not doing. Definitely not. But now I wanted to know how Gene happened to know the answer to that question. No, I didn't. But I did. Really? No. He must have sensed the turmoil as I argued with myself and he nuzzled my ear to calm me.

"George's friends down at the station were gratuitously graphic about it when I was down there answering their questions."

"Eeuw." But then I couldn't help myself. "Pants off?"

"In his shorts."

"Which doesn't put Claire clearly in or out of the picture."

"No. What does Angel of Death mean and why is it crossed off?"

I told him about Bitsy and the Angel of Death Mafia Theory. After a few minutes he was able to stop laughing.

"And she's never figured out you made the whole thing up?"

"No, and at this point she wouldn't believe me if I told her. Who'd've thought, though?"

"What?"

"That sleeping lies would start dogging me now."

"Serves you right." He nuzzled my ear again. That served me about right, too. "Mmm, you know what I think?"

"What?"

"You should either get rid of your list or give it to George."

"Hmm, how romantic. I'll think about it. You know what I think? We should either invite Leona to join us or you should go home and have a cup of cocoa with her."

He looked across the yards to see Leona in her lit window gazing unsubtley in our direction. "Or, we could give her something worth looking at."

"Mr. Mashburn," I said, standing up, assuming my most Bitsy-like pose, "I feel responsible for my elderly cousin's health and well-being and I take my responsibilities seriously. I'm not sure she can handle that much excitement."

He grabbed me and bent me back in a swooning embrace, planted a resounding kiss on my lips then returned me to the upright position. "But can you?"

He chuckled his way through the dark to Leona's house. She, I noticed, was no longer standing in front of the window. She was peeking around the edge of the curtain. For her benefit I breathed an exaggerated sigh with hands clasped to my heaving bosom, eyes fixed heavenward. Then I blew her a raspberry and went inside.

Loath though I was to abandon it mid-read, I ignored my bedtime Hiaasen that night and went in search of something else on my shelves. The orderly system for shelving titles I follow in the bookstore doesn't carry over to my personal books upstairs. I know where things are, generally, and can usually put my hand on a book quickly enough, but the books tend to sort themselves out organically, their order not always apparent to the casual or uptight observer.

Bitsy, chief uptight acolyte for the muse of methodology, has mentioned the lack of plan on my shelves. (And chairs and tables and sofa or wherever else my books congregate.) I tell her that I treat my books as old friends. They're free to associate with whomever they wish and the startling combinations that sometimes result are a source of surprise and joy. She hasn't said anything lately, but I've been noticing the occasional alphabetized shelf.

I found what I was looking for on the bookcase in the hall. A slim, green volume, roughly five inches by eight, published in 1916. *A Walk Through Time* by Harker Grundy. It and a book of walking tours through the British Isles had been communing with *Stalking the Wild Asparagus* and *A Wrinkle in Time.* I promised to return it to its companions in a day or two and took it off to bed with me.

Settled into my pillows, reading light adjusted, quilt pulled up under my chin, I discovered the sad fact that *A Walk Through Time* is not fascinating reading. It made me wonder if my family isn't distantly related to Harker Grundy, Bitsy inheriting his gene for exhausting exactitude.

The book's dry-as-dust tone was a shame. Grundy could have taken the reader for a pleasant stroll down Main Street on a bright, sunny morning in 1850. A breeze might have played along at our heels, bringing with it the scents of horses and people who bathed less frequently than we do today. Merchants could have stepped out to greet us, inviting us into the cool depths of their stores and extolling the virtues of their various wares. The man in the mercantile might have given us peppermints to suck. But none of that happened.

What had Doug been looking for? Despite its gripless narrative, the book was a treasure trove for anyone with an interest in the antebellum businesses along Main Street and the staying power to slog through it.

But what had got Doug so hot that he stole the Historical Society's copy? And why did that word "treasure" now jog my memory? I couldn't remember.

I read awhile longer, trying to be fascinated by Grundy's memories, but I couldn't lose myself in them and found my mind drifting back to current events.

Should I take Gene's advice and turn my list over to George? The more I thought about it the goofier the idea seemed. What could my list have on it that the police hadn't already thought of and thoroughly looked into? And if it was a question of the list somehow being dangerous because it exposed a villain, then the damage was already done. People had seen it. Maybe I was being recklessly modest, but I didn't see myself as much of a threat to anyone.

Still, it was nice to have somebody worrying about me. In a way. In another way it pushed my perversity buttons. Tell me what to do, eh? We'll see about that. I know I react that way to Bitsy, sometimes, but it was interesting to see that I might be reacting the same way to Gene's bit of paranoia. If it were paranoia. Maybe by holding onto my list and my curiosity, I was stepping from the pan into the fire, proverbial or otherwise.

I dreamt that night of dancing in the flames of good intentions.

CHAPTER 28

"Why do you have to make everything so melodramatic and complicated, Margaret?" That was Bitsy complaining at high volume into the phone the next morning when I tried explaining my reluctance to go with her and Cousin Leona to Doug's funeral. "And what makes you think you're any more sensitive than anyone else? Do you think anyone enjoys going to funerals?"

"Sure, Bitsy, some people do. You know that old lady who shows up at every one we've ever been to? She's like a funeral groupie."

"I meant normal people."

"All I know is, I'll be disappointed if she isn't still alive to come to mine."

"I'll pick you up at ten."

Well, it wouldn't kill me. And, if it did, then it couldn't happen in a handier place. On that note of cheerful efficiency, I pried myself out of bed and took a shower, attempting a verse or two of Phil's anthem as needles of steamy water massaged my shoulders. I couldn't remember most of the words so I substituted pseudo Russian lyrics and emotive gestures. It was a pleasing effect but in the end didn't make me feel any more like going to the funeral.

Every funeral I go to brings back memories of previous funerals. They're like layers of sorrow, with each new layer adding its weight, making the emotions that much harder to handle. And because I hadn't liked Doug much these days, anyway, today I'd be feeling guilty for that as well as soggy.

Over a bowl of cereal, I came up with another reason to avoid the funeral. How would Diane feel about seeing Bitsy and me there, reminding her of her drunken indiscretions? Assuming she even remembered them. Maybe I should offer to cover the store so Fran could go instead. Maybe I should give lessons in straw grasping.

Leona, in her spinster's weeds, tottered over a few minutes before ten. I had on the skirt I'd worn the night of the date-by-ambush and was beginning to think it was getting pretty weedy itself. As we waited for Bitsy, I idly wondered if, now that there was an itinerant architect in my life, I should take more interest in my clothes. But I promptly lost interest in that idea when Leona said she hoped William was able to hold up during the service.

"How do you mean, hold up?"

"His nerves, dear. Apparently he's taking the situation terribly hard. Eleanor says he and Doug were quite close. It's been a shock for him and a further shock to see how much it's affecting poor Diane."

"He seemed his old self when I saw him yesterday."

"Of course he's putting up a good front, but Eleanor is worried he won't be able to keep it up. He always has been sensitive."

"That sounds like a polite way to put it. Hey, wait a second, didn't you tell Gene I was 'a sensitive creature'? I don't know if I like being lumped in with William."

"That was merely for Gene's benefit, dear. And yours. It never hurts to show a little feminine vulnerability." She patted my arm then picked a stray crumb from my sweater.

"Cousin Leona, you know, I've never asked you. Did you ever have a sweetheart?"

"Don't be silly, Margaret. I couldn't be bothered."

Bitsy pulled up in her respectable car and gave a respectable wave. She drives a new-ish, dark green Honda sedan and keeps it washed and waxed and the interior free of clutter. It's a more suitable vehicle for attending a funeral than mine. Leona's car is too, but Bitsy and I avoid riding if Leona is driving.

I handed Leona into the front seat and climbed into the back and we made our sedate and respectable way to the DeAngelis Funeral Home. I distracted myself from the coming ordeal by picturing myself arriving in Gene's far from sedate speedster.

"No one would've missed me, Bitsy," I whispered to her when we got to the funeral home and saw the crowd. "Besides, why didn't Rodney come with you?"

"He's one of the pall bearers."

"Oh." I started to take Leona's arm but she brushed me off.

"Bitsy will take my arm," she said.

That surprised both me and Bitsy. She'd already turned away to mingle with the other mourners but Leona snatched her back, smiling sweetly at me. And Gene. She must have seen him crossing the room toward us.

"You do funerals, too?" I asked after he'd greeted Leona and Bitsy and Bitsy had marched Leona off in the other direction.

"Seemed like the right thing to do. We were working together, after a fashion, and he was my landlord. Besides, I found this

314

great tweed jacket at the thrift shop for five bucks and I should try to get my money's worth out of it." It was a lovely warm brown tweed. To show him how much I admired it I linked my arm in his. "Why don't you fill me in on who some of these people are?" he asked.

So we started a slow circuit of the parlor where everyone was gathering before filing into the chapel for the service. He already knew Nancy Umphrey and the McKinneys, of course. We nodded at Bertie. Ray Jenkins and George were talking but we didn't interrupt them. Rodney gave a discreet wave. It was good a turnout. Duckie had lived his whole life in Stonewall. And he'd lived a very social life, belonging to so many organizations it would make me tired just to list them.

"You ask and I'll tell," I said.

That plan seemed to work until I realized the people he asked about all happened to be attractive young women.

"Window shopping?" I asked.

"What? No, but aren't there an unusual number of pretty young women here?"

"It's the onion rings at Bertie's. They have this astonishing side effect."

"So I noticed." He gave me an unrespectable leer. "But isn't it interesting to see how many of them showed up here? Maybe Doug was more of a stray tom than we thought."

"Now there's a thought. And that might be something the police haven't considered. Hang on a sec." I'd put my list in my bag before leaving, just in case. Just in case what, I wasn't real clear on, but I pulled it out now and scribbled another note.

"Capturing the *mot juste,* Margaret?" a voice asked over my shoulder, startling me so the pen took an uncharted jag across the paper.

"Just taking notes, William, so I'll know what to ask for when I plan my own funeral."

"Ah, yes, I will be happy to help you toward that goal in any way I can. Call on me sometime. Or perhaps I'll call on you. By the way, your Valkyrie is conspicuous, don't you think?"

"Eunice is here?" I did a dizzying three-sixty but didn't see her. "Where?"

"By her absence, Margaret," William tutted. He put a hand on my shoulder and leaned in closer, as though offering comfort, but his next words jarred. "Was she dabbling with our Duckie, do you suppose, and now she's gone into seclusion to assuage her abject grief? Or perhaps she's on the

316

lam as the guilty party."

I pulled away from him and stared. His face was a lugubrious blank if there can be such a thing. My mind was a madhouse.

"The service begins in ten minutes," William said, bowing slightly, "if you will please start moving into the chapel." And he oiled away as soundlessly as he'd arrived, greeting people and giving them the heebie jeebies as he went.

"He can't be right," I said, turning to Gene. "He can't be."

"Not knowing Eunice, I couldn't say. From what we're learning about Doug . . ." he shook his head and shrugged.

Did *I* know Eunice? I put my pen and list away without making note of that question.

The service passed much as they all do. It was better than some because there was no question of an open casket. I tried concentrating on that point to hold the tears at bay. They came anyway. Gene noticed and put his arm around me, which only made it worse. There's no logic to sorrow.

At the end, Diane and the girls followed the casket out. Diane looked like a zombie and she had a right to. The girls just looked lost.

■ ■ ■ ■

"Are you sure you want to go to the burial?" Gene had given me a minute or two alone afterwards to mop my face into some semblance of order.

"Oh, yeah. Believe it or not the cemetery doesn't affect me this way." I blew my nose one last time. "Have you been to our cemetery?"

He shook his head.

"It's very pretty. Hilly, big old cedars, huge oaks. Some beautiful markers. It's full of old friends. Let's find Bitsy and Leona."

They were outside in the incongruous sunshine talking quietly with Bertie.

"I don't know whether they're serious or not," Bertie was saying when we joined them. She was dressed decorously in a shapeless dark suit. She also had on one of those hats with the veils that women used to wear to church years ago. Quite a change from either the Bertie of white floury aprons or the Bertie of flowing pink caftans. Something else was different about her. She looked worried.

"Sometimes I wonder if they have the brains to be serious about anything," Bitsy said. "But here's your solution. Margaret

318

has taken up sleuthing and she's going to beat the police at their own game."

"Shhh, Bitsy, for heaven's sake, I am not." I looked around to see who might have heard her. I should have said that Bertie and Leona were the ones talking quietly. Bitsy rarely does.

"That wasn't your list of clever clues you snatched away from Claire last night?"

"You don't have to broadcast it," I whispered.

"Margaret," Bertie asked earnestly, "what have you found out?"

"I'm sorry, Bertie. I haven't found out anything."

"Except that we had better be going or we'll be late," Leona said. "Gene, if you had your car here I would ride with you. As it is you'd better ride with us. Bertie, we'll see you there. And go talk to George Buckles. He'll give you a straight answer."

"What's Bertie worried about?" I asked when we were all tucked into Bitsy's car.

Bitsy waited to start up, tapping her fingers on the steering wheel while Gene groped for a seat belt down the back of the seat. I was amazed Bitsy let her seat belts get away with that sort of behavior in her otherwise orderly car and almost said something about it. But I could see her mentally tallying the delay in Gene's debit column and decided not to make matters worse. Instead, I watched her watching him in the rear view mirror. Her lips were drawing up in anticipation of some biting remark when an amazing thing happened. She closed her eyes, took a few deep breaths, then smiled. Wanly, but still she smiled.

"Mr. Mashburn, how did you arrive here that you are now traveling with us?" she asked.

"I, uh . . . ," His arm was buried up to the elbow between the cushion and the back of the seat. He gave a tremendous yank and the belt popped out like a newborn boa constrictor.

"Congratulations, Doctor, I think it's a boy," I said.

Gene buckled himself in. "I rode my bike. Thanks for letting me hitch a ride with you to the cemetery, though."

"My pleasure," Bitsy said, wheeling out of the parking lot.

"Really?" Gene looked at me.

I shrugged. "So what is Bertie worried about?"

"Apparently the police are checking into Doug's business relationships," Leona answered. "Including, of course, the Bank Tavern."

"I don't see you taking notes, Margaret," Bitsy said.

"Gene's trying to convince me to desist and hand my list over to George."

"Oh?"

"Besides, I already had questions about the Bank Tavern on it."

"But not about his other businesses?" Leona asked.

"Well, the school project." I gave Gene a quick glance. Nothing in particular showed on his face. "But other than that I only know he was busy around town. Doing what, I don't know. Do you?"

"No. You might speak to Ed McKinney. And William. And Eleanor for that matter."

"Leona?" I tried interrupting the to do list she was creating for me.

"Doug's parents, too. Though, it might be too soon to impose on them, perhaps. And Nancy Umphrey, of course. Go have lunch with her and see if she'll tell you anything. Probably not, but you never know. Certainly worth a try."

"Leona, really, I'm not playing detective."

"Of course you're not, dear."

Evergreen Cemetery lies on the east edge of town. There are other, newer, cemeteries but Evergreen is old enough to have grown comfortable looking. The markers don't march in raw looking rows across shadeless lawns. They shelter in the gently rolling landscape, with trees bending close, ready to commiserate with the newly grieving and welcome back familiar faces. The bouquets and arrangements of flowers left behind are mostly real.

Meandering gravel lanes invite visitors deeper into Evergreen's acreage, around small hills, past the reflecting lake with the island in its center. There is no parking lot. Visitors are expected to pull slightly off the gravel onto the grass verge. Bitsy, following in the long line of cars, pulled off behind a white Cadillac.

"That's Hattie and Ed," Bitsy said. "Got your pencil sharpened?"

"Yeah, sorry about the shavings all over the floor back here, though."

"Hush," Leona told us.

We joined the stream of people heading in groups of twos and threes and fours for the green tent set up over the new grave. This time Leona took Gene's arm and I further irritated Bitsy by taking out my pen, casting furtive glances left and right, and pretending to make notes.

Doug was being buried on a hillside overlooking the reflecting lake, in an area shared by other Everetts, a few Ledfords, and the Pickle family. I remember being disappointed as a child not to find a Catsup, Onion or Relish family anywhere. There is a Mayo, though. And a Hamburg. It was getting too close to lunchtime for me.

Leona must have directed Gene to take her right up front because they disappeared into the crowd. Bitsy went looking for Rodney. I nodded at people I knew and decided to stay on the outer fringe.

"The better to spy on people?"

I barely avoided whiplash, turning to see who had snuck up on me this time. Claire. Wasn't it rather indelicate of her to show up?

"Those were a strange couple of questions about me on that piece of paper of yours I found last night," she said. "Do you really think I'd stop to take a shower if I knew Doug was dead in the sofa? Unless what you meant was did I know he was dead because I killed him? And then there's that whole thing about Grandma and me wanting the building and would I kill him if I couldn't get it or would I kill him *to* get it? You're really pretty nosy, you know? Not that I hold that against you." She smiled. "Actually I've been making a list of my own and you're about the only one not on it

323

because you're almost never anywhere but your bookstore. Want to compare notes?"

Several people near us turned to shush her. Claire winced exaggeratedly, smiled conspiratorially, and blended into the crowd. Was she just tweaking me? Shouldn't there be some old adage about too many amateur sleuths spoiling the scoop?

But I shook off that image because it was a beautiful day for a burial. The reflection in the lake, when I turned to look, was nearly perfect. The lone mausoleum on the island in the center and the arched bridge spanning the distance from the shore fairly sparkled. The scent of mown grass hung in the air. A mockingbird sang somewhere in a treetop. As they lowered Doug into the ground, I ignored the preacher's hollow words and wandered down to the lake's edge.

We used to tell a story about this lake when we were kids at slumber parties or on overnight campouts. Mostly it was older children telling shivering younger ones. Maybe it's a story told about any lake or pond or body of water in any graveyard, but to us it was the absolute and terrifying truth.

If you squint your eyes just right and just long enough, and if the day is calm and the water is clear enough, there is a spot a few feet out from the edge of the lake, and a few feet off from the side of the bridge, where you can just make out the face of a drowned woman. She's not easy to see. You have to lean out just far enough.

She's been there more than a hundred years. Her long black hair waves slowly back and forth in invisible currents and sometimes covers her face so then you can't see her no matter how hard you look. But her eyes will open when she knows you're looking at her. Although, she's not looking back at you. She's looking for the face of her murderer. Her name is Adele Pickle.

I hadn't looked for Adele in years. Actually I'd never really looked too hard for her at all because the whole idea scared the hell out of me as a kid. Come to think of it, it didn't appeal to me all that much as an adult, either.

What nonsense, I scolded myself. And just for that I put one hand on the end post of the bridge and leaned out for a look, squinting as best I could. How bizarre, someone or something was there. Out of focus, but . . . Something brushed me. Then shoved.

Who would have thought the lake bottom was that muddy or the water that cold? I suppose my yelp when I went in alerted people. Or maybe it was the gurgles I made when I pulled my head out of the mud. In any case, when I'd cleared the mud from my eyes and stopped blowing bubbles, I saw there was no end of helping hands reaching out to save me from two feet of water. But only two hands gallantly came in after me. They were Gene's. And as he helped me out, I wondered which of the hands still on shore had pushed me in.

CHAPTER 29

Gene whipped off his lovely new five-dollar tweed jacket and draped it around my unlovely, sodden shoulders. I'd provided an interesting but graceless note to the conclusion of the burial service and he walked me back to the car amid sympathetic murmurs and a few twitters. Nancy and Bitsy met us there. Bitsy clearly didn't want to let us and our pond scum in her car.

"You're alright, Margaret, thank goodness." Nancy gave my arm a quick squeeze.

"But your skirt is absolutely ruined," Bitsy said. "And look at your shoes. And the sweater. Not that any of them are a great loss. But you are completely covered in mud. How on earth did you manage to fall in head first in the first place?"

"I was looking for Adele Pickle."

"Oh for heaven's sake."

"I think I saw it, too," I said, trying to dredge the memory out of the lake bottom.

"Or her. Or whatever. Someone, anyway."

"Bitsy," Gene said urgently, looking from me to her in a worried way that was sweet but unnecessary, "she's clearly suffered a trauma of some sort, maybe hit her head on a rock. Why don't you unlock the car and let her sit down and warm up. Maybe we should take her to the hospital."

"Why?" Bitsy asked.

He stared at her in disbelief. "Your sister fell head first into two feet of mud and water and is spouting gibberish about seeing dill pickles and you question whether she should be seen by a doctor?"

At that Bitsy and I fell into hysterics and would have collapsed into each other's arms except I noticed her shying away and just in time remembered I was still covered in mud. Leona arrived then, shushing us both.

"It's enough we have one spectacle in the family," she said, giving me a withering look, "must we have two? Bitsy, we should take Margaret home immediately. Harriet said she keeps a blanket in her trunk for emergencies. We can wrap that around her so she doesn't ruin your seats."

Bitsy reluctantly unlocked the doors. Gene still looked concerned or confused or both. Nancy went to collect the blanket from Harriet who fluttered around looking upset.

"I'm all right," I told Gene after they'd wrapped me like a newly wallowed pig in the blanket. "Thank you, Nancy."

"Look, I need to get back to the bank," she said. "Call me this afternoon, though, will you?"

"After I get the mud out of my ears." She hugged me gingerly and departed. I turned to Gene. "I really am okay." He didn't look convinced. "I'll tell you about the Pickles, but later. Not while Bitsy's driving. We don't want her running off the road. And there's something else . . ." Over Gene's shoulder I saw George moping his way over.

"You all right, Margaret? What happened?"

"She was looking for Adele and she slipped," Bitsy sputtered, her hysterics threatening to ignite again.

"I didn't slip," I said with as much dignity as I could, wrapped in Harriet's fleecy yellow blanket and my hair smelling strongly of algae.

"You trip?" he asked.

"Why don't you come by later, George? I just want to go home and take a shower."

He shrugged. "It's no big deal, Margaret. Either you slipped or you tripped or you went for a dip, but as long as you're all right."

"That was very poetic, George, but I didn't slip, trip or dip." I looked around to see who else was listening or watching, then lowered my voice. "I was pushed."

"What?" Only George, Bitsy and Gene had been within earshot, but all three gave voice to that incredulity. I don't know whether Bitsy or George was the loudest. And of course they attracted more attention than if I'd shouted in the first place.

I closed my eyes, hoping maybe they'd all go away. I opened one eye again and said to George, "I'm going home. Come around later if you want to." And I eeled my way into the car.

Bitsy continued being incredulous, at volume, most of the way home but that didn't keep her from remembering to stop back at the funeral home so she could put Gene out. I was tempted to escape with him but didn't especially relish the idea of riding on the handlebars of his bike like a mud-encrusted figurehead. Leona was strangely silent the whole way.

"Thanks, Bitsy," I said when she'd thoughtfully delivered me around back so I could bypass Fran and any curious customers. "Don't think it hasn't been swell." I closed the car door on another variation of "I can't believe you're going to tell people you were pushed" and let myself in the kitchen door.

A convenient feature of this house is the back stairs. I trudged up them, shedding bits of drying mud. Trying not to shake from anything other than being cold and damp.

I was sitting in the kitchen, newly showered and cleanly dressed, having a restoring cup of tea with honey and ginger, when George and Gene blew in. They wore similar expressions. Concern? Disbelief? I didn't know, couldn't tell, and wasn't sure I was up to finding out.

"Hi. I was sitting here marveling at the number of new and putrid scents I've washed out of my hair lately. What do you think I should try for next?"

They both started to pull out the chair next to me. Gene won. George took the chair opposite us and crossed his arms. His expression had gelled more definitely into disbelief. Gene's still wavered.

"Tea?" I asked, getting up to refill my own cup. They eyed each other, probably trying to figure out which response would give them the advantage. If he says no, should I say yes? Should I answer first, or make him? I poured them each a cup, anyway, while they tried to figure it out. Then I established my own bit of advantage by not sitting back down. Instead, I leaned against the counter and sipped my tea.

"Margaret," George said, then cleared his throat, "was anyone with you at the edge of the lake?"

"Before I was pushed, when I was pushed, or after I was pushed?"

He scrubbed his hand over his face and took a big swig of the tea. It was too hot for that kind of action and in reaction he banged the mug back down on the table. "Do you know who pushed you?"

"No."

"Why would someone push you in?"

"To drown me."

"In two feet of water?"

"It's possible."

"But why would someone want to drown you?"

"Because I know something about Duckie's murder."

His look of disbelief sharpened into something closer to derision. "What do you know?"

"Nothing as far as I can see. But maybe they think I know something."

He took time out to massage his scalp. I looked at Gene.

"Maybe it was a warning," Gene said, "so you'd stop asking questions." Ah, finally a true believer.

"And maybe it was her imagination," George said.

I put my hands on my hips and produced a credible Bitsy-like scowl. We aren't sisters for nothing.

"Okay, okay," he rushed on, "maybe it wasn't your imagination. *Have* you been asking questions? Come to think of it, maybe I'd better see that paper you were so quick to grab from Claire last night." He held out his hand like a schoolteacher asking for the note I'd passed.

"George, it was in my purse."

"Yeah?"

"My purse went in the drink along with me. The contents are goo."

"Good. Then that takes care of that. Don't try to recreate it, whatever it was, and don't go around asking people any more questions, and if you hear anything that might be relevant, call the station."

"And that's it? End of investigation?"

"Investigation into what? If someone was out to kill you, Margaret, there are more efficient ways than giving you a shove into Adele's mud puddle. Now, if they'd strangled you first and then pushed you in,

333

it might have ended with better results. Kind of a public place for that kind of thing, though, don't you think? Unlike Mashburn's apartment, which was so conveniently vacated by him." He drained his mug and heaved himself up from the table. "I'd ask you to keep an eye on her, Mashburn, just in case there is someone out to get her, but I don't really know if you're the right guy to do that." At the door he turned around. "Margaret, it occurs to me that you should read more Nietzsche." And he left.

"Nietzsche?" Gene said.

"I didn't like to ask."

"I didn't like his attitude. What the hell? You might be in real danger."

"Except that I think he's probably right. What a dumb way to try to kill someone. It would've been taking a ridiculous chance. Anyone could have seen it happen."

"Except no one did," Gene said. "Are you saying now you weren't pushed?"

"Oh, no, believe me, I, who have made a profession out of being either pushed or pulled around by one or another of my female relatives, know a well-placed hand in the back when I feel one. No, the more I think about it, the more I think you might be right and it was a warning." We looked at each other and nodded.

"This is a more exciting town than I'd bargained for," he said. "You have been locking the kitchen door, haven't you?"

"And flossing my teeth every night."

"I'm allowed to worry about you, you know."

"But only up to a certain point."

"Oh?" he said, getting up and crowding me in an interesting way. "And what happens after that?"

"Unfortunately I start acting like my sister." He shuddered deliciously. "Want a sandwich?"

Over a couple of peanut butter and jelly on toasts I told him the legend of Adele Pickle.

"Ranks right up there with the Angel of Death Mafia Theory of Arson," he said. "Was there ever a real life Adele Pickle?"

"You're not supposed to ask rational questions about a story like that. But to tell you the truth, I don't know. We all thought there was. I figured she suffered from the same kind of parents Ima and Ura Hogg had. Hey, wait a second. I bet I know why I was thinking about her today. Be right back." I ran up the back stairs and returned, flipping through *A Walk Through Time*.

"Here," I said, sitting back down. "Arthur Pickle had a butcher shop on Main Street from 1884 until 1896. He married Adele McCoy in 1888. That's a relief, anyway. She wasn't born a Pickle. She just married one. But it doesn't say anything about her being murdered. Then again, if it didn't happen on Main Street, apparently old Harker wasn't interested in it." I passed the book to Gene.

"Or it hadn't happened yet when he wrote the book. Why was Doug so interested in this?"

"Something to do with one of his buildings, I guess. I can't picture him digging his way through it, though, to find what he wanted."

"Digging?"

"Yeah, deathless prose Grundy did not write. It's pretty turgid stuff."

"Old buildings, though, huh? Mind if I borrow it?"

"What do you think you'll find?"

He shrugged. "You never know. Old buildings."

"Oh yeah, that's your bag, isn't it? You know, Leona mentioned Doug's buildings and businesses this morning. I wonder if they're worth checking into?"

"Have you already forgotten what George said?"

"He said not to go around asking people

questions. So, okay, A, I'm not going to 'go around.' That implies aimlessness or at least random action. I'm more organized than that. And, B, I'm not going to ask people questions. There are other ways to get information."

"And you think that's a good idea?" he asked.

"Who's going to know?"

"I see you like to lead a devious life as well as a dangerous one."

I wiggled my eyebrows at him. "Two of my more delightful qualities."

He laid Harker Grundy aside and was exploring some of my other delightful qualities when he suddenly pulled away, the worried look back in his eyes. "Out at the cemetery you said there was something else you wanted to tell me. Just before George came over. What was it?"

I reluctantly dragged my thoughts back from wherever they'd floated. What was it? "Oh yeah. I saw something. When I was looking for Adele there was something in the water. It really was a face. But it wasn't right. It wasn't where I expected it to be. Like, it wasn't under the water. It looked like it was over my shoulder." We looked at each other. "It was the person who pushed me in."

CHAPTER 30

"So who was it?" Gene asked.

"I don't know."

"Man or woman?"

"I was expecting to see a woman," I said with a shrug.

"You were *expecting* to see Adele?"

"Let me put it this way, I wasn't expecting to see anyone else. Now what're you muttering?"

"I'm wondering if life is too short to get involved with certifiable lunacy. Your family seems to go in for that." He got up and stacked our plates in the sink. "I hate to say it, but I've got to go to work. What are your plans for the afternoon?"

"He asked, with poorly attempted nonchalance."

"Hey, look, you're the one who got dumped in the drink. And, if that's because someone thinks you know something, then the important thing to remember is that person is a murderer. And that should be ringing a few alarm bells, not exciting you to further ill-considered action. Why don't you spend the afternoon trying not to agitate the murderer any more than you already have?"

What a bossy guy he was turning out to be.

I wandered out front and helped Fran with a minor lunchtime rush, then spelled her for an hour or so. She goes home and does things like make a sandwich for Jim, hang sheets on the line and ride her exercise bike for half an hour. Not my idea of a break from work, but as long as it keeps her happy and she comes back to the bookstore afterwards I don't psychoanalyze it. When she got back, during a lull between customers, I filled her in on the morning's adventures.

"I'm surprised the grapevine hadn't already delivered that splashy bit of news," she said. "We're usually more in the swim of things than that. You must be in a real pickle over that skirt, though. You might just have to take the plunge and buy something new."

"Got that out of your system?"

"Sorry, almost," she said. "I couldn't help it. I had to dive right in. There."

"Sure?"

She nodded.

It's amazing the slack you have to cut to keep good staff. "This really could be serious, Fran."

"I know. Are you worried about the bookstore?"

"And the people working here. Damn, I forgot to tell George what William said about Eunice. He can't possibly be right, though. No way Eunice was involved with Doug."

"Doug might have been attracted to Eunice, but Eunice . . . No, that's pretty far-fetched."

"It is. But then the whole thing is. Duckie, the fire. It's unreal. And I really don't see how something I've written down on a crummy piece of paper could be a threat to anyone. How could I come up with anything the police wouldn't already know? Still, I thought you should know."

"Who's seen your list?"

"That's something I need to sit down and figure out."

"A firebug might like the idea of all this flammable material."

"It doesn't bear thinking of. Give me a holler if you need me."

I left her looking uncharacteristically serious behind the counter. Then the bell over the door jingled, and as I turned the corner of the stairs I heard her chirrup a cheerful hello to whoever had come in.

Upstairs I retrieved my purse from where I'd dropped it in the bathroom. I took it down the backstairs to the kitchen and dumped it out on the counter. I'd told George the truth. The contents were goo. What I didn't tell him was they were mostly recoverable goo. I set about rinsing off what could be rinsed, wiping what needed wiping and then copying what needed, once again, to be copied. The list was gooier than my lip balm, or my wallet, but not so irretrievably wad-like as my ex-packet of tissues. And it was still legible.

So, I wasn't recreating it. Not strictly speaking. I was making it easier to read. Besides, there were a few new things to add. And that, I told myself, was surely the act of creation rather than re-creation, hair-splitting being a skill I'm happy to practice.

This time around, I didn't relegate the list to a stray napkin or the reverse of some other work of genius. It got a clean eight-and-a-half-by-eleven sheet of paper all to itself. If I possessed some key piece of information, then it was high time I figured out what it was in a logical, business-like way. I wasn't going to "go around" or ask questions. I would sit here at the kitchen table and analyze the information I had. I would cogitate, ruminate, meditate, draw flow charts if need be. Whatever it took.

What it took was the better part of the afternoon and most of my spare brain cells. I ended up with several more lists with headings like "Who Saw the List" and "Who Heard About the List." That one had an appended listlet labeled "Who Might Have Heard About the List."

Then there was the list of people at the funeral and its sub-list of people standing around, gaping, at the scene of my rescue. I called that one "Friends I Maybe Don't Need" because I was getting slaphappy.

The most interesting list, though, was the one showing the dichotomy of the spate of vandalism around town. I gave that one the heading "Dichotomy of Vandalism" because it's not often I get the chance to use the word dichotomy, much less put it in bold, black letters at the top of a page with such flourish.

I wasn't at all sure the vandalism had anything to do with Doug's murder, but it was interesting to note there seemed to be two distinct types of event. There were the episodes you might call whimsical, and then there were the attacks you'd definitely call deadly. On the whimsical side were the guerrilla crosswalk, the manure in the dumpster, the altered welcome sign, and the goat infested field. On the deadly side were the dead pigeons, Harriet's dead garden, and Doug's exploding fishpond.

So, was there a clear line between the two sides? Were there two perpetrators or maybe two groups of perpetrators? And was there another line between the acts of vandalism and the arson/murder, or had there been a rather major escalation on the deadly side of the dichotomy?

But after hours of scribbling, and pages and pages of questions and lists, I'd gotten nowhere. Except maybe more confused. Even the flow chart looked more like a rat maze.

"Margaret, dear, you shouldn't scowl like that." Leona poked her head in the kitchen door.

"How about like this?"

"Mph. I sometimes wonder what Gene sees in you."

"Not for any lack of trying from behind the edge of your curtain. Would you like a cup of tea, Leona?"

"I don't think so."

"Won't take a minute. It's already made."

"Oh, all right then." She sat down and started straightening my haphazard piles. "Are you writing a book, dear?" I didn't answer and she began reading the new copy of the original list. "Dear, dear," she said, shaking her head, "he stole a book from the Historical Society. Now, why doesn't that surprise me? And that might make one angry enough to feel like slamming a sofa bed shut on him. Perhaps not strangle him, though. Or set fire around him."

"Cousin Leona."

"I'm just thinking aloud, dear. What book did he steal from the Historical Society?"

"*A Walk Through Time.*"

"Why, I haven't thought of that book in years. I used it every year in the fifth grade for our community unit."

"Doug had you for fifth grade."

"Oh, yes."

"So, he would have been familiar with the book." I wasn't asking questions. I was making leading statements. More hair splitting, but I ran a quick check of my conscience and found it resting easy. I smiled at Leona, inviting her to continue.

"He might have remembered it. Possibly not. He wasn't the most inspired student and I didn't let all the children actually get their hands on the book. Only if they were

344

particularly interested. And washed their hands first. Quite frankly the book is a boring piece of drivel and couldn't hope to capture the imaginations of ten-year-olds. It would more likely choke them. The book is full of information and was a wonderful idea. But Harker Grundy was the most officious, pretentious, sententious, self-satisfied prig I've ever seen in print."

"I see you put some thought into your critique."

"Have you tried reading it?"

"It driveled me to sleep last night."

"I took Grundy's information and turned it into something more palatable for fifth graders and then had the children do their own, abbreviated versions, based on Main Street as they knew it. And at the end of the unit we made a scale model of Main Street out of cardboard boxes."

"I always wished I was in your class instead of Miss Klepinger's. I would have loved doing that project."

"Most of the girls did."

"You were a good teacher."

"Of course I was."

"Doug was interested in old businesses on Main Street for some reason. He came in the bookstore, which was unusual for him, looking for information about what businesses were in which buildings before the turn of the century. Then he stole the Historical Society's copy of Grundy."

"Perhaps he'd been bitten by an amoral history bug," Leona said.

I thought that over. Some of my best customers are local historians. They aren't always the sanest people but they're generally pleasant in their zeal. Then I thought about how Doug had been when he came in the store. By comparison, the light of the enthusiast hadn't burned in his eye. He was just peevish.

"No, it was more like he was frustrated and looking for some specific bit of information. But whether that's got anything to do with his murder, I don't know."

"Perhaps he found something in one of his buildings, in an attic or cellar, and he was trying to identify it. Of course, if that were the case, it would have made sense to take whatever he'd found over to the Historical Society to see what they could tell him."

"That's true, but it didn't even occur to him to go there first. He came here. And in fact, it was like he didn't want anyone to know what he was really asking about."

"That was Douglas. He was secretive and

enjoyed keeping information to himself."

"You're right. I remember that from when we were kids. He was always slightly superior, as though he knew more about everything than anyone else. Or at least he wanted us to think he did. It was kind of appealing. Made him mysterious. We usually let him get away with it, anyway."

"But then most of you outgrew it."

"Yup, it just got annoying. I wonder what information he was keeping to himself this time?"

"Or, turn it around, dear. What information did he want someone to think he had?"

"Huh. And, who got more than just annoyed?"

Leona started sifting through the piles of paper with more interest now. "Where's your list of suspects?" I found it and handed it to her. "Hmph. I don't see my name on it."

"Oh, give me a break."

"Bitsy's is."

"That's artistic license." Saying that was better than explaining Bitsy's name being on the list because my mission in life didn't allow me to assume she was innocent.

"You've got Harriet and Ed. Your friend Nancy's on it. And that looks like Eunice in that crabbed scribble. Gene's name is here.

347

You've even got William and Diane. And Eleanor. I feel snubbed."

"Oh, all right, you want your name on it?" I grabbed the paper from her and wrote her name at the top in big, block letters. "There. Now you're the chief suspect."

She looked pleased. Then she looked over my shoulder and my scalp prickled.

"Margaret Welch, my book angel, always so thorough. I thought I would find you here."

I turned to see Eleanor DeAngelis standing in the kitchen doorway. Fran was peeking around her at about the level of Eleanor's right armpit, mouthing a contrite apology for letting her slip past.

Time to move Eleanor's name from the list of people who might have heard about the list to the list of people who definitely knew about it.

CHAPTER 31

"For some things you just need a man. Do you not agree?"

How to answer a question like that? With a resounding, feminist no? A nudge and a knowing leer? The life of a bookseller can be tricky maneuvering. Fortunately, Eleanor never expects anyone to answer. She is secure in her opinions.

I'd left Leona to see herself out and ushered Eleanor back into the bookstore. Now we were standing in front of the self-help books and Eleanor was letting me in on one of the secrets of life while trying to explain what kind of book she was looking for.

"I will tell you, Margaret. It is for William. He is so tense. So worried. Over Diane and the children now that Douglas is gone. Do you know what I might be looking for?"

Leona had said something along those lines. About William, or about Eleanor being worried about William. Huh. Maybe he was more sensitive than I'd ever given him credit for. Shows how insensitive I am.

"Would a book of daily meditations be what you're looking for? We have this one, for instance, *Restful Recipes for Men with Too Much on Their Plates.* It's been fairly popular. Or there are collections of inspirational essays and stories."

She took *Restful Recipes* from me and looked it over. She seemed taken with the cover which showed a man in a leather armchair, eyes closed, serene smile plastered to his face, an empty plate in his lap. To me he looked like most men sitting in front of a TV except he wasn't in a recliner with a beer in one hand and the remote in the other.

"No, this, I think, is perfect. This picture reminds me of William's father, a man who was always the happy, silent type. Yes, I think it will remind William of him, too, and help him to be calm."

We started toward the counter, but she put a hand on my arm and stopped me.

"Diane will need William, now, you see," she said, "and he must pull himself together. For their sake."

Heartfelt personal statements made in the course of business transactions tend to leave me at a loss. Maybe there's a self-help book on the subject I've missed. About all I can do is fall back on sympathetic facial expressions, hoping to convey compassion and support. Bitsy told me once that it looks more like I'm waiting for a root canal, but at least in this case, Eleanor appreciated whatever was there.

"I knew you would understand, Margaret," she said, patting me on the arm. "You are magical with your books."

How could I not love this woman? Even if I did have her name on my list of suspects. Could she have strangled Doug and stuffed him in the sofa bed? Physically, there was no question. But would she have? And why? Maybe she'd always harbored a secret desire for William and Diane to end up together. I shuddered on Diane's behalf.

"You are cold, my Margaret. I see you still shiver from your unfortunate experience this morning." Eleanor put her flapping, black clad arm around my shoulders as we finally made our way to the counter. "Your lucky star was with you this morning. You must be careful. Take no risky chances. Do nothing foolish. We do not want to lose you, too, do we?"

Fran kindly took over ringing up the book for Eleanor. I was feeling a tad wobbly. And was still in the embrace of that black arm.

"That sounded a lot like a veiled threat to me," Fran said after I'd seen Eleanor to the door. "Where exactly is she on your list of suspects?"

"I think that was just Eleanor being Eleanor," I said carefully.

"But you can't be sure."

"I'm not sure of anything right now, except that I'm glad tomorrow isn't another day off because I need the rest that comes with a full day's work." I sat in one of the rocking chairs and closed my eyes.

"Why don't you go upstairs and relax. Then doll yourself up and go out for the evening. Do something with Gene. Take your mind off all this."

I didn't answer her. I didn't like to think I was getting paranoid, but the idea of leaving the house and the bookstore alone for the evening gave me the jim-jams.

"Or you could invite him over here. Make a simple dinner, watch a movie, sit together on the sofa. . . ."

"He's on my list of suspects, too."

"All the better reason for him to come over. Get to know him better. Keep an eye on him. Who knows? Maybe in the process you'll end up . . . ," she trailed off dreamily.

"End up what?"

"Eliminating him from the list."

"You might be onto something, Sherlock."

"Oh, I was hoping I was more like Aunt Bea."

"Keep working at it. You want help closing up later?"

"No, you go on."

I headed upstairs, but not to doll myself up or relax. Nancy had asked me to call her and I needed to rehearse my end of the conversation first. Being suspicious of one's friends and relations is not a rest cure.

Nancy had been at the edge of the lake when I sputtered out of the mud. Along with a dozen others, true, but she was also a partner in the school house consortium. Were these a couple of mundane facts or two tick marks against her name in the suspect column? She was also retiring and leaving town. I had no reason to disbelieve her explanation of feeling liberated after her mother's death and drawn to the Southwest. But what if she and Doug had been in some kind of financial or philandering cahoots? What if her retirement plans included Doug running off with her, then she caught him with Claire, and . . .

How in heaven's name could I call her to make lunch plans with thoughts and questions like those running through my head?

Luckily I didn't have to. The phone rang and it was one of Eunice's neighbors.

"This is Chris. You left a note in my mailbox?" The caller sounded male but it was hard to tell through his or her tremendous yawn. "Sorry. You wanted me to call you?"

"Yes, I . . ."

"Good. So can you come get him?" Definitely male. Not happy.

"Come get who?"

"The cat. I've gotta go to work and he's gotta go. I can't do this anymore."

"Where's Eunice?"

"Hell if I know. I'll be here for another twenty minutes. Then we're both out the door."

"I'll be right there. Which apartment?"

"Up the back stairs. Two B. You're not here in twenty, it'll be the door with the cat skin nailed to it."

I slammed out of the house and jumped into the car. Who was this guy to threaten a cat like that? Put Archie out on the street, would he? Nail his skin to the door? Not if I had anything to say about it. I drove over there faster than I should have and pounded up the back stairs to snatch Archie from the jaws of the cretin. Far easier to be furious with Chris than to stew over the increasingly worrying question of where Eunice was.

A stringy young man opened the door of Two B. "You the bookstore woman?" he yawned. "Eunice told me about you. I don't read much. But books are cool. Come on in. Watch he doesn't get out."

"Watch he doesn't get out? I thought you were planning to *put* him out." I followed Chris into an efficiency decorated in laundry and smelling of stale beer and tuna. Archie hopped from his perch in an empty pizza box and came to twine around my ankles.

"I was desperate. I work weird hours. I'm allergic." He sneezed to prove it. "When's Eunice getting back, anyway?"

"She didn't tell you?"

"She didn't tell me she was leaving. Little dude was crying outside her door. He must've slipped out and she didn't notice. Or maybe she was in a hurry and didn't have time to look for him."

"And you took him in?"

"He was crying."

"When was this?"

"Day and a half ago? Yeah, morning after that fire. I put a note under her door in case I didn't see her, what with my weird hours and everything." He squatted and rubbed Archie between the ears. "You go with the nice book lady, little dude. Your girlfriend will come home real soon." He picked Archie up and put him in my arms. "He likes sardines and tuna." He sneezed. "And pepperoni pizza. I think Eunice feeds him some kind of dry organic shit, though."

"Probably. Thanks for taking care of him. Do me a quick favor? Write another note telling her I've got him. I'll put it under her door on my way past."

"Oh, sure thing." He spun around, found a pen under the pizza box, then turned in a slower circle. "Paper, paper, paper . . ."

"That's okay, I've got it. Hold on a minute, Archie." I handed him back to Chris and pulled a notebook from my bag, tempted to write something along the lines of "I've got your cat. If you ever want to see him or your job again, call me." I settled for brief, without the terse or threatening, and re-gathered Archie. "Thanks, again, Chris."

He sneezed and shut the door.

I slipped the note under Eunice's door and stood for a moment at the top of the stairs looking across the alley and the creek at back of Bertie's Bank Tavern. Now that I couldn't be angry with Chris, there was plenty of room in my head for worries about Eunice. Where was she and why didn't she call?

Bitsy, Gene, and George all said they saw her at the fire, so I knew she'd made it home from Asheville. But what then? William hinted she'd been involved with Doug, a suggestion I couldn't believe. And yet I'd entertained the same notion about Nancy. William had gone one nasty suggestion further, though, by wondering if Eunice killed Doug. And, again, I'd gone and wondered the same about Nancy. At least William gave Eunice credit for some kind of human feeling by supposing she ran away afterwards. Did I really believe Nancy could kill Doug in a jealous rage and torch a building, then act and appear completely normal? What kind of friend was I if I could believe that? The kind who wasn't assuming anything. But, no, I wasn't buying any of it. Not about Nancy, not about Eunice. But if Eunice hadn't run away, where was she?

I stopped at the grocery store on the way home. Archie was either used to riding in cars or exhausted from his stint as a swinging bachelor with Chris. He was curled up, fast asleep, on a sweater I'd left on the seat. The words "poor little orphan" ran through my mind. I shook my head to dislodge them and dashed inside for kitty supplies.

Back at my place, I swaddled Archie in the sweater for the trip between the car and the house. Less chance of his escape, that way, in case he was becoming doubtful about this adventure. We went in through the kitchen and up the back stairs to avoid questions and explanations. I gave him a brief tour of my living space, then put him, still loosely wrapped in the sweater, on the sofa. He cast an appraising eye around the room, slipped out of the sweater, and leapt down to investigate, sniffing delicately at furniture, rugs, and books.

"You're a houseguest, so make yourself comfortable," I told him when I showed him where I put the litter box. "But don't get too comfortable. You're only here temporarily and we don't want any separation anxiety when you go home."

He followed me down the back stairs to the kitchen, tail high, and gave me an appreciative blink and a twine around the ankles when I put bowls of water and kibbles down for him.

I hadn't had a cat for several years as there was no replacing my last old boy who'd been the best cat in the world. But in the way cats do, Archie sensed the vacancy and moved right in. He was sitting on my lap taking a little bath when I called Gene and invited him for supper.

I conveniently forgot to call Nancy while

admiring Archie's beautiful eyes and soft, tawny coat.

CHAPTER 32

Cooking for one lost its appeal long ago. Pretending I'm four people and freezing the leftovers in individual portions works well enough. And the sandwich route, as a path of least resistance, is one I tread often. But cooking for two still holds magic. Particularly when the two are an interesting single man and me. Which, to tell the truth, happens rarely.

When George and I were trying so hard to be an item, I occasionally whipped up a romantic dinner for two. But more often than not, we resorted to the tried and true Bank Tavern or I'd heat a can of soup and fix grilled cheese. George never seemed to notice the difference in the amount of effort it took to put together a crab quiche, or pick up a can opener, or take the paper off a straw down at Bertie's.

One night I outdid myself, both in trying to bring out the gourmet in him and in trying to put a last gasp into the relationship. I pulled out all stops, borrowed an expensive French cookbook off the shelves out front, and prepared a glorious cheese soufflé. It puffed up into sheer magnificence. It was beautiful to behold. The night, the heavens, would be ours.

But, before my eyes, the soufflé took a turn for the worse. "Stop, stop," I yelled, frantically dancing around as it slowly collapsed in on itself. "Stop," I whispered along with its last puff of air. My efforts didn't make any difference to the heartless soufflé, of course. Or to George who didn't notice either the flat soufflé or the flat state of our relationship.

I was taking no chances on prophetic recipes with Gene. Cousin Leona's salmon loaf is practically perfect for any occasion. It's simple and it's delicious. It's salmon; it's a loaf. If it falls apart it's salmon hash and it still tastes good. That, rice pilaf from a foolproof box, and a green salad make a fine meal, no strings or emotions attached. Any salmon leftovers are guaranteed to please a furry houseguest.

I promised Archie tasty tidbits later if he'd lie doggo for the evening. I wasn't entirely sure why I didn't want to reveal his presence just yet, but he seemed happy to conspire. He winked and I closed the door at the top of the stairs.

"You went to a lot of trouble. This is wonderful," Gene said, helping himself to seconds.

"You're too kind. Tell me more."

Such a pleasant, and for all intents and purposes, normal evening we were having. Conversation that didn't include any mention of murder. No gratuitous allusions to inadvertent swims. No growing list of worries or grilling of suspects. Just the gentle dance of two people finding their way toward each other.

My alien kitchen basked in the glow of candlelight gleaming off its still furbished surfaces. Looking around at it and admiring its clean lines, I was tempted to make myself false promises about keeping it that way. But I know better than to kid myself about things like that. Especially considering it wasn't thanks to my efforts that it looked so good in the first place. Though maybe I could do something about keeping the responsible party around.

"Seriously, I'd like your recipe."

"But then you'd know how easy it was."

"Nothing wrong with an easy recipe. Everyone needs them from time to time."

He shrugged his appealing shoulders. "I like to avoid disasters if I can."

"I can think of plenty of recipes *for* disaster."

"And I've tried a few."

I took a sip of iced tea and let my end of the conversation lapse. If he wanted to follow up on disasters he'd known and lived through I'd let him without prying. But he seemed content to leave it with his allusion.

"No dessert, sorry."

"It's a warm night," he said. "We could walk downtown for ice cream."

"We could, but I'd rather not leave . . ." But no, that wasn't the conversation we were having. Had I meant Archie or the house?

"Leave what?"

"Nothing, I just had a better idea. You could teach me the Texas two-step."

"Really?"

"Yeah, I think so. Why, is there something wrong with it?"

"It's just that often people don't want to."

"That sounds ominous."

"It might be the music. You got any Bob Wills and His Texas Playboys?"

"No."

"Kinky Friedman and the Texas Jew Boys?"

"Sorry."

"Well, let's see what you do have. Come on."

He took my hand and we left the kitchen with nary a backward glance at dishes or leftovers. So much for turning over new leaves.

"You've got a lot of Celtic dirge material, I see." He flipped through my shoebox of CDs. "Are you depressed a lot?"

"What? No. What are you talking about?"

"My ex-wife used to call it that. Probably still does. She said listening to stuff like that was part of why I drank. She says Irish and Scottish music comes from societies that tend to be alcoholic and depressed."

"What a bunch of baloney. I don't think I like your ex-wife."

"Turns out I didn't much either."

"Then stop talking about her."

He pulled out one of the CDs. "Sounds good. We'll try this."

I mulled over whether the "sounds good" went with the CD or the not talking about his ex-wife while he put on the music. He'd chosen a bluegrass album we play occasionally in the store.

"Okay, here we go." He held out his hands to me.

"Aren't you going to demonstrate first?"

"Oh." He scratched his ear. "Is that the best way, do you think?"

"You've never actually taught this to anyone before, have you?"

"But I'm sure I can. It's not exactly Bolshoi-grade stuff. Okay, how's this?" He stood next to me and performed a move or two. "See?"

I mimicked his steps. He stopped and gave me a sour look.

"And you say you've never done this before?"

"Nope, why?" I asked, continuing to step around in a lively way. "Looking good?"

"Looking remarkably like a two-step ringer."

"Nope." I added a flourish. "Quick study. Also, this is a lot like a Scottish country dance I can't remember the name of off hand."

"Possibly the Scottish two-step?"

"No, really. In fact," I danced over to the CD player and stopped the bluegrass. "Try this." I pulled out an album of Scottish fiddle tunes.

"Hey, not bad," he said when he realized his feet didn't want to keep still.

This time when he held out his hands I joined him and together we stepped out around the bookstore. There's not a lot of open floor space, but as it turns out that doesn't matter with a dance like the two-step. We had a perfectly good time dancing our way around and up and down the aisles.

"So where did an architect like you learn the Texas two-step?"

"Texas. Want to see what else I learned there?"

"Sure." You'd think I'd have been around long enough by now to spot a line like that coming. Then again, maybe I did.

His other gleanings from Texas were proving interesting and I was showing my appreciation for them when a distant noise caught my attention. He was busy and hadn't heard it, but if I wasn't mistaken, it was the sound of a . . . yes, Bitsy. *Agitato.* She came bursting through from the kitchen.

"Margaret, have you heard?" she yodeled. Then she pulled up short. "Oh. My goodness. What are you doing?"

"Exactly what it looks like," Gene said through bared teeth.

"Honestly, Margaret, I should think you'd have a better sense of decorum."

"We were alone," I pointed out.

"Anyone can see in." She walked over and peered out the front windows. "George, for instance."

"Why should I care about George? Wait a second," I joined her at the window. "Is he out there?"

He was, sitting in his own car, not the patrol car. All three of us stared out at him and he obviously saw us but did a good job of pretending he didn't.

"What's he doing out there? I'm going out and ask him."

"No, Margaret, wait." Bitsy grabbed at my arm. "You haven't heard about Eleanor, have you?"

"What about her?"

"It's so terrible." She let me go and put her hand to her cheek. "Eleanor was sitting at home, minding her own business, listening to *Madame Bovary* on CD. Did she buy it here? I didn't think you stocked foreign language audio books." She looked around as though she might suddenly be in the market herself. "I wouldn't think you'd have much call for them."

"I don't. Bitsy, forget the audio books, what happened to Eleanor?"

She looked at me out of the corner of her eye, the urge to take offense warring with her need to be the first with breaking news. News mongering won out.

"She must have had her headphones on, or maybe she'd fallen asleep, which certainly wouldn't surprise me. Anyway, the point is, she probably didn't hear whoever it was, but thank god that awful little dog of hers was out in the yard and started yapping and wouldn't shut up and the neighbors went over to complain because by the time they would have noticed any smoke, it might have been too late."

"For what?"

"For Eleanor."

"Sum it up in twenty-five words or less, Bitsy."

"She was attacked, Margaret. She was hit on the head and the house was set on fire."

CHAPTER 33

"Have you noticed that, for some reason, my sister is always the first to know about these things?"

"She's obviously guilty, then," Gene said.

"Makes you wonder, anyway."

We were back at the kitchen table, feeling pummeled. It would have been a good time for a beer, but considering the man sitting across from me and his problems, I abstained.

Bitsy had been short on details, though she made the most out of the ones she had, being in turns animated by excitement and choked with the horror of it all. It was exhausting just listening to the little she knew.

Eleanor was in the hospital, unconscious, condition unknown. The fire had been discovered quickly, before much damage was done. William had taken refuge at Diane's.

I let Bitsy out the front door when I couldn't stand listening to it one more time. She wanted to commune with George on her way to spread the news to Leona. I didn't go out with her. I didn't want to see George. He was either out there keeping an eye on his favorite suspect, or after the attack on Eleanor, he was taking my dunk in the lake more seriously. George as guard dog. I didn't want to think about either scenario.

"What time did she say it happened?" I asked.

"I don't think she did."

"Oh. I wonder how long George has been sitting out there?"

"A while."

I looked up from the fascinating grain of rice I'd found on the table.

"He was there when I got here," Gene said. "He was further down the street, but I think he's been out there most of the evening."

I drummed the fingers of one hand on the table, ran the others through my hair. Should I ask? Why not? The evening had already jumped the tracks. "So, where were you this evening before you came over here?"

"I liked it better when you were suspect-

370

ing your sister."

"And I guess if you'd bashed Eleanor and set her house on fire you'd want to keep it a secret, anyway, wouldn't you?"

"That's certainly the approved method. Look, I'm probably George's favorite suspect because he can't get over you." He stopped wiggling his eyebrows mid-wiggle when he caught my expression. "If it makes you feel any better, I don't fit the profile for an arsonist."

"Don't worry about it. I don't really think you did it. George probably doesn't either."

"I think he's obsessive. Or at least obsessed."

"Nah. He's just a good friend. But if he's out there because all of a sudden he's worried about what happened this morning, and now he thinks he's somehow protecting me, then it seems like he should've let me know."

"Want me to go out and talk to him? Invite him in?"

"Wait a second. That's an odd thing to know about yourself. How do you know you don't fit the profile for an arsonist?"

"My ex-wife and her classmates used to practice giving personality tests and I was their guinea pig. I've been told many odd things about myself."

"Oh. Her again. Maybe we should introduce her to George."

"I wouldn't wish that even on George."

He got up and started clearing the table. Nervous reaction to too much thinking about his ex-wife? I watched and wondered if it was ethical for me to take advantage of this neurosis. Yes, I decided, because it seemed to do him good. And it certainly did the poor old kitchen some good. I got up and started a pot of coffee. Leona came knocking at the back door as I was pouring it.

"A bit late for you, isn't it, Cousin Leona? And since when do you knock?"

"Bitsy warned me." She had an evil smirk.

"I'm sure we don't know what you're talking about."

"Speak for yourself," Gene said. He handed his cup to Leona and I poured another for him.

"Besides, I'm too upset about this business with Eleanor." She sat down and warmed her hands on the cup.

"It's awful," I agreed.

"Particularly because there doesn't seem to be any sense to it. Why Eleanor? Douglas was at least offensive in one way or another. Eleanor is just a buffoon."

"Cousin Leona."

"Of course she is, dear. She is entertaining and perfectly harmless, but for heaven's sake, who else do you know from Pulaski who dresses or acts like Eleanor?"

"Pulaski?"

"Pulaski, Tennessee, born and bred. Why, where did you think she came from?"

Pluto would have been more like it if I'd ever given it any thought. "At least I can take her off my list of suspects, now." Oops. I looked over at Gene. He sat, mug halfway to lips, giving me the fish eye. I smiled. "If I still had a list of suspects, that is."

"Why? What did you do with all the pages you were working on this afternoon? And Gene, you can wipe that look off your face right now. Women in this family do not sit at home waiting for dubious cavalry to come to their rescue." Leona the fifth-grade tyrant strikes again.

"Yes ma'am." Gene sat up straighter and folded his hands in front of him on the table.

"I saw George sitting out front," she went on.

"Poster boy for the dubious cavalry," I said.

"I sent him home."

"Was that a good idea?" Gene asked anxiously, then, under a quelling glance from Leona, he pretended a ticklish cough and looked at the ceiling.

"It was a perfectly sound idea," she said, "for several reasons, which I outlined for George and with which he could not argue. First, he was about to fall asleep. Second, if that unfortunate incident in the cemetery this morning were indeed someone's idea of a warning for Margaret, then it was duly delivered and quite publicly received. Third, for whatever reason, Eleanor was obviously more threatening to the murderer than Margaret. And fourth, if the police seriously considered you a suspect in the attack on Eleanor, they would have acted more efficiently and would already have picked you up."

"That's oddly comforting, Leona, thank you," Gene said.

"So Eleanor comes off the list," I said, "but the attack on her raises new questions."

"It does," Leona nodded. "For instance, why hit Eleanor rather than strangle her like Doug? The strangling was much more effective. And that reminds me. George told me something that I knew would interest you."

"What?

"Something I was supposed to tell you. I'm trying to remember."

"Well, while you're trying to remember that, do you remember if you took my notes with you this afternoon?"

"I left everything right here on the table where you had it when Eleanor barged in."

I looked around the kitchen. Where had I put them? I must have tidied them away somewhere before Gene came over. In a drawer? Upstairs? No. I ran upstairs to look, anyway. And came back down more slowly.

"You didn't take them with you?" I asked Leona again, wanting to make sure, hoping she really had forgotten.

"Why would I? This is your project. No, they were here when Eleanor came in. You left with her. I left through the kitchen door. Your lists and charts were on the table."

"I bet Fran found them and took them out front." But if she had, I couldn't find them. I called her. She was sorry; she hadn't seen them. "Not to worry," I told her, "they'll show up, probably in some unexpected place like right where I left them." She chuckled and I hung up.

"Find them?" Gene asked when I rejoined them in the kitchen.

"No, but you know me, I can't keep track of paperwork unless it's stapled to my forehead."

"You feign unconcern poorly, Margaret,

and you lie even less well," Leona said. "If I asked you where the receipt is for that coffee maker you could produce it instantly. The papers are gone. Someone must have taken them."

"Was the door locked?" Gene asked.

"You needn't look at me," Leona said. "I wouldn't know."

They looked at me. I sighed. "This is Stonewall. It was broad daylight. I lock the door when I go to bed at night."

To confirm my casual way with doors, Archie appeared at the bottom of the stairs and introduced himself by jumping to the middle of the table. He shook a back paw and licked a front one by way of greeting.

"Not on the table, Archie," I said reaching to push him off.

Gene got to him first and cradled him in his arms. "Is he Archie as in Archie Goodwin? The name suits him. I like his attitude." The two rubbed noses and made friends, Gene looking enchanted, Archie knowing and smug. Gene looked from Archie to me. "So what's the story? Are you two-timing me with this guy? Can't say I blame you."

"He's Archie as in Archbishop Desmond Tutu."

"Good lord," Leona said.

I shrugged. "Desmond Tutu is one of Eunice's heroes. This is her cat." And I told them about the call from Chris and Archie's status as houseguest.

"What a lot for a small cat to live up to, with a name like that," Leona said. "But perhaps he's already doing it. I've remembered what I was supposed to tell you and this is good news for you and him. George says Eunice is either back or she never left. He saw her car."

"What? When?"

"I should have asked that, shouldn't I? You see how you're more astute at detecting than I am?"

I brushed that aside, impatient now. "And where? And how does he know it was her car? I'm not sure I believe it."

"Her tag number?" Leona said. "He seemed fairly certain."

I was already trying her number again and let it ring as I started pacing. And ring and ring. Still no answer and by now her message box was full. "I don't know what to think," I said, hanging up but continuing to pace. "Except that this is weird. I don't think she's been home since Tuesday night, certainly not since Wednesday morning when Chris found Archie outside."

"Why?" Gene asked.

"She would've found Chris's note under her door. She'd have found the one I put in her mailbox *and* the one I put under her door. She'd have cleared out her phone mailbox. She wouldn't . . ."

"Did George say he saw her car or her *in* her car?" Gene interrupted.

"He said he saw her car," Leona said. "There is a difference, isn't there."

"She wouldn't abandon Archie. She . . ."

Gene got up and stood in my path. "Here." He put Archie in my arms. "I pass to you the cat of peace. Settle down. There are bound to be logical explanations. There usually are."

I buried my face in Archie's fur, then straightened and took a deep breath, trying to ground myself in the sanity of not assuming anything, especially the worst. Unfortunately, it also meant I couldn't assume the best. "Okay, here are a couple of things to think about. Eunice is seen the night of the fire and then disappears. Then she, or her car, is seen the same day Eleanor is attacked. That doesn't look good, does it, if she's at all a suspect? But what about this? What if she hasn't been home because she's scared? Because she's hiding?"

"From what?"

"You can see the back of Bertie's from her apartment. What if she saw something the night of the fire?"

CHAPTER 34

"That sounds melodramatic, though, doesn't it," I said, putting Archie on the floor. He strolled over to the refrigerator and looked over his shoulder at me. "Still, something doesn't smell right."

"Archie obviously thinks the leftover salmon loaf smells right," Gene said. "But maybe we should call George."

"He'll say I'm meddling and then accuse me of cat snatching."

"Then we could go over to Eunice's and see if she really is back and this has all been some weird misunderstanding."

I sat back down and thought about that, came up with nothing. "I don't know."

"We should call George," Leona said.

"You're the one who sent him away," I pointed out.

"Which made perfect sense. And now it makes perfect sense to call him. Your concerns about Eunice are valid and the disappearance of your lists is suggestive."

"He'll say they're suggestive of delusional meddling."

"They're suggestive of a connection, even if you don't see one," she said. " 'You're onto something' is how the professionals like Sherlock Holmes put it."

"Holmes isn't a professional. He's a figment of Conan Doyle's imagination. George will draw the obvious connection between that and my lists."

"But considering the attack on Eleanor," Leona pressed, "perhaps you really are in danger. Especially if someone has already been in the house and taken the lists. We should call George."

I felt like banging my head on the table. "But I don't know anything and my lists prove that. George will say I shouldn't have been making lists to begin with and then he'll say the murderer was obviously more threatened by Eleanor than by me. Then he'll ask what was on the lists and when I tell him, he'll laugh and say the murderer is probably feeling pretty safe right now knowing I'm on the case."

"But maybe you're underestimating yourself," Gene said.

I looked at him. I looked at Leona. I looked at Archie who was cleaning his toes but stopped to blink at me. I was tired and I gave up. "Come on Archie, let's go to bed. You two do what you want. Call George. Call the marines. I don't think anyone is coming after me, but if you're so sure they are, then you just do whatever you think you need to." I picked up Archie and started up the stairs.

"She gets cranky when she's tired," I heard Leona say, not as quietly as she might have.

"I've noticed."

"I heard that and I resent the implication, whatever it is. Good night and lock the door behind you."

I don't know how long they stayed in the kitchen discussing what to do. I climbed the stairs, climbed into my pajamas then into bed and proceeded to sleep like the dead. Which is an inapt turn of phrase considering the situation, but there you are.

In the morning, feeling only slightly better, but possibly more kindly towards interfering friends and relations, I showered, dressed, and ambled down the hall only to discover Gene and Archie snoring together on the sofa. I thought about suffocating Gene with my See Rock City throw pillow, but why look a gift cavalryman in the mouth, dubious though he may be.

He opened his eyes while I was standing over him. He smiled, the devil in his baby blues waking up early.

"How do you manage that first thing in the morning?" I asked. He patted the sofa next to him, the devil now wide-awake. "Never mind. I see exactly where it comes from. Breakfast in fifteen minutes. One if you like cold cereal and cat chow."

They wandered down as I finished my cereal and the story about Eleanor in the paper simultaneously. There were no new details. No leads at press time. I tipped kibble into Archie's bowl and gave him fresh water. He chirruped and rubbed my ankles in thanks. Gene scratched his beard, looking a bit ragged.

"You sleep alright?"

"The Archbishop needs to learn more peaceful ways," he said. "He has a thing for toes."

"Oh, yeah, so Eunice says. Glad yours are more interesting than mine. Here's the story about Eleanor." I handed him the paper.

"Seems like we've done this before."

"With a role reversal, though. Last time I was rescuing you."

"Oh yeah."

"And it was by invitation."

He sat down warily.

"Don't worry." I shrugged. "I still don't think it was necessary, but it's okay you stayed. I was just tired of talking about it last night. I'll call George this morning and tell him everything, see if he thinks it's anything. I'm sure he won't think so."

The bit of blue sky I could see through the window over the sink was bright with promise, erasing the worst of last night's fears. Solid, dependable George had seen Eunice's car. Gene was right and there must be logical explanations for her absence and failure to communicate.

"I talked to George last night," Gene said.

A cloud slipped in, blotting my scrap of blue. "What?"

"You told us to do whatever we thought best so I called him. And it turns out you were right. He pretty much gave me a raspberry over the phone. Anyway, Leona and I still thought you must be on to something, even if George didn't, and even if you don't know what the hell it is. So the next thing we decided was I should spend the night. You know, 'just in case.'"

"I'm surprised you two didn't think it would be even better if you were right on top of things, so to speak, and that I didn't find you sleeping across the end of my bed.

Or in it."

"We discussed that at some length, but in the end I decided not to take a chance because Leona couldn't remember whether it's you or Bitsy who has a black belt in karate."

"Bitsy."

"I definitely won't climb into bed with her."

"You have no sense of adventure. What kind of cereal do you want?"

"What have you got?"

"Grape-Nuts."

"Or?"

"That's it. Want me to get it for you?" I corralled the box, a bowl, a spoon, and the milk and dumped them on the table in front of him. "Well, anyway, thanks for staying."

He saluted with his spoon and dug in. I leaned against the counter and considered the day ahead. Saturdays are often busy. It'd be nice if this one was. I could stand to lose track of my thoughts for seven or eight hours.

"If," I said, feeling my way tentatively toward that goal, "if George says there's nothing to worry about, I'm going to try very hard to believe him. And you should, too, because what you should know about George is, if there is even the hint of a downside to a situation, he will festoon it with black crepe and clasp it to his bosom. So, Archie can spend the day upstairs getting to know his new digs and I'm going to spend the day with the book-buying public. I'm going to forget all about all of the rest, except maybe I'll think of a book Eleanor might like in the hospital."

"That sounds somewhat reasonable and pleasant enough," he said.

"We'll see, anyway. So, will you be at the school all day? Want to come back by here for lunch?"

"Mm, might not have time. Thanks, though," he said without looking up from the paper.

"Got other plans?"

"Hm?"

"Hot date?"

"Just something I have to do."

I raised my eyebrows, but as he was still reading, they didn't elicit further details.

"Well," he finally said, re-folding the paper and pouring a second bowl of cereal, "there's not much more here than what Bitsy told us last night."

"I'm sure we'll hear it first from her if there's anything new. I wonder how she heard about it in the first place, though."

"I think I'm happier not knowing."

"I wonder where Claire and Bertie were yesterday afternoon? Or Diane? I wonder if she was home when William went to take refuge with her? And where was William?"

The crunch of cereal ceased. I looked over.

"Oh, sorry, must be force of habit. Don't worry, you can go off and draw pictures to your heart's content. My mind will be on books."

And it was because after all, that's what puts the cat chow and Grape-Nuts in the bowls.

It was the people who came in the bookstore who kept bringing up everything else.

Hattie McKinney was first to arrive, drifting in on a scent of honeysuckle, soon after I opened. She hesitated at the door. She dithered at the magazine rack. When she finally approached the counter, wringing her purse in her hands and warbling my name, I'd been smiling warmly for so long I must have looked reptilian and predatory. I pretended to cough so I could cover my mouth and massage some feeling back into my lips.

"How can I help you, Mrs. McKinney?"

"Oh, please, will you call me Hattie?" She actually waited for an answer.

"Of course, Hattie, thank you. What can I

do for you?"

She looked at me, shied away and looked again. Her lips worked at something, either trying to get words out or trying to keep them in. I wondered if she had this much trouble dealing with weeds in her garden.

"Would you like a cup of tea, Hattie?"

"Oh, yes," she blurted, "I would love it."

Duly plied with cup and saucer (I went so far as these, thinking they might make her feel more at home) Hattie seemed to relax. She didn't loosen her grip on her purse, but her eyes stopped darting toward the door in alarm every time it opened. She took her tea over to one of the rocking chairs and I pretended not to watch her as I waited on other customers and she pretended not to watch me.

I've only ever known Hattie from afar, not being in the garden set. She's a small, solid woman, given to wearing wrap around skirts and giving a good impression of being dotty. But judging from her position on one or another committee and her seat on several boards in and around town, she is far from it. During a lull, she approached the counter again.

"Thank you for the tea, Margaret."

"You're welcome." I took the cup and saucer from her.

"I want you to tell me what you have found out about my garden." This time she didn't break eye contact. There was sharp metal in her voice.

But her abrupt request caught me off guard and I found myself dithering in her stead. "Oh, well, Hattie, that was a terrible thing someone did to your garden."

"It was nasty, vile, and cowardly. You saw it?"

I nodded.

"If they'd dug plants up and carted them away I might have understood it," she said. "I wouldn't have liked it, but I could at least have pictured someone somewhere enjoying the plants in their own garden. It would have made some sort of sense. What they did do was plain evil. So, I want to know what you have found out about what happened to my garden."

"Hattie, I haven't found out much of anything. I'm not really doing any detecting, if that's what you're hoping." I peered at her. Somehow she was looking larger and even more solid.

"Leona led me to believe you had."

And less friendly, too. I was beginning to see how Hattie was a force to be reckoned with. She used the dithery act to good advantage, then pounced.

"Really, about all I've done is jot down questions that came to my mind. Very few answers. I made a few lists of suspects, if that's what you want to call them. Pretty lame stuff, Hattie, I'm sorry. If I knew anything, I'd tell you."

"Exactly what questions have you been asking? Let me see the lists." She held out her hand.

For some reason, I was glad I didn't have them to give to her. I also didn't feel like telling her they'd been stolen. "I'm sorry, I haven't got the lists on me. Some of the questions were about your garden. But they were pretty basic, like, do you know what was used on it? Could it have been gasoline?"

"Gasoline? Heaven's no. You really aren't a gardener, are you? It was a mix of weed killers, a very lethal mix and a very heavy application. The garden was drenched in it. We were away for a long weekend, not that we could have saved it if we'd been home. When we got back late on the Monday, I smelled something vaguely awful but we were both too tired and we decided to wait until morning to find out what it was. And you saw it. You know what we found. It was too horrible. I'm sorry. It still makes me cry."

At this point in my encounter with Iron Hull Hattie, the tears surprised me. I looked around and was glad to see the other customers were happily oblivious to the waterworks. Which says something about my sense of compassion, but after all, my business isn't called Books and Bewailing. I made some clucking noises that were supposed to be comforting and pushed a box of tissues across the counter to her.

"I'm sorry I don't have any useful information for you, Hattie. Are you going to start over again on your garden?"

"Oh, I don't know," she said. "Ed has thought for years it's too much for us, anyway, the house and the garden. We do rattle around in the house, I suppose. We'd probably consider selling up, but now, with the garden like it is, I don't know." She fluttered her tissue to show her indecision.

"If I hear anything, would you like me to call you?"

The tissue stopped mid-flutter and her eyes slued round to meet mine. "Yes. I definitely want to know what you find out. And I have another request."

"Yes?" I waited while she reverted to dithering mode, her lips working hard again to either hold in or put forth.

"Don't tell any more people," she finally

spit out, "that you were pushed into the lake. And tell anyone you've already told that you were mistaken. Do you understand?"

She must have interpreted the look on my face as comprehension. She nodded, and if I'm not mistaken, winked at me. She left, then, and the honeysuckle fragrance she left behind turned vaguely malevolent.

CHAPTER 35

Was Hattie more than an intense gardener? There was definitely something going on with her. Had she suspected Doug of murdering her garden, gone off the deep end, blown up his fishpond, and then taken him out, too? That was a bizarre scenario and, after that wink, I wasn't sure I'd ever feel comfortable turning my back if she were wielding a pair of pruning shears. But Hattie as homicidal?

I didn't have time to dwell on that image, though. Unlike the day after Doug's death, when odd bits of gossip floated in rather aimlessly, there were now people streaming in, eager to share their news and views. It was so busy, in fact, I called in reinforcements.

"No Eunice?" Fran asked over the phone. I floundered. Couldn't answer.

"See you in a few minutes," she said.

When she blew in fifteen minutes later,

she was suitably impressed.

"Did Christmas come early?" she whispered to me as she hurried to help the next person in line.

"Looked more like Fourth of July when Bertie's went up," the sharp-eared customer said. "Insurance money will come in mighty handy, though."

"I'm sure Bertie would rather have the business back," Fran said. "Don't you think so?"

The customer took his bag and shrugged. "It's what I heard, anyway. Wouldn't be the first time someone took that way out of financial difficulties. Happens all the time in New York. Or so I hear. See ya."

Fran gave the man a wave, and though my fingers itched for pen and paper, I willed them to do their tap dance magic on the cash register keys, instead.

"Did you find everything all right?" I asked the woman in front of me.

"I only wish you issued blinders so I could make it out the door without finding one more thing."

"Sorry, it's against store policy."

"What that man said, though," the woman nodded her head toward the door, "the way I heard it, it wasn't Bertie having financial difficulties at all. And, you know, I don't like to repeat anything malicious, but I heard it's kind of a black widow thing. Or maybe it's a praying mantis. Anyway, the way I heard it, Bertie's granddaughter was having the affair with Doug Everett just to get the building from him."

"But now she hasn't got either," Fran pointed out.

"And there you have it," the woman said. "Crime doesn't pay like it used to."

"Like it used to?"

"Sure. There was that Mafia business years ago. That was hushed up all the way around. You hear the stories but you never hear about any arrests in that case, do you?"

"You never do," I marveled.

"Scot free, that's what someone got off," she said.

"I think she was getting sort of nostalgic," I said to Fran as we watched her go.

"For the good old days when crime paid," Fran agreed.

"By the way, thanks for coming in."

"My pleasure."

A couple came in eager to find books by Brian Jacques for their grandson and to spread a tale they'd heard of revenge and mistaken identity. It sounded almost as exciting as a Jacques adventure. Their story didn't endear them to me, though, involving a certain architect the way it did. But their purchase of the first six Redwall books in hardback, and a promise to return for the rest, went a long way toward making up for it.

The bell over the door jingled a few more times before I got back to the counter, but the customers I could see were browsing contentedly. Fran was showing someone the travel section. A voice in the other room was exclaiming happily over something.

"Crime seems to be paying pretty well for us, today, anyway," I said to Fran when we'd finished with the next mini rush.

"Did you hear what Tom Dulaney said? He said yesterday it was even money but today you're the odds on favorite."

"For what?"

"Over the Stonewall PD, for catching the bad guy."

"That is so completely absurd." I half closed my eyes. This had the double benefit of showing my pain and blurring Fran. She's much less pleasant-looking when she smirks. "So that's what this is all about. Now we're known as Books and Bloodhounds. For god's sake, I'm not even doing any detecting." I closed my eyes all the way. "And won't George be pleased if he hears the odds." I stood back and let Fran catch the next few customers and weighed the situation. Then I did pick up pen and paper.

Fran clucked.

"Okay, this is the way I see it," I said. "We've become the clearing house for any speculation or hypothesis going."

"You," she interrupted. "I think it's you. The bookstore and I are innocent sidekicks."

"Fine. The situation isn't all bad, though. If there's a free exchange of ideas, then I won't have any exclusive information. It removes me from the ranks of amateur sleuths who discover key clues and don't divulge them in time."

Fran considered that and shrugged. "Probably a moot point, anyway. Your part in this seems well advertised already. Might be hard to back out, now."

"All the more reason to be open and above board, then," I said, flourishing the pen. And, in between customers, I started once again making note of the news coming through my front door.

"Say, ya'll aren't really thinking of moving the store, are you?"

One of our faithful magazine browsers and I were exchanging head shakes over a report that William was threatening to kill whoever had attacked his mother when that question popped up, startling all of us.

"Absolutely not," Fran told the young man who'd asked. "That will be $10.79, please, and where on earth did you hear that piece of baloney?"

"Someone in the bakery this morning. Said something about something else moving in here and the bookstore moving out."

"Well, it's news to me," I said, "and I'm pretty sure I'd be the first to know."

"Yeah, I guess you would at that."

We watched him go and I debated, then went ahead and jotted down that tidbit, too, snorting as I did over the gullibility of youth.

"What are you writing down now, Margaret? Jokes?"

"Oh, Claire. Hi." I glanced down at my latest batch of notes, suddenly not so convinced they were a good idea. "What can I do for you?" I asked, my voice too high and bright. I folded the paper and shoved it in my pocket. Goose bumps rose on my arms despite the blush I felt glowing on my face.

Claire smiled, didn't answer. She turned in a slow circle, surveying the room, as though checking ceiling heights and measuring square footage.

"Grandma?" she called. "Come in and talk to Margaret."

Bertie came slowly out of the other room,

nose buried in an old cookbook. "How much you want for this, Margaret? I think I'd like to buy it."

"Really, Grandma?" Claire squealed. "You like the idea? You really want to do it?" She looked like she wanted to jump up and down but Bertie's words grounded her.

"I was talking about the book, Claire, not Margaret's house. Oh, and now look, you've upset her."

That was an understatement. I held onto the counter in case my knees were more shocked than my brain. I know I was slack jawed, a look I try not to mix with intelligent business transactions. My house? My place of business? My life's blood? Claire wanted them?

"The book, Margaret." Bertie waved it under my nose like smelling salts. "How much? I haven't seen a copy of this since the sixties."

Words failed me. I fumbled with the book and showed her inside the front cover where I price used books in careful pencil.

"But you like the idea, don't you, Grandma?" Claire persisted. She turned to me, eyes starry, obviously not registering the dopey look I couldn't seem to wipe off my face. "It's sort of small, Margaret, but it would be a start and that's what I've been telling Grandma we need to do. We need to make a start on the future of Bertie's. And this could be so darling. What do you suppose it would take to knock out that wall?"

"My dead body?" When I do find them, I have such a way with words. "What I mean is, my house isn't for sale. Aren't you planning to reopen in the bank building?"

The stars in Claire's eyes looked more like something left to smolder now. "But the bank building is ruined, Margaret. It burned up and I almost did, too."

"For Pete's sake, she knows that," Bertie said. "Go take another look at that fireplace in the other room you're so mad about. I'll talk to Margaret." She shooed Claire off with an indulgent but tired smile. "I swear. Did I ever have that kind of energy?" She laughed and leaned on the counter across from me. We might have been a couple of old mates ready to raise a jar.

"Bertie . . ."

"Don't worry, Margaret, I'm not after your house. She's just got this bee in her bonnet. Had to come down here. Had to look the place over. She's got no real concept of money yet, I'm finding out. But she's got her dreams and she can sure dream up some doozies."

"She sure can." I laughed, but only faintly.

"How serious are you about moving out of the bank building?"

"Not very. But even if Claire's over enthusiastic about spending my money, she's no dummy. And I'll listen to her, but if Diane is either fixing it up or fixing to sell, I plan to be right back there."

"You'd buy it? Have you talked to her yet?"

"Maybe too soon for that just yet."

"Oh, of course, no, I wasn't even thinking. So Bertie," I said, moving smoothly into nonchalant mode now that we had the business of my house remaining my house out of the way, "have you heard anything from the Fire Marshal or the police?"

"From them, no. I've said a lot *to* them, I can tell you that. But I can't get any answers. Not yet. But I'll tell you, I'm about tired of some of these rumors. Mafia. Have you heard that one?"

"Mm, yeah, I think I did. Are you worried about the rumors?"

"Mostly not. When we're back up and running, like as not, the rumors will bring in more people. People are a curious bunch." She stopped and shook her head. "And a morbid bunch."

"A winning combination."

"For business it often is. I notice you're

not doing too badly yourself today, and I'd better be getting out of your hair. See if I can corral my galloping granddaughter. If you wanted to sell I might talk to you about it. But don't worry." She waved and wandered off, looking for Claire but looking around with a more appraising eye than I thought was necessary.

"Breathe, Margaret," Fran said, "breathe."

"How long have they been here?"

"I think they came in while you were showing Ed Tidwell the photography books."

"Maybe we've been looking at it all wrong," I said. "Maybe everybody has. Maybe Claire burned the place because it was the only way she could think of to get her grandmother to move the restaurant and update business."

"But then why kill Doug? Because he caught her in the act?"

I shuddered and couldn't think of any answer better than that, so I went to straighten the children's area. Books are so much less complicated than people. After a calming dose of Drs. Seuss and De Soto and their colleagues, I returned and waited while Fran finished with her last customer.

"Cheer up, Margaret," she said, patting

me on the shoulder, "Claire and Bertie are gone."

We settled our backsides against the shelf behind the counter and were silent for a minute or so.

"Okay, here's another question," I finally said. "If Claire burned the Bank Tavern and killed Duckie, then why did she attack Eleanor and start a fire there?"

"You don't believe she did any of that, Margaret."

"I don't know. I might. Of course, earlier I was sure it was Harriet McKinney."

"It is true that someone did it."

"Someone did," I agreed.

"But no one we like, Margaret."

"What about someone for whom we have deep affection but about whom we often wonder?"

Fran looked confused. The bell over the door jingled.

"Hi, Bitsy," I said.

CHAPTER 36

"I'm not sure I trust you when you're smiling like that, Margaret. And why did Fran just bolt for the kitchen?" Bitsy had marched in but stopped half way between the door and the counter. Phil came in behind her, carrying a box he couldn't quite see around.

"Oh, sorry, Bitsy," he said, bumping into her.

"Oh, sorry, Bitsy," I echoed. "It's just that the sight of you unexpectedly brightened our day. I think Fran went to make tea."

"Oh." She processed that through skeptical eyes and tight lips then appeared to shrug it off. She must have been in high agenda-mode because she wasted no more time, instead introducing the first topic of discussion by clearing a space on the counter.

"Put them here, Phil. Margaret likes to highlight special items by putting them in the prized position next to the cash register."

"I usually like to pick them myself, though, Bitsy." I smiled. She smiled. "What have you got there, Phil?"

He smiled and unfurled one of what he carried. "The T-shirt," he sang on a triumphant note.

It was a cream-colored shirt with Gene's design of two hands cradling a patch of lawn in the shape of a policeman's badge, sprouting a thatch of wildflowers, centered below the words "Lawn Order" in an organic, art nouveau script. The whole thing was rendered in vibrant green, magenta, blue, and black. A number of remarks swam past my eyeballs as they took in the full effect of the shirt. *How did you get them made so quickly?* was one. Another was, *My, aren't they colorful?* What eventually came out of my mouth was, "And you want me to sell them?"

"You could at least make an effort to sound enthusiastic, Margaret."

"Sorry, your efficiency boggled my mind for a minute. So why aren't you guys each wearing one?"

"We just now picked them up. We thought we'd give you the honor of being the first place in town to have them for sale."

"Oh." I stretched that out into an enthusiastic sound.

"And we'll buy ours from you," Phil said.

"And you can, too," said Bitsy. "And Phil, you can put the poster up on the front door. We've got to get the word spread fast. Margaret, can he borrow your tape dispenser?" she asked, having already handed it over to Phil.

"Word about the shirts?"

"About the rally tonight at the courthouse. It's a candlelight vigil to draw attention to the violence. We want everyone who's suffered an attack or a loss to be there and up front. I'm going to talk to Diane this afternoon. I wish Eleanor could be there. I wonder if we could check her out of the hospital for the evening and bring her over in a wheelchair? But how would we get the wheelchair up the courthouse steps? Why did they put the handicap ramp all the way around back? It's so inconvenient. Anyway, we'll all be wearing the T-shirts and we'll introduce Phil's anthem and pass out copies. It will be a very powerful statement."

All of that really did boggle my mind. Bitsy didn't notice, though. She was busy refolding the shirts into a crisp pile.

"So Bitsy, who are you counting as victims?"

"Well," she cast a glance toward the door where Phil was in earnest conversation with someone. Maybe he was making a T-shirt sale. "Phil and I had a bit of a philosophical disagreement over that."

"Really."

"Yes, here I thought he was just a quiet, mild man who enjoyed gardening. Turns out he has very strong opinions about green spaces. Among other things."

"Probably why he was able to put so much emotion into the anthem."

"It's an amazing piece of music, isn't it? Anyway, he doesn't think things like the manure in the dumpster or the goats in the field count as violence. He says the goats were merely agents of civil disobedience and therefore there were no victims."

"Except they did a pretty good number on George's squad car."

"Exactly. Not to mention the trauma suffered by the bulldozer driver. He's clearly a victim, too. You don't happen to know who he was, or better yet, have his phone number, do you?"

"No, but do you really think the poor guy wants to stand up and be counted as the big, brave bulldozer driver who was bullied by a gang of goats?"

"We'll all be there for him, Margaret. That's what this whole event is about. Community support."

"Oh, yeah. And I'm sure he'll appreciate

it. Call George. He'll have his name and number. So how did you and Phil resolve your differences?"

"I was able to talk him around."

"You can be very persuasive."

"Why, thank you, Margaret. As I told Phil, it just makes sense. If we're trying to forge a spirit of solidarity in the community, we need to adopt an inclusive definition of the word victim. Ray Jenkins is a victim because he wrecked his truck when he went gaga over the welcome sign. And William should be counted as a victim, even without his peripheral victimhood due to the attack on Eleanor and his being Diane's cousin, because it was his lot with the goats. Have you noticed that he seems to be taking all of this personally? What a loon. I swear."

"Being a victim might have that effect on someone. According to Eleanor, he's very sensitive."

"And if you believe that, you'll believe dead pigeons fly," she snorted.

"Anyway, it's good of you to support him, Bitsy, even in his lunacy. How many victims are you expecting to show up tonight?"

"All of them."

"Surely not Doug?"

"Margaret, I thought you were taking this seriously." She sighed to illustrate her taxed patience. "All of them with a few exceptions. It probably is too much to hope that we can spring Eleanor from the hospital for the evening."

"Probably."

"Oh." She stopped, brightening, with her forefinger raised artfully to her cheek. "Perhaps minus one other, as well." She played that line with the skill of a fisherman placing her fly exactly where she wanted it.

And I bit. "Who?"

"What's-his-name." She continued smiling.

Too late to spit the fly out and retreat. "Who, Bitsy?"

"I guess I forgot to tell you when I came in. I was downtown, earlier, and I saw George pull up to the old mercantile in his squad car. The mercantile's door was open, which is suspicious because the place is supposed to be empty, and George went inside, checking it out, I guess. Anyway, he came back out with that Mashburn character."

"And?" There was so clearly an "and" to this story.

"And he was in handcuffs. It looks to me like that just might be the tidy and satisfying end to Mr. Mashburn's sojourn in Stonewall."

CHAPTER 37

I didn't gasp. I didn't swoon. I didn't leap up and rush to the rescue. Bitsy had caught me on her hook, but I didn't give her any satisfaction. I thanked the sanity instilled in me by my recently and fortuitously chosen mission in life, assumed nothing about the reported incident, ignored her gleaming gloat and turned to Phil.

"How would you like to pay for your T-shirt, Phil? Cash, check, or credit card?"

"But, Margaret, don't you find that piece of information fascinating?" Bitsy prodded.

"Fascinating? No. More like sad. You want a bag with that Phil?"

"No thanks, I'm going to wear it." He pulled the T-shirt on over the one he was wearing and struck a pose.

"Right on, Phil," I said. "You wearing yours, Bitsy?"

She looked at Phil, probably assessing the layered look and the statement she'd be making if she didn't immediately join him, then pulled one on, too. The bright colors clashed with her peevedness.

"I must say I'm surprised, Margaret. You've been quick enough to rush to that man's defense up until now. That you haven't done so over this latest development, I find quite telling."

I shrugged. "Who knows, Bitsy? Maybe it's just a case of easy come, easy go. Speaking of which, you'd better go and get busy if you want a big turnout tonight."

"Right on, Margaret," said Phil. "Lawn Order waits for, uh, no person. You coming, Bitsy?" He took her arm and hustled her out the door. He was beginning to grow on me.

Fran returned from wherever she goes when Bitsy comes. She didn't return with tea and I didn't ask her what she'd been doing other than avoiding Bitsy. If avoiding Bitsy keeps her happy and in my employ, that's something I'll accept, knowing that every bookseller must be allowed her private peccadilloes. I showed her the T-shirts.

"Good god."

I told her about the scene with George and Gene as reported by Bitsy.

"Dear god."

"You've become a woman of few words."

"And you a woman oddly lacking a normal reaction."

"I did, briefly, think of throwing up." She backed up several steps. "Only briefly, Fran, then I considered my other options. I could assume Bitsy was right about what she saw and what it means, in which case I was mistaken about Gene Mashburn and there's no point in rushing off in a lather. Or, I could assume Bitsy is wrong, in which case Gene will wander in at some point when I least expect him, as he is wont to do, and so once again there is no point in rushing off."

"You could call George and find out which it is," Fran said softly, kindly.

I thought about that then shook my head. "Thanks, Fran. I know I could. But I can also hide behind my mission in life and go about my business day. Unassuming serenity, that's the key."

She had to leave soon after that, but by then the late-afternoon doldrums had set in, anyway. People were picking children up from soccer games and play dates, thinking about evening plans, and winding up their own work days. I was just as glad to be left alone with the sanity of my books and any sense of serenity I could dredge from the slough of despond my spirits were sinking into. And then William shrieked in.

"Is your sister certifiable?"

"Oh, blow it out your bagpipe, William." Turns out, far from being serene, I was snappish as hell. "What do you want?"

He waved a candlelight vigil poster under my nose. "I'd just like to know what your sister thinks she's going to accomplish with this ridiculous gesture." He emphasized his desire for information with a ridiculous gesture of his own. Talk about overwrought. If Eleanor had been worried about his state of mind before, she should see him now.

"So ask her."

"What?"

"Ask Bitsy, William, and leave me alone."

"She is apparently too busy organizing this charade, this travesty, to answer her phone. She also is not at home and I don't have time to traipse all over creation tracking her down. Besides, you've got one of these ludicrous posters on your door and you're selling these." He picked up one of the T-shirts as though it were infested and dropped it back on the counter in a pathetic heap. "You can't be totally clueless, Margaret."

It is not for nothing that I am my sister's sister. I swept up the T-shirt and pulled it over my head in one swift, elegant move.

"William," I said, struggling a little with

413

the sleeves, "I'm surprised at your lack of community spirit. The candlelight vigil is going to be a tremendous outpouring of support for your poor mother, you, Diane, the children, and all the other victims of this spate of senseless crime. If you're objecting, I don't understand why. In fact, this will be a profoundly powerful statement against whatever villain or villains have been preying on our community. I plan to be there front and center. Wearing my T-shirt. By the way, how is your mother?"

"She is only as well as can be expected. But your solicitude for Mother brings up another point. Are you also going insane? Or is it the people who think you know something about what's been going on in this town who are insane? Because if you know something, anything at all, then you should have told the police so that my mother would have been spared having her brains dashed out and her house set on fire . . ."

"William. Get a grip."

He drew in his breath sharply, drew himself up as though I'd slapped him with my glove and challenged him to a duel.

"Calm down, you're alarming the few customers you haven't scared off. Now, is there something I can actually help you with?"

"Oh, like you helped my mother with that asinine book?"

"Which asinine book would that be, William? I specialize in asinine books so you'll have to be more specific."

"*Restful Recipes for Men with Too Much on Their Plates.* I found it insulting. I find your attitude insulting."

"William, I'm sorry. Don't you think we're all just a little on edge? But I think your mother was genuinely concerned about you. And you know my policy has always been if you don't like the book, you're welcome to bring it back. Now, if you don't mind, I have to help other customers." I turned away from him to ring up a magazine and apologize for the wait and the scene. William stewed a minute or two then turned on his heel and left.

"Hi."

I knew that voice. I looked up. Gene materialized from the mystery section.

CHAPTER 38

Gene looked to be unfettered and unescorted by local constabulary. I raised my eyebrows. In question? In surprise? I wasn't sure which.

"How do you do that?" I asked.

He looked confused.

"Slip in so silently. So unannounced."

"I must have come in while you were concentrating on not beaning William. You handled that well, by the way."

"Not really."

"Well enough. No blood, anyway. How about I make us some supper while you finish up here and then we spend a relaxing evening playing with Archie and watching a movie or something? I've got that idea for a new dessert I'd like to try out and I bought this for the little guy." He showed me a cardinal red mouse with tartan ears. "Choicest catnip."

"Supper and mousing around sound good.

The relaxing bit is out, though. Turns out I have other plans." I spread my arms, exposing the glory of Lawn Order spread across my chest.

He wiggled his eyebrows.

"The T-shirt, hot shot."

"Spiffy. They got their act together fast."

"You like the colors?"

"Not bad. Maybe not what I'd've chosen, but they're eye-catching as hell. You selling them? How many you sold so far?"

"With the one you're going to buy, four."

"Any discount for being the artist?"

"Nope."

He forked over the fifteen bucks Bitsy had decided on as a fair and profit-making price. "So what are your other plans? Hawking T-shirts on Main Street?"

I explained about the candlelight vigil I'd planned on skipping until William started ranting.

"I think it's nice of you to stand up for your sister like that. Even if it does dash my evening's hopes and dreams. Shows a sense of loyalty."

"Yeah, too bad my loyalty takes the form of a perverse reaction to an asshole, but that's just me. You should be there tonight, too, though, you know. You lost your apartment. You're a victim."

"As long as victims aren't required to make speeches. I don't want to make a speech."

"Someone will probably say something. Probably Bitsy because she's got a lot to say about everything. But I sort of think she's not even expecting you to show up so you should be safe. Oh, and they're unveiling Phil's anthem tonight. But if you really want to be on the safe side, you probably shouldn't sing, either."

He turned with a hmph he must have borrowed from Leona and flounced off to the kitchen. For my part, I was glad I hadn't given in to Bitsy and her groundless rumors. Gene in handcuffs. Hah. I shook my head at such foolishness and congratulated myself on living up to my mission in life so well.

"I got arrested this afternoon," he tossed out while cheerfully tossing more croutons on his salad.

Unfortunately, I'd just taken a bite of the spaghetti he'd made and now some of it went down my windpipe and another few strands hung from my chin.

"At the mercantile?" I choked.

He nodded.

"Well, hell. That is just so irritating."

"Don't worry, it was all a mistake."

"You can't even begin to know how damned irritating it is."

"It's alright. George and I are buddies, now."

I buried my face in my hands and gave vent to a throat-wrenching growl.

"Hey, hey, now." He got up and came around the table, put his arm around my shoulders and stroked my hair. "It's okay, it's okay. Tell me what the problem is."

"It's Bitsy."

I'll give him credit for holding on during that explosion. I seethed for a few more minutes during which he rubbed my shoulders. Then I took a deep, cleansing breath and sat up straight.

"Better?" he asked.

"Much. Thank you."

"You want to tell me what that was all about? In fact, wouldn't you like me to tell you what the arrest was all about?"

"You said it was all a mistake, right?"

He nodded.

"Then the answer to both questions is no. I'm sorry you had that unfortunate experience, but as long as it's over, I'm moving on." I took another deep, reviving breath. "So, what's this dessert you've invented?"

"I'm not buying it."

"I know. You said you were going to make it."

"Not the dessert. Your lack of curiosity. I'm not buying your disinclination for questions and answers. You've been up to your eyeballs in questions and answers for days. You've got questions and answers coming out of your ears. In fact, I think I see one leaking out of your left ear right now. Oh, no, that's just a piece of spaghetti on your shoulder." He reached over and tidied it away.

"Okayokayokayokay. What happened?"

"I borrowed the key to the mercantile from Diane so I could look around inside and George thought he'd caught me red-handed burgling the place."

"With a key in your hand?"

"He thought I might have gotten it off Doug after strangling him. But after he talked to Diane, he apologized for being overzealous. And you can hardly blame the guy. Everyone's jumpy these days and there I was creeping around tapping on walls."

"Yeah, I guess that would have me reaching for the handcuffs, too. Creeping and tapping, huh? What is that? Skills architects share with cat burglars?"

"And treasure hunters."

"Oh yeah?"

"Some of these old building have odd nooks and crannies that have been walled off over the years, eaves in attics, places like that. I occasionally find them in buildings I'm working on and old stuff in them, too. More often than not the stuff is junk. But not always."

"That night at Bertie's, you said you gave Doug tips on treasure hunting."

He nodded.

"So did you find anything?"

He nodded, again. "A likely space, anyway. Might not be a thing in it, of course. George is going to see about opening it up, though. He's a different guy when he's excited, isn't he?"

"It's nice you noticed. Not everyone can detect the difference between normal George and excited George. So, forgotten spaces, hidden treasure, are these clues that might help find the bad guy?"

"Beats me, unless Long John Silver is alive and well and stalking the streets of Stone-wall."

"It's got good rumor potential, though, even better than the Mafia. Pirates have real entertainment value. Now, how about that dessert?"

But he said there wasn't time for his dessert if he were going to do it right and we still wanted to make it to the candlelight vigil. He wouldn't tell me anything about it, either, merely smiling a sly smile that almost had me abandoning the candlelight vigil altogether. But in the end, he was keen on seeing the Lawn Order committee in action and I was anxious to see Bitsy's reaction when he showed up. After spending a few quality minutes introducing Archie to his catnip mouse, we made it to the courthouse in time to see both.

Bitsy and the rest of the committee were already at the courthouse and organized. Harriet sat at a card table under the willow tree selling T-shirts. Phil stood on the sidewalk looking like a new father, proud and nervous by turns, handing out copies of the anthem. Two other members handed out unlit candles and explained that lit ones would be passed at the appropriate time.

We picked up our anthems and candles and went to stand with Rodney at the bottom of the courthouse steps. Bitsy was busy pacing back and forth at the top of the steps, mumbling and making small gestures. Either William had been right and she was going nuts or she was up there rehearsing a speech. Rodney, resplendent in his size triple X Lawn Order T-shirt and sans-a-belt golf pants, gazed up at her. A look at his face showed him rapt in admiration rather than wracked with anxiety so, using my cunning wits, I deduced she was practicing.

"I'm impressed," Gene said, as the crowd grew by twos and threes. "How did they manage to get the word around so fast?"

"Effort. Something more people ought to put into their affairs."

"Oh, Leona," I said, startled to find her at my elbow. "I'm sorry, we should have stopped by and walked down with you."

"Hmph. Had your mind on more interesting affairs, no doubt." She leered at Gene.

"Leona, may I say how lovely you look this evening? The colors in the T-shirt bring out the blue of your eyes and put roses in your cheeks," Gene said.

Leona took his arm and patted his hand. I left them to their mutual admiration society and turned to look for people I knew or recognized. It was an amazing crowd. Whole families must have turned out. There were easily three or four hundred people ranging up and down the sidewalk, now. The candles had long since been handed out. Phil still had a few copies of the anthem but the crowd had swallowed him up and he held the remaining copies over his head as he swam his way toward the steps and us.

"Mr. Mashburn," he said, finally breaking free, "great to see you. Word was that you were, uh, possibly going to be kept from joining us. Glad you could make it after all. When the time comes, we'd like you to join the other victims further up on the steps."

"I'd rather not."

"Please. It will help to create a united front. Solidarity in the community. All joined together as though one voice raised in plangent song." He shrugged. "You know, that sort of thing."

"All for one and one for all?"

"Exactly."

"How can I refuse? Just give me the signal."

Phil raised his fist in what must have been the Lawn Order power salute and surged off into the crowd again. Then I felt an electric prickle run down my spine and turned to find Bitsy, hands on hips, lips and eyes narrowed in distaste.

"Why am I not surprised to see you?" she said, looking Gene up and down. "Slipped out on some technicality, I assume?"

"If you want to call a misunderstanding a technicality," he said, "sure. Nice turn out, by the way. This is a marvel of organization. Good job and a good idea, too."

Her eyes and mouth made three round Os.

"And on such short notice. It's remarkable. Congratulations."

She actually blushed. "To tell you the truth, I'm a little surprised so many people came," she said. "What do you think it really is, morbid curiosity?"

"Does it matter?" he asked.

"Not for tonight, I guess. But I'd like it to mean something more than that. I'd like it to be the beginning of a new awareness. I'd like it to be the stirrings of . . ." Her voice swelled and her hands went operatic, "stirrings of a true spirit of . . ."

"Oh, hey, Bitsy," I cut in. "Is that part of your speech? Maybe you ought to save it so it sounds fresh." The fervor in her eye turned suspicious. "Sounds great though." I smiled and nodded. "Oh, look, there's Diane and the girls."

With a "wish me luck" and a "join us on the steps, Mr. Mashburn" trailing behind her, she charged off in Diane's direction.

Leona had disengaged from Gene's arm and was talking to Rodney, probably about her violets, of which he seems unnaturally fond. I gave Gene a warm kiss for taming the wild sister and went back to surveying the crowd. Bertie and Claire were pushing

425

their way through to reach the steps. I might have missed them but Bertie's pink caftan glowed like a beacon. Claire followed along in her wake.

"Who's George got his arm around?" Gene asked.

"Isn't that interesting? That's Rosemary O'Grady, the third grade teacher."

"That supposed to mean something?"

"Long story," I said. "I'll tell you some-time."

"He's wearing the wrong T-shirt. His has a kid's drawing of a dog on it."

"So it does. Look's like that story is start-ing a new chapter."

"Do you suppose this is his idea of a fun date?"

"Well, I know I'm having fun." And I was mildly surprised to find I was.

The variety of people in the audience was wonderful. Kids chased back and forth, in and out of legs, at the base of the stairs. Others climbed two or three steps then jumped back to the bottom, arms spread wide. Several families sat on lawn chairs in the beds of pickup trucks parked at the curb, some passing bottles. A couple of teenagers skinned off their Lawn Order T-shirts in exchange for a couple of tens each. Fran and Jim walked by on the other side of the street, arm in arm, eating ice cream cones. I saw Nancy and waved.

"You've been busy," she called as she pushed through the crowd to join us.

"Not me. This is Bitsy's show."

"Oh, I know." She gave me a quick hug and squeezed Gene's hand. "Gene, as ever, good to see you. No," she said, turning her back slightly to him and lowering her voice so she was speaking only to me, "I hear through the grapevine you're developing a sideline business in sleuthing. Not something I expected from you."

I couldn't gauge her mood from her expression and the tone of her soft words was lost in the surrounding hubbub. "It's not something that's entirely true, either. I certainly won't be applying for a P.I. license."

"Just be careful," she said without her usual, easy smile.

Bitsy appeared at the top of the steps, again, framed by the two central columns.

"That's something she didn't think about," Gene said. "A sound system. They'll never hear her."

"It's built in."

"Huh?"

"Listen."

A mere throng of several hundred is nothing for the wonder that is my sister. She raised her arms, raised her voice, and she had their hearts and souls in the first half dozen words.

"Holy cow," Gene said.

"Shhh," said everyone around him.

Chances were I'd regret it later because she might give me a pop quiz on content, but I let Bitsy's words swell past me. I'd gotten the gist of what she was saying, anyway, in the teaser speech I'd interrupted earlier. Instead I watched the people listening to her, thinking their reactions might be more instructive. When my eyes strayed across George, again, it looked as though he had the same idea. We nodded to each other and continued surveying.

I expected to see the rest of the Lawn Order committee members in a group near the bottom of the stairs, ready to lend their support en masse. But they'd spread themselves throughout the crowd. The better to spread the "flame of unity," as it turned out. Bitsy paused while they lit their candles then started passing them from hand to hand.

"That's the signal, Gene," Rodney said.

He tipped his candle to light Gene's, shook his hand heartily, and gave him a shove in the right direction. Diane and the girls were already standing halfway up the steps. They looked small and uncertain. Harriet and Ed crossed to join them and Harriet put her arm around Diane. Bertie and Claire climbed the steps and Claire put her arm around Gene. Bertie went back down to give Ray Jenkins a hand up. He took off his feed store cap and waved like the politician he'll always be.

William sidled up and spoke in my ear. "The architect and the wayward waitress look cozy. You two have a falling out?"

"That's part of the whole unity theme, William." I looked at him. No candle. No anthem. No T-shirt. No sense of personal space. "I'm surprised you came. Why don't you join them on the steps in honor of your mother?"

He made a rude noise.

I moved closer to Leona. "Did you get your T-shirt from Harriet, Leona?"

"Bitsy told me to buy one from you when she called about the vigil," she said.

"And we left without waiting for you. I'm sorry I forgot you."

"That's all right, dear, that's what spare keys are for. I left the money on the counter. Or did I? No, maybe I left it on the kitchen table. Next to an intriguing recipe. One of Gene's?"

"He left the recipe on the table?"

"Shhh. I think it's time for the anthem."

Phil was standing with Bitsy now. The candles were all lit. We were a sea of flickering faces in the gathering twilight. A hush fell and Phil began to sing.

His voice wavered at first, then grew stronger. Others joined in and soon the plangent song he'd hoped for rose from all around.

Phil was right. Old Rousseau knew what he was talking about in remarking on the power of people singing in unison. Phil's solo voice had stirred something in me the other night in the store. But this. This grand noise had a contagion bubbling up within me. I sang with unaccustomed gusto and found myself longing to link arms with my neighbors, march down the streets of Stonewall, scale the green and thorny heights. There were tears in my eyes. I linked one arm with Nancy's and put the other around Leona as we trumpeted another chorus.

Leona leaned closer and said something.

"What?"

"I wonder if I forgot to lock your back door. I might have been distracted by the recipe."

"And you remember this now?"

"The anthem reminded me of it. There

are dangerous things in the night, dear. Maybe you should go check."

"It's dangerous, so I should go off by myself in the dark and check it out?"

"I'll come with you," Nancy said.

"Oh, do go, Margaret," William added. "The last thing we need is for the bookstore to burn down. God forbid we lose what little culture we have in this bourgeois burgh. If it will make you feel any better, I will come with you, too."

"I'll let Gene know where you are if he's through being a victim before you get back," Leona said.

Swell.

And so Nancy and I marched down Main Street followed by a supercilious undertaker.

CHAPTER 39

"Thanks for coming with me Nancy," I said, and after a beat added, "You, too, William," though that part might not have sounded so much like I meant it. "This shouldn't take long."

"Not a problem," Nancy assured me.

"A fool's errand," William said. "But any diversion is an improvement over your sister's silly serenade."

To annoy him, I walked faster and started humming the Lawn Order anthem.

The streets of Stonewall, after dark, aren't what most people would consider danger-ous, even given recent events. William was in greater danger of me smacking him, for instance, if he continued maligning my sister, than I would have been walking by myself. It did cross my mind that walking in the dark with either of these two, alone, wasn't a smart idea. After all, they were both on my suspect list, no matter how tenuous my suspicions. But logic told me the pair of them canceled each other out. Unless they were working together, and that possibility was beyond the realm of reason, beyond even the ozone.

"So, Margaret, you were always the bright one in high school. Inhibited and introverted, it's true, but you could always be counted on to have the right answer. Who do you see as the perverted perpetrator?"

"So many suspects, it's hard to say."

"But I'm sure you've eliminated your sister from your list. Who else? The lush who lusts after you?"

"Grow up, William."

"Merely speaking the truth. What was he looking for at the mercantile today, by the way? He didn't tell Diane when he inveigled the keys from her. That was my building, you know, until Doug cheated me out of it."

"Then maybe you can talk Diane into giving it back to you."

"And what about you, Ms. Umphrey? You're strangely silent. Or perhaps that's not so strange. I hadn't realized you were a partner in the schoolhouse consortium."

"It hasn't been a secret," Nancy said.

"Just something resembling an exclusive club."

"Just private business."

"Come on, William," I said, taking Nancy's arm. "Drop the complaints and pick up the pace. I'd like to get back to the rally before it's over."

It was a soft evening, the kind I like best in Stonewall, when the blanket of night takes some of the rough edges off our town. It hides my rusting garbage cans, for instance. William bumped into them as we rounded the corner of the house heading for the back door. If I'd been thinking, I would have put on the outside light before we left.

"The moment of truth," I said, pulling my arm from Nancy's and climbing the back steps with a twinge of trepidation. If the door was unlocked, should I go in to see if everything was all right? Should I send William in first and Nancy and I could wait outside and see what happened? Or should I lock the door, hot foot it back downtown, find George, and get him to check it out? Check for what? Manure? An infestation of goats and dead pigeons? Stray bodies tucked in my sofa? Eunice? I suddenly felt a little sick.

William tsked impatiently and reached past me to try the door. It was locked. A good surge of adrenaline wasted.

434

"Well, that solves that little mystery," I said, bouncing back down the stairs.

"Ahem. Might I trouble you to use the facilities?" William asked.

"Oh. Sure." I dug out my keys, unlocked the door, and pointed him in the right direction. "Glass of water or something, Nancy?"

"No, thanks," she said, swirling a forefinger around her ear in the universal symbol of lunacy and pointing over her shoulder in the direction William had disappeared.

"A little more so lately, maybe. Your consortium's got him in a twit, that's for sure." I listened for a second. "Hang on. Be right back." I ran lightly up the back stairs and opened the door. Archie met me with a petulant mew. "Hey, little guy, you hear a party downstairs and feel left out?"

I picked him up and took him down to meet Nancy. She had her back to us, staring at something on the table.

"This is outrageous," she was saying.

I hesitated at the bottom of the stairs. But she heard me and turned around with a piece of paper in her hand.

"Is this yours?"

"Er . . ."

"What an outrageously fabulous combination of ingredients."

"Oh, right." I started breathing again and

435

loosened my suddenly too-tight grip on poor Archie. "Yeah, that must be the new dessert Gene invented. He's been keeping it a secret."

"MMmmmm," she said. "Then I'd better not show it to you."

"Trade you a cat for a peek?" I held Archie up to my cheek and batted my eyes. He purred loudly enough for her to hear.

Nancy laughed. "If it means that much to you." She handed me the recipe and reached for Archie. "You're awfully cavalier with your cat, though, if you'll trade him for nuts and chocolate."

"More than nuts and chocolate," I said, scanning the recipe. "Besides, he's a foster cat. No real attachment, yet. MMmmm is right. Dates, crystallized ginger, eggs, bit of flour. Brandy. Hm, I wonder if that's a problem?"

"Oh, sure you're not attached. What a sweetie this guy is. Whose is he, then?"

"You know Eunice?"

"The Valkyrie had a cat?" William had rejoined us.

Archie looked at William over Nancy's shoulder and hissed. He scrambled out of her arms, scratching her hand, and darted under the table.

"What do you mean 'had' William?"

436

He ignored my question and kicked at Archie. "What's that in your hand, Margaret? More of your detective fiction?"

"Yeah, and the first word on it is 'nuts.' "

He skirted the table and kicked at Archie again.

"Hey, quit!" Nancy said. She stooped to cluck at Archie.

As soon as her back was to him, William lunged.

"Hey!" she yelled as he grabbed her. He yanked her upright, his left arm across her throat, choking her next words.

"William!" I started toward them.

"Stop!" he shouted at me, jerking Nancy sideways off her feet.

She struggled, kicking, trying to scream.

"William!"

He squeezed with his left arm, pulling her back against him until she hung there, gasping and gulping. Her terrified face fit neatly beneath his chin.

"Don't even breathe, Margaret, or neither will she," he said, squeezing her throat again. "There, see? You're not so clever, are you?"

"I never said I was." I swallowed. "Let her go, William. Please."

"Too late." He lifted Nancy off her feet. She dangled, limp now, eyes closed. "This

437

is the perfect solution, you see. *La solution la plus merveilleuse.*"

"No, no, it's not. Whatever you're talking about, it's not."

"But it's as plain as the nose on our Ms. Umphrey's face." He shook her like a rag doll. "Don't you see just how clever you're not?" He started circling the table toward me, dragging Nancy, his arm still tight around her neck. "Is she dead, Margaret? What do you think? Want to chance it?"

I didn't know what to do, didn't know what I *could* do, made the mistake of darting a glance toward the back door.

"You're not listening, Margaret!" he shouted. "If you run out the door, I'll burn your bookstore with her in it. Whoosh! Almost as satisfying as Everett's fish folly or Bertie's Burnt Bank Tavern. I have gas cans waiting out back!"

I had to believe him. Had to breathe. Think. I couldn't take my eyes off him and I couldn't think clearly seeing Nancy in his . . . she half opened one eye, closed it, opened it. A wink? I stared. She did it again. She was bluffing to stay alive.

So could I.

Drawing on every ounce of strength in me, I pulled myself up into the best imitation I could muster of the staunchest, steeliest, most commanding figure I know.

"This is ridiculous," I pronounced, sounding exactly like Bitsy, adopting the set of her shoulders and the tilt of her imperious chin. "William, if your goal was to burn the bookstore, you're too late. The vigil is almost certainly over by now. Gene and Leona will be back any minute and George, probably, too. You've stupidly wasted your time with a poorly thought out plan."

"Watch what you say, Margaret."

My back was to the table, now, and he'd continued circling so he was between me and the back door.

"What happened, Willy? Doug wouldn't lend you money? He kept you out of the schoolhouse consortium? Was that the problem? He wouldn't let Wee Willy play?"

"Shut up."

"I will not. What's the matter? Did Doug cheat you out of the mercantile, too? Did he tell you, that night at Bertie's, that he'd found a forgotten hidey-hole and hoped to find a fortune in it? And did he say he wasn't going to share with Wee Willy?"

"I said shut up!"

"I will not." I took a deep breath, then, but couldn't quite keep my voice from shaking. "You killed Eunice, didn't you?"

A smirk flashed across his face.

"She saw you that night and you found out. And you killed her."

"And I cremated the bitch and buried her with Everett."

I fought back a sob and barely managed to turn it into something that sounded like a laugh. "Well that was completely stupid, Wee Willy. You're an idiot."

"Shut up!"

"You're an ass Wee Willy. Hah, Wee Willy, Wee Willy, what an *utter ass.*"

"Shut up!" he howled. He dropped Nancy and came for me.

He was faster than I'd expected and he got his hands around my throat. Who knew those fish-belly-white undertaker fingers were so strong?

Unfortunately, it is Bitsy who has a black belt, not me. George showed me a few self-defense moves, so you could say I have a pink belt because they're moves useful to women in my current situation. I wouldn't call it a pink belt because I'm not fond of pink, although that's beside the point. I'm rambling. But apparently that's what I do when the life is being choked out of me.

Enough of that.

I gave William a terrific instep stomp. He yelled and briefly loosened his grip on my throat. I took advantage of that with a brain-jarring head slam. Thank god my forehead only slammed into his sternum, though. Encountering a chin, according to George, can raise a mean lump. But the head slam wasn't enough to break the strangle hold. I clawed at his hands and kicked his shins and together, we danced sideways into the kitchen table. I made a grab and managed to get hold of a candlestick and then I performed a perfect, ten-point, adrenalin-laced skull crush.

It was fairly awful. But effective. And left William moaning and bleeding on my shiny kitchen floor.

I hit him again.

CHAPTER 40

"It was me, in the kitchen, with the candle-stick," I said when Gene and Leona came in the back door a moment later. I was still standing over William. He was still moaning and bleeding on the floor. I looked for Nancy and saw her in the corner, holding onto Archie, sobbing. "He killed Eunice," I said, and then I closed my eyes and fell apart, too.

I was aware of hands and a shoulder, sirens and more voices arriving. Being shuffled from the kitchen into the shop. A chair. A blanket. Quite a lot of tissues. My neck and throat hurt. I finally ran out of tears, started answering questions.

At some point George was there telling his fellow cops they had enough answers. Leona, Bitsy, and Gene stood off to the side talking quietly together. Nancy'd gone away in an ambulance. I'd refused.

Gene lifted Archie from my arms. Bitsy

put hers around me and took me to her house. In the morning I left her a note and crept back home.

I kept the store closed, shades drawn.

CHAPTER 41

People came and went over the next two days and I did my best to interact, but mostly I ignored them and read. Someone, probably Gene, had straightened the kitchen and scrubbed the floor. He'd brought Archie back and the cat and I retreated upstairs. Leona wisped in and out, bringing tea and soup. I reread *Charlotte's Web* and *The Magician's Nephew*. Gene climbed the stairs to let me know Nancy was bruised but okay. He sat quietly while I lost myself in *West with the Night*. Fran came by and we didn't do much more than hug for an hour. I picked up *The Seven Storey Mountain*, but put it down and read *Blackberry Winter*, with Archie snuggled in my lap, instead. Bitsy tucked a tuna casserole in the oven. I shared it with Archie and reread my favorite Wodehouse and Richard Peck short stories. It wasn't possible to ignore the world completely, but I gave it a good shot for a while.

And then it was time to get up and doing again. Bitsy helped with that. She came around Tuesday morning full of purpose.

"Margaret, I'd like your permission to do something."

I was flapping a dust rag around my neglected shop, attempting a return to normal, steeling myself to unlock the front door and let the public in. "Um, okay. I guess."

"And before you say no," she held up a hand to ward off the no she anticipated. "Before you say no, let me tell you why."

"And what, I hope."

She nodded. "Of course, yes. It's for closure, you see. Something we can all use. The bookstore, too." She smiled and straightened the bookmarks next to the cash register. "So, what I want to do is invite people over here tonight. For a wake. For Eunice. And for Doug, too, I suppose."

I stared at her.

"You're not saying anything."

I didn't know what to say.

"You're not going to start crying, again, are you?"

I shook my head. "Bitsy, I don't . . ."

"You won't have to do a thing. We'll have it here in the store. It's really the heart of your place, anyway, isn't it? This will be just what we need." She was off and running, in high agenda mode.

"Bitsy?"

"Hm?"

"Not a public thing."

"Oh, no. Invitation only."

"And no speeches or eulogies, okay? And not a lot of people."

"Oh, no, Margaret, no. It'll be a quiet, cozy gathering. Friends reaching out to friends. A little music, maybe, and nibbles." She was already heading for the door. "Leave it to me. I'll take care of everything."

I didn't doubt it. "What time?" I called after her.

"Seven."

"Goals are probably good," I told Archie when she was gone. He was steeping in a puddle of sunshine and blinked his agreement. "Yours is to continue being charming. Mine will be making it through the day and keeping myself together this evening."

Gene stopped by at noon to see how things were going and how I was doing. He was more receptive to plans for the wake than I expected.

"Hunh, I think I'm beginning to appreciate the way your sister thinks."

"Really?"

"Sure. Closure, healing, a wake, a memorial, whatever terms you use for it, the outcome should be healthy." He looked at his watch. "Oh, hey, I'd better get going, but I'll see you later." He gave me a quick peck on the cheek. "What time?"

"Seven."

So I found myself, that evening, surrounded by Bitsy's guests and a soft cello concerto. Rodney was there with his arm around Bitsy. Bertie and Claire. Harriet and Ed. Phil. Leona. Nancy sitting in one of the rockers getting reacquainted with Archie. Fran perched on the stool she'd brought from behind the counter. George was there with Rosemary O'Grady and an adoring Lambert sitting on her feet.

The gathering wasn't as cozy as Bitsy had imagined, though. Lambert and Archie were the only ones relaxed and enjoying themselves. The others maybe thought they were smiling as they balanced little plates and cups of coffee. But they either sat stiffly or shifted from foot to foot, no one sipping or nibbling. Conversations hesitated and stalled. Yo-Yo Ma sweated away over his cello in the background, trying to soothe and smooth, but even he wasn't making this work.

Come to think of it, I probably didn't look very comfortable standing behind the counter. Possibly not welcoming, either, with my arms crossed and who knows what strained look on my face. Time to make an effort. I tried relaxing my shoulders and taking a few slow, deep breaths, then joined Fran on the other side of the counter.

"They look as though they're waiting for something to happen, don't they?" I whispered.

"I'm not sure much ever happens at a wake without a massive infusion of liquor," she whispered back. "Do you think Diane is coming?"

I shrugged, but that reminded me and I looked around. "Where's Gene?"

Bitsy's fine-tuned ears picked up my question. "Gene is working on something special at Leona's. Some new dessert creation, apparently. He got a little behind, but he'll be here shortly."

His recipe. Good heavens. I'd forgotten all about it. I looked at Nancy.

"Do you think?" she asked.

"We can only hope."

Our exchange wasn't lost on Bitsy, or anyone else. Interests were piqued. Conversation and movement thawed somewhat. Bitsy peeled away from Rodney.

"Margaret, you haven't got a plate. Why don't you come over here and visit with Nancy and I'll fix you one."

She gave me a little push toward the rocker next to Nancy's and bustled off. Was she playing the attentive hostess or was she was up to something? I couldn't tell, but I sat anyway.

Nancy reached for my hand, squeezed it, and held on. "I should have called," she said.

"No, it's alright. But," I paused and cleared a small lump from my throat. "I should have done something that night. I should have hit him sooner."

"He'll wish you'd hit him harder before this is all over," George said.

Startled, I looked up. All eyes gazed back. Nancy and I were the center of attention. In fact, side by side, facing the other guests, this suddenly looked less like a wake and more like a press conference. I looked for Bitsy. She gave me a little wave. Of encouragement? Victory? Nancy squeezed my hand again.

"But don't worry, Margaret," George went on. "William will be okay. Until they toss him in the slammer. They've got him in the psychiatric ward, now. Suicide watch. You know, though, I told you not to play detective."

449

"I wasn't." I shook my head. "I didn't think I was."

"Just being kind of natural and nosy," Claire helpfully added.

George snorted. "Anyway, what I want to say is, I'm sure sorry about Eunice."

There were general murmurs and probably a few nods agreeing with him but I'd closed my eyes hoping against tears. Someone blew a nose and someone else coughed, then George spoke again.

"And Ms. Umphrey? I'd like to apologize. If I'd seen you two leave the vigil with William, I'd have come after you. We had our suspicions about him."

"What?" Bitsy cut in. "That's the first I've heard of that. And you let him run loose? He could have killed them. He could have burned down the bookstore with them in it. He tried to kill his own mother for god's sake."

I flapped a hand to shush her. "Not to kill her, I don't think. To complicate things. Like Eunice's car. He took it and parked it somewhere, didn't he? So someone would see it and think she was still around?"

George nodded.

"But my garden," Harriet said. "He did that?"

George nodded again.

"For what possible reason?"

"Ed, did he try to borrow money from you?" I asked.

"Yes, and I told him I couldn't accommodate him. He wasn't happy, but it was a business decision. The same with the matter over joining the consortium. He didn't have the money and we declined his membership." Ed stopped. "He destroyed Harriet's brilliant garden for that?"

"His cogs were slipping," George said.

"What he did," Leona said, "was to assume people owed him something, and when told he couldn't have it, he reacted. I take it he was responsible for destroying Doug's fishpond for the same reasons?"

"And if he'd known earlier I was part of the consortium, who knows what he'd have tried at the bank," Nancy said. She turned to me and mouthed what looked like "Oh my god I can't wait to retire and get the hell away from here."

"He's not insane," Leona continued. "He's warped and there is a difference. And you can't possibly believe, George Buckles, that a twisted, destructive mind like that was also the genius behind the crosswalk, the manure in the dumpster, or the goats tap dancing on your squad car."

George swiveled around. "And what do

you know about those incidents, Miss Leona?"

"Not a thing," she snapped and stalked off into the kitchen.

"Any of the rest of you? Phil? Bitsy? I didn't think so and I suppose it doesn't matter anyway."

"Some of it matters," Bitsy said. "There were two murders, George, and at least two attempted murders, and maybe an attempted negligent murder or whatever you'd call it if you throw Claire and her burning bathrobe in, too."

"I should hope so," Claire said. "I don't think I've been able to think straight since then. I mean, can you believe it? I even tried to talk Grandma into buying this poky place from Margaret."

"Ahem."

"Oh, sorry, Margaret. There I go not thinking again."

"So," Bitsy interjected, with a glare for Claire and me, "William, a person we've known all our lives, did these things? Why? How does something like that happen?"

"You wouldn't think a mortician could have money problems, would you?" George said. "It's not like there's anyone out there who doesn't drop dead at some point. But it turns out William's a terrible businessman. Overextended at the bank, credit cards. His investments tanked. He was bitter and getting desperate."

"And dopey Doug rubbed his nose in it one time too many," I said.

"But why the destruction, too?" Bitsy asked. "What was the point?"

"I'm guessing, here," George said. "But I think he was borrowing a line from that ridiculous old Mafia rumor. Taking on a Mafioso persona. Only it turns out William isn't any better at being a Mafioso than he is at being a businessman. Neither Ed or Doug made the connection between the vandalism and the turned down loans or membership in the consortium. Or maybe it's less complicated than that, and like Leona says, it was a warped reaction to not getting what he wanted."

"A big step up from fishponds to murder, though," I said.

"It is."

"So why?"

George shrugged. "You probably got it right. Doug went too far once too often. And we all knew Doug. Geez, William probably could've gotten off by pleading self-defense because Doug was going to aggravate him to death. But then there's the small matter of stuffing the body in the sofa

453

bed and going back to torch the place." He stopped and looked at me, then looked away. "We found a couple of cans of gas hidden around back here, the other night, you know. They yours?"

I shook my head.

Even Bitsy couldn't think of anything to say after that. She came over and put her hand on my shoulder.

The kitchen door opened a crack and Gene's head appeared. "Anyone got a match? Oh. I said something wrong, didn't I?"

"Oh, hell, I've got one. Here," Bertie said. "Claire, find some other music over there. Something lively."

That broke the mood and breathing resumed. Gene waved at me and disappeared back into the kitchen. Claire picked out a CD of fiddle tunes and in another minute Leona came in with plates and forks. She rapped on the counter.

"Eyes up here," she said and Gene came through the door with his creation to a collective gasp.

"Jesus god, Mashburn." George said, springing forward. "You'll have the place burnt down yet." He cleared space on the counter large enough to crash-land a flaming dirigible.

"Got carried away, didn't I?" Gene juggled the flaming platter uncomfortably from hand to hand, and just before his potholders ignited, he set it down. "Whew," he rubbed a hand across his beard, "for a minute I thought I was going up with it."

The flames burned themselves out to the merry jigging of fiddles in the background. Something plum puddingish was left behind. No one approached for a closer look. Neither Nancy nor I needed to because we already knew what it was — a life-giving, spirit-reviving concoction of chocolate, nuts, and ginger.

Gene sliced and handed plates around. Everyone smiled and thanked him and hesitated over taking a bite. Phil sniffed his. Bertie studied hers from all angles as though deciphering a hidden code. Even Leona fluttered her fork over her plate. Nancy and I, on the other hand, dug right in.

"Oh, now this," I said, stopping first to take another bite, "is heaven."

"So what do you call it?" Phil asked, after several rapturous bites of his own.

"I don't know. I guess I haven't got a name for it."

"Sure you do," said Claire. "If you let us use the recipe, that is. Exclusively." She jabbed Bertie with her elbow. Bertie had just taken another bite and looked dazed and in love. "Don't you think, Grandma? Wouldn't this be great?" She turned to me. "I talked to Diane, Margaret. She wants to restore the bank building. We'll be back in business. Isn't that great?"

"It's wonderful."

"So what's the name of the dessert?" Gene asked.

"The Flaming Bathrobe. What do you think?"

The Flaming Bathrobe disappeared quickly after that and Claire and Bertie disappeared just as quickly after getting the recipe from Gene.

Harriet and Ed were next to say good-bye, Ed still muttering over William, though that hadn't stopped him from having two helpings of the Flaming Bathrobe.

"Oh, and Margaret, my blanket," Harriet said. "I'll take it with me if you have it handy."

"Blanket? What . . . Oh my gosh, your yellow blanket. I can't believe I forgot it. I was going to wash it."

"Don't trouble yourself, Margaret. You run get it and I'll take it home now."

"Are you sure?"

She was.

The blanket was still sitting where I'd tossed it on the washer in the basement what seemed like weeks ago. Embarrassed at being so inconsiderate, I tried brushing some of the worst mud off. As I gave the poor fluffy thing a shake, an errant memory gave my mind a twitch but slipped away before I caught hold of it. I folded the blanket slowly, trying to bring the memory into focus.

"You alright?" Gene asked, when I returned.

"Yeah, yeah, there's just something . . ." I looked at the blanket again. Something . . .

"There it is," Harriet said, sending the thought flying off again. "Thank you, Margaret. And thank you for the, er, the lovely evening."

As she reached for the blanket, Gene put his hand in the small of my back. And then I remembered. Harriet tugged, but I held on.

Phil, Leona, Fran, and Rodney were talking and laughing together. George was reading *Officer Buckle and Gloria* to Rosemary, Nancy, and Archie. Bitsy and Lambert were staring at each other. Whistles and an accordion had joined the fiddles on the CD player. And Harriet tugged at her blanket.

"Who pushed me in the lake?"

"What?" Gene and George asked in tandem.

"William didn't push me," I said. "He was overseeing the burial service. But I *was* pushed. So who pushed me?"

Everyone stared at me. Into their silence came a small cough from Harriet.

"I didn't mean to push you, Margaret," she said. "It was an accident. I wanted to ask you if you'd found out anything about my garden. Leona told me you were looking into things. Only, I slipped, and I put out a hand to steady myself. On your back, you see. And I'm afraid I pushed you in. I was mortified. I can't swim. Then I saw that you were more or less all right and I crept off, too ashamed to own up to what I'd done. But I did lend you the blanket."

"Yes, you did. Thank you, Harriet."

Ed had quit muttering about William and was now gaping at Harriet. She tucked the blanket under one arm, tucked his arm under her other and steered him out the door.

"Well, I guess that about wraps it up," Bitsy said. "And, as it turns out, my idea worked like a charm."

"What idea was that?" I asked.

"The candlelight vigil to stop the violence."

"But the vigil didn't stop the violence, Bitsy."

"Of course it did. Everything that happened Saturday night happened because of the vigil. If you hadn't forgotten Leona when you went down, and if she hadn't forgotten whether or not she locked your door, William wouldn't have walked home with you and tried to strangle you or Nancy and you wouldn't have hit him on the head, thereby stopping the violence."

That made sense to her.

"Well, the anthem was a hit, anyway," I said. "You did a great job, Phil. There are a couple of lines in it that haunt me. They keep running through my head, you know? Dah-de-dah, something, 'we'll walk the green paths, the free paths, cross meadows and highways.' Dah-de-dah-dah, 'our four-legged friends will forever safely graze.' And what's that next line? 'Ripe apples and muffins delivered unto our foes,' dah-dah 'the pungent aroma right under his nose' and then something about changing signs and portents, gatherings and great events?"

"Just lyrics that struck me, Margaret," Phil said. He hopped up, suddenly energized.

George got up, too. Somehow, that made Phil nervous.

"Guess it's time to go. Uh, thanks, yeah,

thanks. Bye." And Phil was out the door and in his paint-spattered pickup.

George watched him go. "What was that all about?"

"Beats me, George." I pulled him away from the window. "That was a nice editing job on the third grade T-shirt, by the way."

"I did that," Rosemary said, putting her arm around a pink George, "with the kids' unanimous approval. 'Officer Buckles and Glorious Lambert.' So much better."

"Glorious Lambert certainly looks happy about it."

To prove it, he closed his eyes and leaned his full weight against Rosemary's legs.

"Hey Mashburn, you into irony at all?" George asked. "That walled off space in the mercantile? Empty except for a few pigeon feathers and pigeon droppings. Goes to show how dangerous assumptions can be. Which reminds me, Margaret," he pulled some papers out of his pocket, "here. I highlighted the important parts. Come on Glorious, let's you and me take Rosemary home."

Lambert and Rosemary headed out but George turned at the door. "You know, Margaret, between you assuming you could safely play detective and William assuming he was smart enough to play Mafia or whatever, I'm about beat. But you know what William should've done? What would've gotten him somewhere? He should've blackmailed Doug over the dead pigeons."

Bitsy's ears perked up. If she had a tail it would have pointed. "Blackmail Doug over the pigeons? Doug killed them? I knew it. I knew he killed them. From the very beginning I said he killed those pigeons. I came right here and I told Margaret . . ."

George escaped out the door. Gene, Fran, and Leona jumped up to take dishes to the kitchen. Rodney gathered Bitsy and her purse. He said something to me but I couldn't hear him past Bitsy trumpeting her vindication.

I turned around and there were Nancy and Archie.

"So you're okay?" I asked.

"I will be."

I looked around the bookstore, saw Eunice in so many parts of it, but a lot of other friends, too.

"Um, Margaret, may I have Eunice's cat?"

"Have Archie?"

"Is that his name? I was thinking of calling him Jeb. Please, Margaret. He needs a new start as much as I do. I think New Mexico will suit us both."

I hugged Nancy and kissed Jeb between his ears and locked the front door after them. After all, he was only a foster cat, I told myself. We hadn't really bonded, yet. I blew my nose and was reading through the pages George had handed me when Gene wandered back in.

"What did George give you?" he asked, coming up behind me and putting his arms around me. They felt nice, especially since he didn't attempt anything like a shoulder massage. If he'd put his hands anywhere near my neck I'd probably still go into instant candlestick replay.

"Remember his remark that I should read more Nietzsche? Looks like Nietzsche and I could be pals. He didn't trust assumptions much either."

"George should take a leaf out of his own book. He assumed you were making assumptions."

"And I was. I assumed William was merely the loon I've known all my life. Too bad. It was a perfectly good mission in life and I abandoned it when I needed it most. Although, ultimately, you could argue that abandoning it saved our lives and not only because I assumed what Bitsy would do, but because I actually assumed Bitsy."

"That's practically a nightmare."

"In so many ways. So, how about this for a mission in life? 'Don't confront what you can safely ignore.' "

"Doesn't sound like you, somehow."

"More than you think, maybe. But, okay, how about this? 'Never predict how other people will react.' "

"That sort of has the ring of the old one about assumptions."

"Sort of. But assumptions aren't as concrete as predictions so now I've got wiggle room." I gave a wiggle that he seemed to enjoy. "And to celebrate my new mission, I'm going to jump right in with an assumption."

"Mm?" he said into my hair.

"I'm going to assume Fran left out the back door and that you've already walked Leona home."

"Mmhm."

"And that you're going to do the dishes."

"When?"

"I couldn't possibly predict."

"How about in the morning? Assuming we're not otherwise occupied?"

"You know, I'm almost tempted to make a prediction about that."

We turned out the lights and found our way upstairs.

ABOUT THE AUTHOR

Molly MacRae spent twenty years in the foothills of the Blue Ridge Mountains of Upper East Tennessee, where she managed The Book Place, an independent bookstore; may it rest in peace. Before the lure of books hooked her, she was curator of the history museum in Jonesborough, Tennessee's oldest town. Molly MacRae's first mystery novel, *Wilder Rumors,* was published in 2007. Her stories have appeared in *Alfred Hitchcock's Mystery Magazine,* and she is a winner of the Sherwood Anderson Award for Short Fiction. These days, MacRae lives with her family in Champaign, Illinois, where she pushes books on children at the public library.